". . . tight, compelling, and convincing writing that is also witty and insightful, tossing off a critique of our culture which you can take or ignore . . . My biggest concern here is, does Maddox have some more of these in stock?"

— Jon A. Jackson, author of *Hit on the House* and *No Man's Dog*

"I couldn't put this novel down. *Darkroom* is suspenseful and beautifully written. Kelly Durrell is a deftly drawn, intelligent, and likable heroine. There is humorous relief as well, and the art-world setting adds another dimension to an already fantastic read."

— Daiva Markelis, author of *White Field, Black Sheep: A Lithuanian-American Life*

"The plot is never predictable, the characters are complex and believable, and her prose flows with beauty and clarity. The book has the added bonus of pushing us to ask ourselves: how strong would we be if faced with similar circumstances?"

— Tahlia Newland, author of *The Locksmith's Secret*

"Maddox is a master at using the art world's atmosphere as a backdrop in a solid mystery that involves a satisfyingly diverse range of characters . . . an engrossing story that's filled with surprises right up to the end."

— D. Donovan, Senior Reviewer, *Midwest Book Review*

"[*Darkroom* is a] thriller with unexpected plot twists and suspenseful action. The murder mystery is dark and menacing, and the characters are multi-faceted."

— RT Source

DARKROOM

Cantraip Press, Ltd.
2317 Saratoga Pl.
Charleston, Illinois 61920
www.cantraip.com

Publisher's Note:

This is a work of fiction. Names, characters, places, and incidents are a product of the author's imagination. Locales and public names are sometimes used for atmospheric purposes. Any resemblance to actual people, living or dead, or to businesses, companies, events, institutions, or locales is completely coincidental.

Cover Design by Pete Garceau

Darkroom / Mary Maddox —1st ed.
Paperback ISBN 978-1-942737-04-9
Electronic ISBN 978-1-942737-05-6

LCCN 2016903883

DARKROOM

MARY MADDOX

Cantraip
Press

For Steven James Maddox

Prologue

Some photographs speak for the dead, but their meaning may be elusive. You can't know for certain what's happening outside the frame or what happened before and after the image froze.

Look at these four black-and-white photographs.

In the first, a young man and woman crane their necks at the camera. They sit on a blanket with a Navajo pattern, surrounded by the remains of a picnic—bottles of Corona, a half-eaten hard roll, an open jar of Greek olives, a hunk of cheese on a board, a knife. A metal pipe used for smoking hash. In the upper edge of the frame, beyond the blanket, are meadow grasses and rangy wildflowers. Stalks and blossoms of the wildflowers are entwined in the woman's hair. They have begun to wilt.

The couple are in their early twenties, no older. The young man's head seems too big for his body. He has a round face, a snub nose, and an undersize mouth tight with disapproval—of the bothersome flies or having his picture taken, or something far worse that he would call evil. The woman's mouth, dark with lipstick, hangs open. Her forehead is creased. She gazes beyond the camera to where something has drawn her attention, pulling her out of the framed moment.

She sees it coming and is afraid.

In the next photograph, the couple are gone. A creek flows under a barbed-wire fence. The angle suggests the photographer has crouched on the bank and aimed the camera low over the water, upstream. Close up, the water is transparent down to the riverbed. Beyond the fence, shadowed by trees, the water darkens and winds across the frame, drawing your eye to the edge.

The creek in the third photograph is more narrow, rippling with current as it tumbles downhill. Another low angle, but this time the photographer aims the camera across the water and into trees. No focal point, it seems at first. But keep looking. After five seconds, maybe longer, your eye settles on a cross carved into the trunk of an aspen. The cross is several inches high yet no more prominent than the black knots and threads of lichen around it. But once seen, its wrongness stands out—the single unnatural detail in a landscape too wild to be framed. The knife cuts are fresh.

The last photograph points down at a patch of forest floor that also looks wrong in subtle ways. Pine needles are unsettled, not packed as they would be after lying together for a long time. The scattering of cones and twigs seems deliberate, like coconut sprinkled on a cake. Despite the unusual fluffiness of its cover, the ground looks sunken, as if the cake had fallen while baking. No marker distinguishes this spot from any other on the mountainside. The photographer has led you from the border into the heart of nowhere, trusting you'll care enough to follow the trail.

Manic whoops and a whiff of cannabis seeped into the garage. Daffy Duck was getting high. Kelly shifted a bag of groceries into the crook of her arm and opened the door. Beyond the kitchen and the sunlit dining area, Day sat on the carpet, toking on a hash pipe. An ashtray and several dishes, one piled high with orange rinds, formed a half circle in front of her.

Kelly dumped the groceries onto the counter and considered how to handle the situation. She was scared for Day, but it wouldn't help to let the fear show. She bought a minute by placing the car keys on their hook beside the door and detouring to the hall closet to hang up her coat. Then she went into the living room. "Hey, what's going on?"

Day's face froze in panic and then broke into a grin that lifted her eyebrows in exaggerated arches. A mischievous gleam lighted her eyes. A teenage girl lived inside the body of a thirty-eight-year-old woman. She held out the pipe. "Want a hit?"

Kelly shook her head. "My flight's at 9:10. And you're driving me to the airport, remember?" Her voice was drowned out by the cartoon soundtrack, a blare of horns and violins and Daffy's mocking laugh. She had to shout. "Turn off the TV."

Day fumbled the remote, aiming the wrong end and then dropping it. Finally she turned off the cartoon. The silence filled with the refrigerator's hum and the creak of bedsprings from Day's bedroom, next to the kitchen.

"Who's in there?"

"I was about to tell you. Odette's here."

"Who's with her?"

Day giggled.

"Odette gave you the hash."

"Don't be pissed."

"I'm not. It's just, you know what could—" She met Day's unfocused gaze and stopped. They could talk later. She went back to the kitchen and put the groceries away. She hesitated with the lamb shank. The plan was to show Day how to make curried lamb, but maybe not tonight. She put the meat in the fridge.

Voices from Day's room. Odette and—big surprise—a man. The door opened and Odette came out, her face haloed in Pre-Raphaelite curls. A T-shirt emblazoned with a pink butterfly showed off her breasts. "Hi, Kelly." Her boyfriend ventured out behind her. He was thin and tall, with a large head and a cherubic face. Like a lollipop. "This is Marcus."

"Marcus French," he said. "Sorry to bother you."

"No problem." Kelly put on a polite smile. "You guys are welcome to stay for dinner."

"Marcus is vegan," Odette said. "There's so much stuff he doesn't eat."

Day lurched to her feet and gathered up the dishes, stepping on the pretzel crumbs scattered over the carpet. She carried the stack into the kitchen and retrieved her camera and back-pack from a chair at the dinner table.

"You're going with them?" Kelly said.

"Just taking them back to Boulder."

"You're driving the Corolla? The brakes are shot."

"They work. Kind of."

Kelly grabbed her car keys. "Why don't I take them?"

"You don't have to. I mean, I can . . ." Day's voice trailed off and her gaze wandered.

Odette and Marcus followed Kelly to the garage and piled into the backseat of her Jeep Cherokee. She backed out of the garage. The Corolla, rust-pocked and dented, was parked at the curb in a different spot from where it had been that morn-ing. The car was a deathtrap, but Day had no other way into town.

"This place," Marcus said. "It's soulless. Everything is the same. Tan brick, perfect lawns. I wonder how many trees they cut down to build this chancre on the mountainside."

The kid wanted to start an argument.

Kelly wasn't crazy about Ash Mountain Estates, but she couldn't afford anything this nice closer to town. The subdivi-sion had a social center with a gym and a pool. She drove past the basketball and tennis courts, where half a dozen players were enjoying the last hour of the bright autumn day, and then through the entrance gate—more bland brick—and onto the road.

Marcus cleared his throat. "So, Day says you're curator of the cowboy museum."

"Assistant curator. You going to give me shit about that, too?"

"It's Eurocentric."

"Not entirely. It's not just cowboys. It's the art of the American West, including Native American art. Plus we have community programs and shows of local artists. Day knows that."

"Your founder is a fascist."

Kelly laughed. "That's harsh." The Museum of the Rockies did somewhat reflect the worldview of J. Elroy Jorgensen, a libertarian businessman, now deceased. He might have conceived MOR as a stiff middle finger to Boulder's progressive image, but things hadn't quite turned out that way.

"You're comfortable working there?"

"Damn straight," she said in a John Wayne drawl.

Marcus looped his scrawny arm around Odette and snuggled his cheek against hers. "You're gonna tell him, right?"

"I don't know." Her voice trembled a little.

"Come on, Odette. It makes me sick when I think about him with you."

Kelly glanced at their faces in the rearview mirror, his rapt and hers frightened. Lost in each other. Sex kitten and sanctimonious vegan—one more example of the old rule that opposites attract. Only their fear seemed wrong.

The road descended into a narrow canyon and wound through foothills planted with expensive houses before intersecting Broadway at the north edge of town. "Where can I drop you guys?"

"Downtown at the mall," Odette said. "Take Marcus home first."

"Just let me out here."

"I'll take you home." Kelly slowed behind a line of cars waiting as students crossed the street, a stream of backpacks and bobbing heads mostly clad in baseball caps.

"This is great, thanks." Marcus pressed his mouth against

Odette's before hopping from the Jeep and dashing to the curb as the light changed.

Kelly drove toward downtown. "What happens when your husband finds out about Marcus?"

"It's not like he gives a shit. He's out of town anyway." In the mirror her eyes darkened in unhappy thought.

"Do me a favor," Kelly said. "You know Day's bipolar. Don't give her drugs."

"She can handle it sometimes. When she's feeling centered."

Day tried to get by without medication. For the last eight months—the time Kelly had known her—she'd been all right, but a few puffs of hash might launch her into mania and land her in the psych ward.

"Just don't, okay?"

Near the Pearl Street Mall, Odette hunkered down and peeked out the window. "Turn left at the next street. Let me out anywhere but the corner."

"Who is it you're hiding from?"

"My bodyguard. Stuart says it's for my protection, but that's bullshit. He just wants to know what I'm doing every second of the day."

"You ditched your bodyguard?"

"In Banana Republic. I took a bunch of clothes to try on and gave the girl a twenty to let me out the back."

Kelly spotted the bodyguard, the only person not strolling along the sidewalk or gazing into store windows. He scanned the traffic in both directions, his shoulders and chest freakishly wide in a bulky lambskin jacket. His arctic gaze stuck to the Jeep as if he sensed Odette crouched in the backseat. "Where do I let you off?"

"Around the corner."

Kelly turned left alongside a municipal parking garage. "If Stuart doesn't give a shit, why are you hiding?"

"I don't know. Because I want my privacy? For once." Under the sarcasm, her voice trembled. She was afraid of her husband. Maybe for good reason. When the Jeep stopped, she ducked out and strolled toward the garage. Reeking of hash and carrying no shopping bags. The bodyguard wouldn't be fooled.

⬥

D ay waited at the dinner table sipping chamomile tea from a Japanese cup. She filled another cup for Kelly from the matching teapot. Except for bloodshot eyes and a subtle thickness in her voice, the high seemed to have worn off.

Kelly sat facing her. "The house stinks. Couldn't you get stoned in the car?"

"Your next-door neighbor was, like, peeping out the window again. He's such a weird little dude."

Owen worked at home and looked for things to complain about. Like Day's Corolla. He called it an eyesore. But Kelly wasn't in the mood to poke fun at Owen. "You know what can happen if you get stoned."

"It was just a couple tokes. I'm stable."

"That could change in a split second."

Eyes lowered, Day traced the ideogram on her cup with her forefinger. "I've never had a friend like you. And I don't wanna fuck it up. I mean, it's just sometimes like I don't know what's normal. What's okay with normal people?"

Help me to be better, teach me. Day had made the same appeal before, several times, the reliable key to Kelly's sympathy. Manipulative but also honest. She was only asking for what she needed.

"I'm not a doper," she went on. "Like, how many times have I gotten high? Twice on grass. Maybe a dozen times on booze. My thing is making photographs, not being strung out."

"No more drugs, then."

"Okay."

Kelly couldn't let go of an uneasiness that covered more than the drugs, but she didn't want to talk about the hulking bodyguard and the fear in Odette's voice. Not now anyway. "Are you up for helping me make curried lamb?"

"Sure."

She put Day to work chopping carrots, onions, and potatoes. She took the shank from the fridge and began assembling spices for the curry.

"Nutmeg," Day said. "You can get stoned on nutmeg. John used to do it when there was no weed." She talked about her father like an old pal. Her parents moved around a lot, and she hadn't been in touch with them for a couple of years.

The doorbell chimed while Kelly was pouring olive oil. "Get that, will you?"

Day bounded down the hallway. She said something, but her voice was crushed by a sharp thud and heavy footsteps. Odette's bodyguard barged into the kitchen. His pale blue eyes fixed on Kelly. "Where is she?"

Day squeezed past him. "This is Yount. Odette's asshole bodyguard."

Fear churned in Kelly's stomach. "Odette? I dropped her off at the mall."

Yount stepped backward, pushed open the door to the guest room, and peered inside. Then he headed for the stairs.

Kelly went after him. "I'm calling the cops."

A smile twisted his mouth. "Go ahead."

Her phone was in the kitchen and she didn't want him to roam through the house without her. She turned to Day, who was watching from the hallway. "Call the cops."

She trailed Yount through the upstairs—bedroom, walk-in closet, bathroom, office. He checked under the bed and behind the shower curtain but otherwise touched nothing. "I told you, she's not here. Get out of my house."

"There was someone with her," he said. "Who?"

"I don't know."

"He didn't introduce himself?"

"I just wanted them gone. I don't like drugs in my house. Day knows that."

He snorted. "Day doesn't listen. You ought to know that." He thrust his face so close to hers that she saw individual hairs in one of his eyebrows. "You seem a little smarter, so I'm telling you. Don't let yourself be used."

"I don't know what you're talking about."

"Then you better figure it out." At the top of the stairs, Yount gestured for her to go down first. His chest nudged her forward, and a hard lump poked her shoulder. A gun inside his coat? He kept nudging. He wanted her to wonder if he was going to shove her down the stairs. And she did wonder, with every step.

Day opened the front door and stepped outside. "Satisfied, asshole?"

He paused long enough to glower and then strode across the lawn to a black Land Rover. Odette sat in the back, her head lowered.

Lightheaded, Kelly leaned against the wall. "Why did you do that?"

"Do what?"

"Call him an asshole."

"Because that's what he is." Day frowned. "You're scared."

"Of course I'm scared. He forced his way into my house and threatened me. He claimed to be looking for Odette, but she was outside in his car."

"He was just fucking with us. He does that."

"Just be sure to tell the cops everything you know about him."

Day avoided meeting her eyes. "I didn't call."

"Why not?"

"Odette would be in worse trouble."

Instead of going back to the kitchen and the curried lamb, they wandered into the dark living room. It was early November and the evenings contracted suddenly into night. "He barged in here with a gun. I'm supposed to let that go?"

"I owe her," Day said. "She helped me when I was my most down."

Yount could park around the corner and sneak back through the trees behind the houses. He could be outside the window right now, watching them. Kelly drew the curtains and switched on a lamp. "Look, Odette's welcome here, but not with Marcus. That includes while I'm out of town."

Odette had been Day's first friend in Boulder. Odette had taken her in and outfitted a darkroom for her in the basement. She still drove to the estate in the mountains to develop her prints. That perk might end now that she'd antagonized Yount.

"You never told me why you moved out," Kelly said.

"Stuart."

"He's hardly ever there, you said."

"Yeah, but his pit bulls are. Every time you scratch your ass, Yount reports back to Stuart. I mean, if you're down with that, no problem."

"Gotta be free," Kelly said.

"Always." A smile, arch and weary, flitted across Day's face. "Hey, I have something for you." She retrieved her backpack from the dining chair and handed Kelly a large envelope.

Inside were half a dozen eight-by-ten prints, multiple developments of two close-ups of Kelly's face. She studied them, so caught up in Day's experiments with contrast and nuance that she forgot she was looking at herself. It came as a shock when she remembered. The faces weren't the familiar one in her bathroom mirror, the woman who dabbed her smudged mascara with a tissue and dreaded going to work. The photographs showed a woman with amazement shadowing her eyes, a woman caught in the world's strangeness. Seeing them, Kelly understood why she couldn't be the daughter her mother wanted, why moving far away from home had been her only hope. She understood who she was. And why she was happy to keep buying Day's groceries and letting her stay in the house rent-free. "Damn, you're good."

Day grinned. "Yeah, I know."

"I'm leaving extra cash in the ceramic bowl in my office in case something comes up while I'm gone. Call me if you need to."

"Have fun in Chicago."

After the conference, Kelly planned to spend a few days wandering through the Art Institute and the Museum of Contemporary Art. She had to trust Day to keep her promise. Whatever drama was going on between Odette and her husband, Kelly didn't want to get caught in the middle. The bodyguard had shouldered his way into her house, armed. Maybe he was all bluff, or maybe he carried the gun because he would use it.

2

At the top of the stairs, Day stopped and listened to the voices. They boomed in the open space above the white geometric walls of the museum. The building's shape molded the sound. A blind person could hear it and know the height of the ceiling and the steepness of its vault. Another kind of sight. But Day was all eyes. Give her scaffolding and she could shoot the maze of gallery walls, the sophisticated rats nibbling snacks and sipping chardonnay. Not her kind of shot, though. She was more the up-close-and-personal, whites-of-their-eyes, breath-to-breath type, going for that flicker of an instant before the lens fogged.

She kept standing there, breathing funny. She couldn't be scared of those fools. Not her, the woman who'd flipped Baba and lived.

She'd felt sorry for one of his child whores and called the girl's parents. He chased her through the house with a blade until she locked herself in the bathroom. He slammed the door, yelling that he would cut her throat, bleed her in the tub and carve her like a chicken, and wrap the chunks in newspaper and toss them in a dumpster behind the supermarket with the other rotten meat. She was too scared to feel herself, like her body had turned into air. Baba had a way with threats. He might have carried them out except for Shawn, his half brother. Shawn calmed him down and told Day to get the fuck out, warning her that if she stuck her hook nose into their business again, he would personally waste her skinny ass and save Baba the trouble.

That was an occasion for terror. *This* was just a crowd of art snobs. No blades here. Just voices, diamond-sharp.

"Going to the party?"

Day whipped around, startled.

Stocky guy in jeans and a lumberjack shirt, not much taller than her. Dark hair streaked with gray. Life stamped in his face, deep impressions around his mouth and eyes. Irony in his smile but no trace of cruelty. He held out a gnarly hand. "Leonard Proud."

She reached out with caution. Not that he seemed like the type who gave women crushing handshakes, but he looked strong. "Day Randall."

His hand closed over hers—no squeeze or shake, but firm—and then let go. "Kelly says nice things about you," he said.

"You're her friend?"

"More like colleague. I'm on the board of the museum."

She reached for the scuffed Pentax hanging from her neck, the first and only camera she'd owned, her longtime crutch and trusty third eye.

He waved his arm. "No."

"It's, like, official. Photos for the newsletter."

"Even worse." But he squared his shoulders and turned his face to stone. Ready for his close-up.

"Dude. I'm not a firing squad."

Leonard clamped his mouth to keep the laughter in. His cheeks puffed a little and his eyes crinkled in amusement. She saw the moment and took the shot. Snap, snap. What she did best. Kelly would never use the photo in the newsletter—members of a board were supposed to look more dignified—but Day might add it to her portfolio if he agreed.

"Let me send you a print," she said. "What's your address?"

He gave her a business card, a plain one with a block font.

"You make Native American art? What kind?"

"Weaving and painting."

"I'd like to see it."

"There's a couple of my pieces back there." Leonard nodded toward the rear of the museum.

"Show me."

"Some other time. I wanna get the meet-and-greet over with."

Day followed him into a gallery of Inuit art. "Would you, like, do me a big favor? Point out the other board members so I'll be sure and get shots of them. You and Joyce are the only ones I know."

"How much is Joyce paying you?"

"She's not."

He snorted. "A new low, even for her."

A glass case imprisoned several small totem animals carved from stone, including a curled-up seal so smooth and dark Day yearned to feel its coolness and weight in her hand. "It's for Kelly. I mean, I'm not paying rent or anything, so I try to help."

"You live with Kelly?"

"Yeah, for almost eight months. She's in Chicago at a conference for curators, so I'm, like, helping her. It's a surprise."

Leonard raised his eyebrows. "You're here without an invitation."

"Do I need one?"

"Hell, no. You're with me."

Day followed him into the reception area, drafting in his wake like she sometimes drafted behind a semi in her Corolla to save fuel. She needed his forward energy to make her entry. She hated coming uninvited among these people wrapped in cashmere. Not hated—feared. *You have to tell yourself the truth because these people are going to lie.* Their smiles were rubbery, like masks.

Leonard veered toward the refreshments, tidbits of food on trays and glasses of wine lined up on the tablecloth beside them. Wine the color of pee after you drink way too much water. Day stopped. Too many people were crowded around the refreshments. She would catch Leonard after he got his food.

She felt something, turned, and caught Annie Laible staring from across the room. She smiled and waved and got a sour smile back. Annie had new and wilder hair, hennaed and spiked. Months ago, Day had asked permission to hang a few photographs for sale in her gallery—she needed money bad—and Annie had blown her off. Just a blunt "No" without saying why.

Joyce was talking with two men in their forties. Older than Day, but not by much. Day was thirty-eight, though she tried hard to forget it. The short guy was wasted, face bright pink, eyes shining and empty. The other was tall and gaunt. *His cheekbones drank the wind.* She remembered the line from a poem she read growing up. She forgot what poem. Anyway, it described this guy. He turned his head as if he felt her stare. Their eyes met. Locked. She recognized him. Not personally.

More like she was an alien species who finds another of her kind among strangers.

She lifted her camera, zoomed in, and took his picture. Then zoomed out and got the whole group. They were probably important if Joyce was talking to them.

He walked over to her. "You're Day Randall. I bought two of your prints."

Day knew which ones. Soon after she came to Boulder, she submitted her portfolio for an exhibit at the museum. Joyce turned down the portfolio but said she had a buyer for the prints at $350 each. A fortune for Day. Of course, Joyce never gave up the buyer's name. She wouldn't want Day to sell to him and cut her out of a commission. Now here he was, this guy whose cheekbones drank the wind.

"What's your name?"

"My friends call me Gee."

She grinned. "Am I your friend?"

"I don't know. Are you?"

"I feel like we're the only ones from another planet."

Gee reached out and stroked her cheek. His fingertips set off a tingling that reached down to her core. "Let's play Find the Magic."

"What's that?"

"This exhibit is called Magic and Realism." He pointed to a painting. "What's magical?"

The painting showed a bird and a cat, the tension between prey and predator. The bird's beak was open in frozen song. The iridescent feathers, intense cobalt and silky green, burned into her mind. "It's like a window into someone's dream."

"We're doing analysis," Gee said. "Notice how the details aren't realistic. The color of the feathers, the way they glow.

Not like any finch in the real world. And the proportions are skewed. The finch is ten times bigger than the cat. It fills the whole room."

"But it's afraid of the cat anyway."

"How do you know?"

"I just do."

"Maybe because the finch is hunched and the cat's kind of batting at it. Check out these claws. The tips are red."

"Yeah, like with blood."

"Exactly."

Day shook her head. "I don't have to take things apart. I see them whole."

"There's nothing whole. Everything is pieces." Gee's gaze played over her face and started her tingling just like his fingertips had. "The universe blew up a long time ago."

Gee tied her up. Anyone else, she would have said no way. With him it was different. The coke launched her head into space, on a course to Planet Elsewhere. Transformed her body into a rush of energy. He bound her wrists together with a silk scarf and threaded a rope between them and then through a metal loop screwed into the wall above his bed. He tightened the rope until she couldn't lie down without four pillows under her shoulders. The loop told on him. He made a habit of playing prisoner-in-the-dungeon with the women he brought home.

He yanked away one pillow and then another. Then another. Her body dangled. Almost at once her elbows and shoulders ached. Day begged him to untie her. Not that the pain mattered—she was too high to care—but she knew he wanted to hear those words. They were, after all, the same species, alien to this world.

His mouth moved over her body. He tongued her stomach, her belly button, her nipples. She waited for him to mention her non-breasts. Guys always said something, a stupid joke or fake reassurance. *I need a magnifying glass to find those. Hey, it don't matter. You're hot anyway, you're scorching.* Not Gee. He treated them like ordinary breasts.

Soon she was screaming with pleasure.

When he was done, he untied her and said he needed to have her arms around him. She pressed her skin against his. Their sweat thrummed with the electricity between them. It made them one. Their body trembled with the pounding of their heart. He bent to her ear and whispered that she was the only living thing in a dead world and please, please bring him back to life. "You're the magic," he told her. "You're the only magic."

◈

They fucked in his plush bed and her plain one. They went dancing. Day could have stayed with Gee forever, but on Sunday morning Odette called, sobbing. "Marcus is gone."

No shit, home for Thanksgiving. Odette could be a drama queen. Day listened to her choke out a story about Marcus's wanting her to leave Stuart. Insisting. "He knew I couldn't. I told him—"

Marcus had been insisting for weeks. Nothing new there. "What makes you think—"

"I texted him. And called. And this morning Yount and his clones drove out into the pasture."

"They patrol there."

"Not that early. And Yount doesn't go with them."

"What is it you're thinking?"

A long pause, filled with something Odette was afraid to put into words. "Just walk back there and look."

"For what?"

"I don't know. Tracks. Anything that—just look, okay? You know the patrol times. And if they catch you, say you're taking pictures. Say I gave you permission."

Day stood outside her bedroom door, naked except for her phone. She wanted to crawl back into bed with Gee, but Odette was her friend and she owed her so much. She went back into the room and kissed Gee, raking her fingers in his loose hair. "I gotta go to the darkroom. You know the film I shot at the exhibition? It's, like, a gift for Kelly, for the newsletter she does."

He gave her a sleepy smile. "Why now? She's not coming back for a few days."

"Yeah, but I can't get in the darkroom unless Odette's around and she called to say she's around this morning. You can, like, hang out here and have coffee."

"It's all right, I have work to do anyway." His hand caressed her thigh and slipped between her legs. "Call when you get home."

On the way to Stuart's, she fretted over the shadowy fear behind Odette's words. A possibility occurred to her—a scary possibility that nudged her heart into high gear—and slowly an idea began to take shape.

She parked on an access road where the Jeep couldn't be seen from the road. She hiked along the electric fence behind the property. She stayed under the trees and listened for the distant growl of an engine. Her boots crunched the pine needles.

A bird's cawing ripped the silence. But no engine. Pretty soon Yount's goonies would begin their patrol around the fence. She had twenty minutes, maybe less, to reach the back of the fence and get out of sight.

Nothing so far. But supposing she found the tracks or whatever and took pictures, Odette would beg her to keep them secret. Even if they could set her free, Odette was so scared and used to being caged.

Stupid—trying to rescue someone who didn't want to be rescued, as she knew only too well.

And yet.

She paused long enough to snap a picture of a tree. Nature wasn't her thing. Faces were. The tree's gnarly trunk had an ancient face.

She moved through the shadows while the meadow exploded with sunshine. The air had the brightness of fall in the mountains—everything clear, sharp, more real. Her camera never caught that light, only its hard shadows. It was wild light, beyond capture. Color film made no difference. Neither would the expensive DSL camera Gee promised her. A camera and a laptop computer to manipulate the images.

Manipulate. The wrongness of the whole digital thing packed into a single word. You don't manipulate negatives, chemicals, and paper in a darkroom. You transform them. Chemistry becomes alchemy. Val's words.

The only kid at the commune, Day had followed Val around like a baby duck. Up and down between the garden rows, she breathed the warm smell of plants growing in the sun. Strawberries, zucchini. A damp-earth smell that lingered even in sleep. Once the gardening was done, Val shot photos with a 35 mm Pentax and developed them in a makeshift darkroom attached to the greenhouse. She taught Day photography. Then it happened, the inevitable shit. Sheila always screwed around, and John couldn't make her stop. They got thrown out of the commune. Day begged to stay without them. Val promised to take care of her, but the commune people said no way. They weren't giving Sheila an excuse to come back. Val gave Day the Pentax and some photography books. Day knew what a sacrifice it was. She tried to refuse. "I'm an old woman," Val said. "My spirit goes with you."

Day cupped the Pentax in her hands. She would keep taking photos with Val's camera—the photos that mattered—and use the digital camera for commercial work. Weddings and whatnot.

She reached the corner of the electric fence and turned. The creek burbled up ahead. She checked her phone. The patrol would start any minute. Her boots scuffed through dead weeds and grass. She smelled water. She scanned the ground ahead, unsure what she expected to see until she spotted it—scraped mud where something was dragged out of the water and onto the bank. Something big. They must have rolled it into the creek and then pulled it under the fence and out of the water. They probably carried it from there. She couldn't find footprints in the rocky outcrops above the creek, but it was the only path. In the mountains, you stayed on the trails, especially when you carried something heavy. Somewhere farther up, they would pick a spot to leave the trail. Day felt confident of finding where. Seeing was her gift.

She squatted and aimed her camera up the creek and took a picture. Then she started up the trail.

Kelly plucked her suitcase from the baggage carousel and rolled it to a spot near the wall, away from the passengers streaming past. She called Day and left a message. "I'm at the airport. Hopefully you're on your way here. Call me." Above the doors, leering gargoyles emerged from suitcases. Kelly loved the art at the Denver airport and wished she had time to walk around and enjoy it.

Twenty minutes into the wait, she sat on her suitcase. After twenty more minutes, she went to the shuttle desk and bought a ticket to Boulder. She took the seat up front beside the driver, a stocky guy who cranked the radio once they were on the road. She called Day and raised her voice above the wail of a country singer. "Where are you?" Day hadn't answered the phone all day. Most likely she'd gone off partying with Gregory Tyson and forgotten about Kelly.

It seemed like a lucky break, Day's meeting Tyson at the exhibition opening. He had money and admired her work. He could be both lover and patron. But the day before yesterday,

Day's voice on the phone, hyped and breathless, had tripped a warning in Kelly. Tyson did drugs. Sometimes at board meetings his eyes had an unnatural gloss.

She tried to read, but the van lurched and bumped. Sunlight glinted off the windshields and roofs of cars, piercing her polarized sunglasses. She caught whiffs of exhaust in the air blowing from the dashboard vents. Then her phone chimed. She rifled through her bag and pulled it out. Her father.

"Hi, Dad."

"Hi, sweetheart." Exhaustion weighed down his voice.

"Everything okay?"

"I'm worried about your mom."

"She's still taking the Prozac?"

"No, they have her on something else that's not working any better. It's been over a year. I'm starting to think she'll never get over Beth."

Kelly said what she was supposed to. "I'm sorry." Sorry she wasn't the one who'd died in the car accident. Of course they loved Kelly and losing her would have grieved them, but losing their younger daughter broke their hearts.

"Your mom needs you, sweetheart. I wish you lived closer."

"I can't live in Morrison. You know that."

"What about Chicago or Indianapolis? You can find a job there."

"Mom's not around?" Somehow Mom was never there when Dad called.

"She's sleeping. She's been sleeping a lot."

"I'll come visit, I promise."

"How about next month, for Christmas?"

"I have too much work. Maybe in the spring." She couldn't explain that the work had piled up during her week in Chicago. Dad would be hurt that she hadn't told him about the trip beforehand. He could drive to Chicago in less than three hours.

As usual after talking with him, she brooded. She used to wonder if the hospital had made a mistake and sent her home with the wrong people. She loved her family but was nothing like them. None of them—sister, parents, aunts, uncles, or cousins—cared about art. To them, her career choice seemed bizarre. They would have understood law school or medical school, even running off to Hollywood to be an actor, but art curator? A career without money or glamour. When she tried explaining how certain paintings were luminous, why others stirred her in ways she'd never before imagined, only Dad listened.

Now he wanted her to come home and take Beth's place.

Kelly had chosen the role of secondary daughter by distancing herself from them. She couldn't change now. Mom might warm to her if she produced a grandchild, but that was an unlikely prospect. She was thirty-five and unattached and had no desire to become a single mother.

The shuttle meandered through Boulder, dropping off passengers. She was the only one left when the driver headed for Ash Mountain Estates, a few miles northwest of town. Early twilight darkened the canyon. She opened the window of the overheated van and let the cold air flutter against her face. She pointed out the brick gateway and gave the driver directions through the tidy winding streets. Most houses blazed with Christmas lights. Today was Thanksgiving and she'd hardly noticed.

"The house with the brown Corolla in front,"

She tipped the driver ten dollars for carrying her suitcase

and laptop case and then unlocked the door and paused at the threshold of the darkened house. A smell . . . some kind of petroleum distillate. Had Day been housecleaning? Leaving her baggage in the hall, Kelly went to the kitchen and started heating water in an electric teakettle. The fridge was empty except for jars of condiments and jams, plastic tubs containing week-old leftovers, two cans of diet soda, a bottle of unsweet-ened cranberry juice, and a carton of low-fat milk. She opened the carton. The milk smelled okay, but not much was left. Day hadn't bought groceries.

The car keys were missing from the hook beside the door to the laundry room. Day had the Jeep. She was probably with Tyson.

While her tea steeped, Kelly hauled her suitcase into the laundry room, stuffed her dirty clothes into the washer, and hauled her toilet kit, jewelry case, and shoes upstairs to her bedroom. The timer beeped. Her tea. She brought the ceramic mug and her laptop into her office. She hadn't checked her e-mail since Wednesday, the day before yesterday, but there wasn't much—another message from Joyce about the Christ-mas fundraiser, a newsletter from the Getty museum in Los Angeles, an electronic receipt from the hotel where she'd stayed in Chicago, and the inevitable spam that slipped past the filter. She began a reply to Joyce and then decided the Museum of the Rockies could wait until tomorrow. Instead, she put away her things, showered, and donned clean clothes.

The washing machine buzzed. Kelly hurried downstairs to load her laundry into the dryer. After double-checking that everything was unpacked, she carried the suitcase into the ga-rage for storage.

The Jeep was there.

Its windows and chrome gleamed, its exterior spotless even at the bottom. Day never washed her Corolla. The Jeep must have been filthy for her to take it to the carwash, and she would go to the trouble only because it was Kelly's car. Afterward she'd gone off with Tyson and absentmindedly taken the keys or left them somewhere other than the hook. Kelly searched the kitchen counter and the dining table, where a week's worth of mail was heaped, unsorted. Then the living room. Finally she went into Day's room.

The Amish quilt was arranged squarely on the bed, pillows and shams plumped against the headboard. The floor planks gleamed. The chemical odor was strong, obnoxious enough to bother anyone sleeping in the room, but Day wouldn't have realized the problem until after using it. She'd gone to so much trouble for Kelly's return—washing the Jeep, cleaning the house—and then forgot to show up at the airport. Kelly was touched and exasperated. She opened the closet to search Day's pockets for the keys.

Her own winter clothes were there, zipped into plastic storage bags and pushed to one side, but Day's clothes were gone. She searched the dresser drawers. Everything belonging to Day was gone.

She sank onto the bed.

An anal personality would scour the room and wash the car. Day was the opposite of anal. When they'd talked on the phone, she was rushing off somewhere and seemed a little breathless. With excitement. Or anxiety. An undertone of sadness haunted her voice. She'd repeated Kelly's flight number and arrival time and promised, "I'll be there."

The Corolla was still parked at the curb, so someone must have helped her move. Odette? Kelly couldn't picture Odette's bodyguard lugging boxes from the house. He probably considered such a task beneath him. Maybe Day had moved in with Tyson. She could at least have left a note. And the car keys.

Kelly's stomach reminded her she needed to buy food. She retrieved the spare key from the ceramic bowl in her office and spent several minutes searching for her bag before spotting it on the chair where she'd dropped it before making tea.

She found the original set of keys on the driver's seat of the Jeep. Day must have tossed them after returning from the carwash. A last-minute chore on the way to her next adventure.

She raised the garage door, backed the Jeep into the driveway, and stopped. Light blazed from an upstairs window of the house next door. Owen, a software designer, worked at odd hours. His office window overlooked her driveway and the front curb, and he complained about the broken-down Corolla spoiling the view. He might have seen Day move out.

Kelly crossed the lawn to his doorstep and rang the bell. A couple of minutes passed, but she knew better than to ring again. Owen wouldn't answer if she rushed him. Finally he opened the door and blinked at her through oversize round glasses, a diminutive man with loopy curls of ash-blond hair. "Hi, Kelly. Did you have a good trip?"

"How did you know I was gone?"

"The woman staying at your house told me."

"You talked to Day? When?"

"A few days ago. I went out on my deck, and she was on your deck. She took my photograph. Without permission." Owen shot nervous glances over Kelly's shoulder, as if the empty street were full of watchers. "She promised to hand over the negative."

"It's cold out here. Can I come in?"

"Oh." Panic welled in his eyes, but he rode the wave. "Okay, sure. Why not?"

Owen led her down the entry hall and halted. She peered over him at the dining and living area. The floor plan of his house mirrored hers, but otherwise they occupied different universes. His living room was dominated by a huge rear-projection TV and a sound system consisting of black boxes of various sizes and shapes, aglow with a complicated array of dials and buttons and LED displays. The media setup occupied most of the longest wall and smelled of heated metal.

"I don't suppose she left the negative with you?" he said.

"Then you know she's moved out?"

"I should've insisted on getting it right away."

Kelly tried a smile. "Why don't we sit down?"

"She told me she wanted to develop the roll because there were some good shots. Now she has my picture."

"When you talked to her, did she say anything about moving out?"

"If she ever shows it in an art gallery, I'll take legal action."

"I don't think she'd do that. Not without asking. Did you happen to notice when she left?"

"People are tracking me." His gaze swept the hallway as if cameras might be hidden in the walls and ceiling. "They'll see my picture in the art gallery."

She tried a joke. "Haven't you been paying your taxes?"

"Very funny. They're tracking you, too whether you know it or not."

"Please, Owen. I just wondered if you saw her moving out."

He folded his arms stubbornly. "Give me the negative and then we can talk."

Kelly took a slow breath, but her exasperation refused to die. He was fixated on the negative and lost in his paranoid fantasies. She was wasting her time. "I've already been through the house. Day took everything."

"I suppose she stole you blind. You know, there's a rule against leaving vehicles parked in the street for more than seventy-two hours. Now that what's-her-name's moved out—"

"Her name's Day."

"*Night* is more like it. You should be more careful. Taking in strangers, trusting them with your house. You could've come back and found the place cleaned out. Or trashed."

"But I didn't."

"Not this time. This time you got lucky." His mouth twitched. "That junk heap of hers parked in front? I want it gone."

Kelly worked in a beautiful building. It had been conceived like a pueblo—an outgrowth of the natural landscape, rising within the sacred circle defined by the curved terraces at its base. The dolomite masonry had been assembled exactly as quarried, so the pattern of the grain was unbroken and the building seemed hewn from one massive piece of rock. The walkway on the outside was constructed of logs and beams of unstained red cedar. The Museum of the Rockies had made a bold aesthetic and political statement. Probably not the one J. Elroy Jorgensen had in mind. But whatever else could be said of MOR's founder, he put architecture before ideology.

She parked in the underground garage, in the area reserved for employees, and rode the elevator to the lobby. Waving hello to Marta, the receptionist, she passed the gift shop and a huge triptych depicting Custer's Last Stand.

The art downstairs was devoted to the romance of the Old West—frontier landscapes peopled by cowboys, cavalrymen, and noble savages. Its quality varied. The red hills of Georgia O'Keeffe's New Mexico and Charles M. Russell's bronze bronco rider shared the floor with works that had justifiably fallen into obscurity. Then there was the huge portrait of John Wayne commissioned by J. Elroy.

The offices were upstairs with the Native American art and special exhibitions. Kelly climbed the open staircase and passed an elderly guard at the entrance to the new Magic and Realism exhibit.

"Hello, Kelly."

"Hi, George." She waved and kept walking until she reached a wide beechwood door labeled "Administration." Her office was one of four off the short corridor.

A spider plant, parched and brittle, hung high in the narrow window like a sacrifice to the sun god. She'd ignored it for weeks. She filled her coffee mug at the fountain in the corridor, climbed onto the wide sill, and stretched her arm to reach the planter.

"That Marta's job." Joyce stood in the doorway, arms folded, scowling.

"You know Marta. She's kind of a space cadet."

"A nice way of saying she's incompetent."

Kelly watered the plant. "She's too short to do this."

"There's a stepladder in the janitor's closet."

The last thing Kelly wanted was to get Marta in trouble. "That's a beautiful necklace. Is it new?"

Joyce touched her necklace, a fat silver collar set with chunks of turquoise. "Yes, it is." Her voice warmed a degree or two. "Come on, there's a lot to do." She led Kelly into her office and sat behind her Scandinavian designer desk, its inky glass agleam in the sunlight pouring through two windows and a skylight.

Kelly settled into her usual chair. "Did the Magic and Realism opening go okay?"

"Day showed up and took photos. You know we can't pay her."

"She did that on her own. I didn't ask her to."

Day must have planned to surprise Kelly with the photos. A week ago she wasn't going to leave. Something happened that changed her mind.

"Well, we can use them in the newsletter," Joyce said. "If she's willing to donate them."

"She's gone."

Joyce raised her eyebrow in a studied way. "Really? Where?"

"I don't know. I came home last night and her stuff was gone. She's been seeing Gregory Tyson. I'm wondering if she moved in with him."

"I doubt that very much. Gee's a player." Joyce iced the word with bitterness. "Anyway. While you were gone, your big plans for the fundraiser have been falling apart. Two artists have withdrawn their donations. Barney Factor threw a tantrum because we're not featuring that insipid line drawing of his in the program. I told him . . ."

It had been Kelly's idea to stage a silent auction as part of the holiday fundraiser. Artists would donate their work. The museum would display it and showcase a few pieces in the newsletter and in fundraiser invitations. Joyce brushed aside the idea when Kelly proposed it and then presented it to the board as her own brainchild. A classic Joyce move.

She groused on. ". . . cares about Barney. He's a nobody and I'm tired of catering to his overblown ego. But it's too bad about Serena Carlyle." Her mouth twitched in something between a smile and a grimace. "I was hoping Day would donate a photograph. Oh, well."

"We still have twenty-one pieces," Kelly said. "That's enough."

"If everyone keeps their promises. Six pieces haven't arrived yet. By the way, I want you to pick up Annie's and Leonard's pieces. They're board members. It's the least we can do."

The pickups would take half an afternoon. Leonard lived thirty minutes outside town, and Annie's glass sculptures were so fragile that driving over a pothole could shatter them. "Can't one of the workmen do it? Or Marta?"

"No. I don't trust any of them."

"I'm so behind schedule already."

Joyce peered from beneath lowered eyelids as if taking aim. "Maybe you shouldn't have skipped off to Chicago right before our biggest event of the year. You've been gone an entire week."

"Yesterday was Thanksgiving. The museum was closed anyway."

"When did the conference end? I'm guessing last weekend. What was it about?"

"Art and war in the twentieth century."

"It's not really relevant to your work here, is it?"

Kelly gave up trying to justify the trip, her first real vacation in over two years. She loved art and working with artists, but her job at MOR was eroding that love. Joyce treated her like a flunky, not a colleague. The woman knew her stuff, but she cared more about money and community politics than art. The museum mattered because she was the curator. If Joyce ever found another position, she would walk away and never think of MOR again. Kelly's nightmare of the future was watching helplessly as she warped into Joyce's Mini Me.

The morning dragged while they reviewed details for the party—whether to pay the string quartet from last year the higher fee it demanded, how much to spend on the catering, whether to host an open bar or just serve wine. Matters that Kelly thought had been settled. The fundraiser was fifteen days away.

Finally she escaped to her office and started to work on the auction program. She needed an image for the cover. She studied photos of the donated pieces—oil and acrylic paintings, wood and glass sculptures, mixed-media collages—much of their impact and subtlety lost in reproduction. Kelly imagined donating one of the portraits Day had given her and putting that on the cover. She chuckled at the idea. Joyce would be furious. Even though Day had more talent than Barney Factor and Serena Carlyle combined, she was a nobody.

Day had shown up last March after MOR publicized its annual exhibit to showcase local artists. Kelly was in the curator's office at the time and started to leave, but Joyce signaled with a pointed look for her to stay. The interview started badly. Day slouched. In her fuzzy snow boots and pink satin parka she looked like a downscale ski bunny. Her talk was stuttered with "uhs" and "likes" and "kindas." What Joyce called junk language.

Joyce's face hardened in judgment before she opened the portfolio. She flipped through several pages and stopped, gazed for a long moment, and then slowly turned the page. She went on gazing. "Could you leave this for a day or two?""

Day was wide-eyed. "Sure."

"Is there a number where we can reach you?"

"Not really, but—I could, like, come back day after tomorrow?"

After she was gone, Kelly said, "There's no way we can take her stuff. The deadline's passed."

Joyce turned another page. "I know."

"Then why lead her on?"

"Because I may have a buyer."

"She's that good?"

"See for yourself."

Day shot in black and white and developed her prints in a darkroom, a rare skill in the age of digital photography. Her sense of composition seemed effortless and unerring. Some of her photographs were stereotypes—brazen street kids and elderly men with cartographic faces, derivative of the street photographers of the '60s and '70s. But her best photographs broke through all preconceptions and discovered the secret of each face, its elusive life, so that each became the portrait of an intimate you had yet to meet.

She caught the souls of her subjects the way super-fast shutters caught raindrops in mid-splatter or hummingbirds in flight.

Several pages were devoted to two women as they partied with different men in the cluttered rooms of a bungalow. The most compelling shot showed the women alone, a fleshy blonde and an emaciated redhead. The blonde sprawled on a sofa, one leg flung over its low back and the other dangling. Her thighs bulged beneath her skimpy shorts, and one huge breast had slipped from her halter top. Eyes staring upward, unseeing, her face echoed the slackness of her breast. The redhead knelt on the wide sofa arm opposite the blonde's head. Damaged by too many days on the beach, her skin was lined and blotched with freckles coarsened into age spots. The skin identified her hair as red, even in black and white. She gazed at the blonde with a faint contemptuous smile. Her eyes gleamed with hatred.

"Remind you of someone?" Joyce had said.

"Larry Clark." These photographs had the same rawness, the

same disturbing intimacy. A sense that the artist, more than a chronicler, was implicated in the scene.

Joyce nodded. "She could be great. If she doesn't self-destruct first."

❖

Someone cleared his throat. Startled, Kelly peeked over the computer screen. Gregory Tyson stood in the doorway. "Can we talk?"

The question startled her. She knew Tyson from board meetings and other museum functions, but they were hardly friends. He wore the usual black leather motorcycle jacket. His hair was pulled back at his neck in a ponytail, except for a thin braid laced with beads dangling by his left ear. A diamond stud sparked his left earlobe. The guy watched too many pirate movies.

"Come and sit down."

He shot a glance toward Joyce's office. "Let's go somewhere. I was thinking the Dushanbe Teahouse."

"I have too much work."

"Joyce says it's cool."

Of course Joyce would. Tyson gave a lot of money to MOR, and being polite to him was part of the assistant curator's job. "I can't be gone long."

Kelly followed him downstairs, past the grandiose painting of Custer, and out to the street. The sun blazed in a hard blue sky, warm for November. His Jaguar sedan waited at the curb. She climbed into the passenger seat and he pulled into traffic.

Tyson drove a few blocks in silence. "You and Day must've talked while you were gone on your trip," he finally said. "Did she say anything about what she was doing?"

"She talked about you."

"Nothing else?"

"No, just you and how much she liked you. Why? What is it you think she might have said?"

"Why she was leaving. Where she was going."

"Nothing at all. She was supposed to pick me up at the airport."

He hesitated a moment. "You've known her since she came to Boulder."

"Not really. She was staying somewhere else when I met her. Then she had to move out, and I offered her my spare room."

"Who was she staying with?"

Kelly's shoulders ached with tension. "A woman she met in a bar. Courtney Lamb."

"You know her address? Phone number?"

"No. Sorry." His cologne overwhelmed her. Something with sandalwood, expensive, not quite strong enough to hide the reek of cigarettes. "Why all the questions?"

"She left without saying good-bye." Tyson turned in to the parking area for the teahouse and pulled into an empty spot.

The moment she left the car, her head cleared. Her sense of oppression probably meant nothing more than a cologne overdose and too many hours hunched over a keyboard, but her response to him felt deeper. It made her wary. "I doubt Day got in touch with Courtney," she said as they walked. "They weren't getting along by the time she moved in with me."

The teahouse was a local landmark and work of art, built in Tajikistan, transported in pieces, and reassembled in Boulder. The wall panels, moldings, and canopy were carved with arabesques and painted Persian blue, fretted with red and gold. A woman in a flowing skirt led them past the bronze Fountain of the Seven Beauties to their seats.

"I love this place," Tyson said. "It's like you're a genie inside a magic box."

"Do you bring your dates here?"

"Hey, I need all the magic I can get."

They assessed each other across the table.

"Joyce called you a player."

He laughed. "That's accurate."

"But you cared about Day after knowing her a week."

"Day wasn't like anyone else. We talked a lot. In a few days, I told her shit I never told my ex-wife. But she was—scared, I think, of getting too close and becoming dependent." Tyson fiddled with a puzzle ring, three bands entwined like snakes on the forefinger of his left hand. "I think she felt the same about you. She told me you were like the big sister she never had. But she had trouble accepting love. From anyone."

Their server showed up with water and menus. His spindly body and pinched mouth reminded her of Marcus, Odette's lover. Tyson ordered some kind of white tea without opening the menu, and Kelly said she would have the same.

"Odette Helm might know where Day went," she said. "Day had a darkroom at her house. She probably went there to pick up her negatives and prints."

Tyson shook his head. "I talked to Odette. Everything's still there."

"You know her?"

"Her husband and I are partners in a couple of business ventures. So yeah."

"What kind of business?"

"Nothing relevant to this."

Their silence filled with people's voices and the wheedling of flute music. Kelly faced what she wanted to avoid, the possibility that Day hadn't grown restless and moved on, that something had happened. A tiny fear caught at the bottom of her throat, a seed she couldn't swallow.

"Do you think Day's all right?"

Tyson glanced up from his puzzle ring. "Don't worry, she's a survivor."

"When was the last time you saw her?"

"Day before yesterday. We went for a drive in the mountains. She got a headache and wanted to go home. So I took her home."

The server brought their tea and told them to let it steep for another minute.

Kelly understood how women might be drawn to Tyson. He tried to appear dangerous. His strong nose and dark eyes reminded her of Caravaggio. She felt an unwilling response to something in his face, a yearning that reminded her of Day. She found it hard to look away from him. Then she spotted the red flag—his nostrils, bloody on the insides. He probably woke up every morning with blood on his pillow.

"You gave her coke."

He shrugged. "It's not like I forced her."

"She was bipolar. Your coke could've triggered a manic episode."

"So I'm supposed to feel guilty."

"If you care about her."

"Guilt won't help Day. It only hurts me."

"This isn't about you."

"Of course it is. I'm the central actor in my life, the hero of my own story. Anything I experience has to be 'about me'. It can't be any other way. The same goes for you. And Day."

The perfect philosophy for a guy who blew coke and wore his hair like a pirate. He probably cared about Day as much as someone like him could, enough to want her back but not enough to worry.

Tyson removed the basket of tea leaves from the pot, set it in the bowl provided, and poured the tea. "What about other artists? She must've known some."

"Annie Laible. Day asked about displaying photographs in her gallery, but Annie blew her off." Kelly and Annie were friends, the kind who meet occasionally for drinks, but the sculptor began avoiding Kelly after Day moved in.

"She lived in Boulder over a year," Tyson said. "Counting the time at Stuart's place. She had to know more than a half dozen people."

"I'm sure she met people. She did some freelance work while she was living with me."

"For who?"

"I don't know. The point is, her only friends were Odette and me. And she didn't . . ."

"Didn't what?" He jumped into the pause.

"Confide in me."

"Something just occurred to you. What?"

Kelly sipped the tea while she put together an answer. "Maybe Odette didn't tell you everything. You're her husband's business partner."

"So?"

"Maybe there's something she doesn't want her husband to find out, that's connected to why Day left."

"Like what?" Tyson threw down the question as a challenge.

"I don't know. But Odette might open up to me. Give me her number and I'll call her."

"I don't know her number."

"You said you talked to her."

"I was at their house."

"Where does she live?"

He shook his head. "The Helms are very private people."

So private that Odette had brought her lover to Kelly's house but wouldn't allow Kelly's to visit hers. "Don't you want to find out where Day went? You bring me here, you pump me for information, but you won't do the one thing that might help find the answer."

"Pumping you?" He laughed derisively. "Is that what I'm doing?"

The uneasy feeling was still there, the seed in her throat, and somehow Tyson had planted it. Until that moment she hadn't been ready to involve the police. "I'm going to report Day missing."

"Seriously? Sic the cops on Day and she'll get busted."

Tyson no doubt worried more about getting busted himself, but that was his problem. "We can't find her. Maybe they can."

"They won't give a shit about someone like Day. And you'll look stupid when she turns up stoned."

"So you're not worried about her?"

"Don't give them Odette's name."

"Why not?"

His face hardened into a mask. "Stuart doesn't like being bothered. Don't mess with him."

"Okay. Fine." She wasn't promising, only acknowledging his order. And it was an order, not a request. Tyson assumed that he could boss her around, that since she worked for the museum and Joyce, she also worked for him. He was welcome to go on thinking that.

The police station smelled of heat ducts and unwashed people. In the sunlit lobby a woman chatted with a girl holding a toddler, and a man in ripped jeans leafed through a *Time* magazine. They could have been waiting to see a doctor. A bulky woman in front of Kelly leaned over the counter. "Why can't I see him now?" she pleaded.

Kelly couldn't make sense of Gregory Tyson. He wanted to find Day, but he waved aside the possibility of her being in trouble and refused to help Kelly contact Odette. And why track down everyone Day knew? If she kept a secret from her friends, why would she confide in an acquaintance? Courtney was the only one she might have talked to. The two women had been close for a while. When Day had submitted her work for the exhibit at MOR, she had to give contact information, and because she'd been staying with Courtney then, she must have put Courtney's address on the application form. It would be on file.

The bulky woman walked away. The cop behind the counter began writing on a clipboard. His hair was combed to cover his bald spot.

"I'm here to report someone missing."

The cop looked up. "Okay."

"I was out of town last week. When I came back my room-mate had moved out."

"And when was this?"

"Yesterday. She was supposed to pick me up at the airport."

"With adults we don't take reports until they've been missing seventy-two hours. Come back Monday if she hasn't turned up." He went back to his clipboard.

Kelly doubted he was writing anything. He just needed a way of dismissing her. "At least give me the form to fill out."

"We don't—"

"I'll take this, Bob."

She turned.

The man behind her thrust out his hand. "Cash Peterson." Calluses ridged his palm beneath the fingers. A badge was clipped to his belt, and a gun bulged beneath his jacket. His bluff face and unruly blond hair suggested hours spent out-doors in the sun and wind. He wore scholarly glasses, square with black frames, and from behind them his eyes stared straight into hers. Green eyes like trees reflected in water, too pretty for a cop. "Come on back. I'll take your report."

"You do that, Cash," Bob said.

Kelly winced at the smirk in Bob's voice. He seemed to think Peterson planned to ask her out. She was pretty much over her ex-boyfriend, a divorced art professor with a five-year-old daughter. After several months of baby-sitting the kid while her father threw pots in his studio, she'd worked it out: He was too cheap to pay a baby-sitter. She felt a spark from Peterson and told herself it meant nothing. She wasn't ready to start a relationship.

He led her down a hallway to a room crowded with desks. Cops, most of them men, worked at computers or strode from place to place, looking purposeful even on the way to the restroom. Peterson had a desk by a window with a view of the street. He held out a chair for Kelly and then sat and began typing at a keyboard. Of course, the report went straight into the computer. Bob probably had no missing-person forms to hand out.

Peterson gathered the basic information: Day Randall, female, thirty-eight years old, medium brown hair, hazel eyes, five feet six inches tall. He took down Kelly's address and phone numbers for home and work.

"Day," he said. "Interesting name."

"She was named after a '70s rock band, It's a Beautiful Day."

"Never heard of them."

"Me either."

His gaze played over her face until the silence began to feel awkward. "Were the two of you getting along? Lots of times people just leave. You know?"

"Day's like that. A free spirit. But she promised to pick me up at the airport, and she usually keeps her promises."

"Usually."

The cynicism annoyed her, but what did she expect? His job was busting bad people. "Day's a good person."

"I'm sure she is. Why don't you tell me what happened?"

She gave him the whole story—the chemical smell in Day's room, the freshly washed Jeep with the keys on the seat, the Corolla still parked in front of the house.

"Why wouldn't Day take her car?"

"The brakes are shot."

"So she apparently used your vehicle to move her things and then got a ride from someone." Peterson rocked back in the desk chair. "She have a boyfriend?"

"His name's Gregory Tyson. But he doesn't know where she is."

"The businessman." His sarcasm cut into the word, suggesting something ugly.

"You know him?"

"We've met."

"Did you bust him?" She made the question a joke, but Peterson didn't laugh.

"Why would I bust an upstanding citizen like him?"

She decided not to mention that Day was bipolar and using coke. Peterson seemed judgmental, the type who might think mentally ill druggies were trash, not worth finding.

"Someone gave her a ride," Peterson said. "Who are her friends besides Tyson?"

"Odette Helm."

He blinked, his face expressionless.

"You know her," Kelly said.

He moved back to the computer. "What's her address?"

"She lives somewhere in the mountains. I've never been out there."

"Phone?"

"She's Day's friend, not mine."

Peterson studied Kelly with his incongruously pretty eyes. "You don't like her."

"It's not that. She just—" If she told him how the armed bodyguard barged into her house, he would ask why she hadn't called the police. The answer would make Day look worse. "I don't have much in common with Odette, that's all."

"Other friends?"

"Day lived with you for how long?"

"Eight months."

"But you know next to nothing about her associates."

Kelly bristled. This cop thought she was stupid. "Day didn't have associates. She was a loner. An artist. She lived with me and had a darkroom at Odette's house."

"An old-fashioned darkroom? No kidding?"

"She's a romantic. A very talented romantic."

"Do you have a recent photograph of her?"

Kelly shook her head. "She was always behind the camera."

"What about family?"

"She has parents. John and Sheila Randall. I don't know where they are."

Peterson added their names to the report. "You're not giving us a whole lot to work with." He turned back to her and his face softened. "I'm sorry, but I have to be straight with you. We probably won't find her. The police don't go looking for people unless they're minors, they've broken the law, or we have evidence they're in trouble. I get the idea your friend just took off." He reached into his jacket and offered her a card. "Call me if you have any new information."

◈

Coming home dead tired after a ten-hour workday at MOR, Kelly decided Tyson was right. Day would show up in two weeks or two months and she'd feel stupid for filing the missing-person report. She cringed at the thought of calling Peterson to explain.

When she hung up her coat in the hall closet, it immediately slid off the hanger onto the floor. Of course it did. A bad day couldn't have too many minor irritations. As she bent to pick it up, a patch of green caught her eye—the wool coat she'd given Day less than two months ago.

Day had asked to borrow the Jeep so she could shop for a winter coat at Goodwill. Kelly owned half a dozen that she seldom wore. "We're about the same size. I'll give you one of mine." She pulled coats out of various closets and spread them out on the sofa. "Take your pick." Day put on a khaki duffle and sashayed across the living room in a parody of a runway model. Kelly stuck a CD of pulsing electronic dance music in the stereo and paraded in a suede cowboy jacket with extravagant fringe—one of her more stupid purchases but fun to twirl around in. Day shed the duffle and slipped on a long black coat without skipping a beat. Kelly changed into the green coat, a sleek mid-thigh style that was unfortunately the wrong color for her. They vogued around the room in one coat after another, modeling all of them several times, and finally collapsed onto the carpet, breathless and giggling.

"So which one do you want?"

"The nice-girl coat."

"The green one? Not the cowboy jacket?"

"Nah. I'm gonna, uh, make an effort to look professional." Day pressed her mouth into a serious frown and then crossed her eyes and tilted her head sideways.

Kelly bent over laughing. She hadn't acted that goofy since high school. She'd thought she was no longer capable of such lighthearted fun, but it came easily to Day.

Now she fingered the coat that her friend had left behind. Maybe Day felt guilty about fading from her life and decided to return the gift. Or she'd simply forgotten it. Or someone else had moved her clothes, someone who didn't know about the green coat.

The uneasiness came back, the seed stuck in her throat. There was nothing big, nothing definite to prove Day hadn't gotten tired of Boulder and moved on, just a lot of small things that felt wrong.

Kelly remembered Owen with his arms folded stubbornly. *Give me the negative and then we can talk.* He knew something.

After last night he probably wouldn't come to the door, so she found his number in the Ash Mountain Owners' Association directory and called. His phone rang several times before he answered with a curt "Hello."

She talked fast. "Hi, it's Kelly. I want to apologize for last night."

After a long pause he said, "I apologize, too."

"I looked all over for the film roll with your picture on it. Day must've taken it with her. The only way we can get it back is to find her."

"Good luck with that."

"I'm going to try anyway. Look, if you saw anything —"

"Come over. They could be listening."

Kelly put her coat on again and walked across their front lawns to Owen's door, where he was waiting to let her in. This time he ushered her into his living room. "Want a cookie? I baked them myself."

"Thanks, Owen. That would be nice."

She settled into a butterfly chair. He brought a plate of cookies dabbed with red jelly and placed it on the table beside her. She popped one in her mouth, chewed slowly, and swallowed.

He perched on a chair across the room from Kelly and waited expectantly.

Kelly nodded. "Really good."

"I do a lot of baking."

She wanted to ask for water to wash down the dry cookie, but Owen's cooperative mood could shift to paranoia in an instant. "When did you see Day move out?"

"I didn't see her. I saw a guy shoving something into the hatch of your Jeep."

"When did you see this?"

"Last night. I was working and heard noise."

"What time?"

"Late. I don't live by the clock."

Day had moved out less than twenty-four hours before Kelly came home. "Did you see anyone bring the Jeep back?" she asked.

"I must've been asleep by then. I don't get up until afternoon except on Monday, when I check in with the company."

"The guy—what did he look like?"

"I just saw his general shape. He was taller than me, but who isn't? Not by much, though. He was stocky. I think he had on a baseball cap."

The description didn't match Tyson, who was thin and about six feet tall. "Did you notice anything else?"

"I saw a Jag parked out front, but I never saw the driver."

"What kind of Jag?"

"A black sedan. But Jags haven't been authentic since Ford bought the company, and now they're Third World junk."

Tyson's car. "When was it there?"

"Uh." Owen's eyes rolled upward, giving him a comical prophetic look. "Right after dark."

According to Tyson, he'd brought Day home after a drive in the mountains. He must have hung around for a while. "Was the Jag still there when you saw the guy in the baseball cap?"

"I'm pretty sure it was gone then." Owen squirmed on the edge of his chair. "That's all I saw. Honest."

"Thanks for your help. I really appreciate it." Kelly pushed herself out of the low-slung chair and started for the door.

He scurried after her. "Don't forget to find the negative. And get that Corolla towed."

⬧

Before calling Peterson with the new information, Kelly microwaved a bowl of soup and sat down to eat. She spread the *Boulder Daily Camera* on the table and checked the ad for MOR's holiday gala and silent auction. No matter how many times she proofread the copy, she fretted that a mistake had escaped her scrutiny. Joyce, of course, would notice. So she read through the ad again, searching for misspelled words and commas pretending to be periods and sentences where words had gone AWOL. The ad looked fine. Relieved, she turned the page and saw a news story.

Student Missing

Marcus A. French, a junior at the University of Colorado, Boulder, has been missing since November 24. He was last seen by his roommate, Alan Schwartz. "I thought he went home," Schwartz said.

His mother, Penny French of Grand Junction, expected him to arrive home on November 25.

According to Det. Cash Peterson, French stopped attending classes several days before he was last seen. "We're appealing to the community for information. Hopefully someone has seen him." Anyone with knowledge of French's whereabouts is asked to contact Det. Peterson at the Boulder Police Department.

Peterson picked up on the second ring.

"I have information about Day," Kelly said. "And about Marcus French."

"Ms. Durrell. Thank you for calling."

"My neighbor saw a stocky guy in a baseball loading stuff into my Jeep."

"So your friend left with a man. Makes sense. I'll add the description to the report, but it's not much to go on." He paused. "What do you know about Marcus French?"

"Marcus was seeing Odette Helm, and I think her husband found out."

"What makes you think so?" Peterson sounded less than surprised.

"They had sex in my house."

"When?"

"A week ago Thursday. The day before I left town."

He was silent for a moment. "How well did you know Marcus?"

"Hardly at all."

"But you let him and Odette have their trysts at your place. I got the impression you don't like her very much."

"Day brought them without asking me. What's going on?"

"I can't talk about an ongoing investigation. But anything you know could be important."

Kelly sighed. "Odette had a bodyguard. She sneaked away from him to meet Marcus. He showed up after she left and barged into my house pretending to look for her. She was outside sitting in his car. He just wanted to intimidate us."

"Why didn't you call the police?"

"Day asked me not to. She said it would cause trouble for Odette."

"How so?"

"Maybe she worried about Odette's husband finding out."

"But the bodyguard had already tracked her to your house. The husband was going to find out anyway."

"Then I don't know." Was she supposed to justify Day's thinking?

"I appreciate your help, Kelly." He spoke her name carefully, as if she might berate him for using it. "Anything else you can tell me about Marcus or Odette?"

"The bodyguard's name is Yount. He had a gun."

"Did he point it at you?"

"No. He just forced his way into my house, that's all."

"Did Yount threaten Marcus?"

"No, but he threatened me if I let him and Odette meet at my house again. Has something happened to Marcus?"

"What's Yount's first name?"

"I have no idea."

The detective paused, probably wondering if he could get more information from her. "Okay then. Thank you for letting me know."

"Will you look for Day now?"

"Yes, we will."

Kelly went on clutching the phone after Peterson hung up. She halted in the living room, where she'd been pacing back and forth during the call. Marcus had a family and a respectable identity as a student, so the cops investigated. Day wandered, cutting ties as she went, so they treated her disappearance as routine—until it became part of the search for Marcus. As much as she cared about Day, Kelly shared the prejudice. She would have reported Day missing and let it go if she hadn't found the green coat.

Peterson would never share information about the case. She would have to find out on her own what had happened to Day. She brewed a cup of Earl Grey and carried it to her office.

Tracking down Marcus French's roommate turned out to be easy. She found three listings for Alan Schwartz in the Boulder area and dialed the first number. Music and raucous voices almost drowned out the voice that answered. She introduced herself as Marcus's friend. "I can't hear you," Alan shouted. Then he hung up. Kelly had already hit "redial" when she got a text.

Who r u?

She ended the call and texted back. *My name's Kelly. I'm a friend of Marcus.*

He's gone

Can we meet somewhere?

Y?

To talk about Marcus.

Talk 2 the cops

I'd rather talk to you, in person.

Half a minute went by before his answer popped on the screen. *Y not*

They arranged to meet the next afternoon at Top O' the Morning, the bar in Louisville where Alan worked, just before his shift started at five. Louisville was a half-hour drive from the museum. She'd have to leave early and hope Joyce didn't catch her sneaking out.

The next day was Saturday. As always, Kelly went to work. At three-thirty she ran an online search of the address in Day's contact information and found Courtney Lamb. Another search yielded Courtney's phone number.

Before she could call it, Joyce barged into the office to complain about the auction program. She wanted margins that were more narrow and different fonts. Bent over Kelly's shoulder, she studied the drop-down menu and pointed to Lucinda Handwriting, a calligraphic font. "Use this on the cover."

Kelly shook her head. "Trite. And all wrong." She felt Joyce bristle.

"Exactly my reaction to your choice. Scroll down."

After a twenty-minute argument, they settled on a compromise. By then it was almost four o'clock. "I'll make the changes first thing tomorrow."

"Start now. You've got half an hour." Joyce swept out.

Kelly peered into the corridor. The door to Joyce's office was wide open, giving Joyce a full view of the exit. After thinking for a moment, Kelly picked up her bag and walked toward the beechwood door leading into the museum.

"Where are you going?"

She held her bag up. "Got my period."

She hurried through the museum, rode the elevator to the underground garage, and made her getaway. She was a mile away before Joyce would get suspicious and make Marta check the restrooms. Once she was out of town and the traffic thinned, she called Courtney, who answered with a bored "Yeah?"

"It's Kelly Durrell. Maybe you don't remember me. I'm—"

"What do you want?"

"Have you seen Day lately?"

"Yeah, last week."

"She moved out without telling me. Did she mention anything about leaving town?"

"Not really."

"When did you talk to her?"

"Last Monday. She invited us to a party."

"That same night?"

"No, the next one." Courtney's voice had an impatient edge. "What's with the interrogation? I don't know where Day is."

"She might've talked to someone at the party. Did you go?"

"Yeah. It sucked."

"Where was it?"

"In the mountains at this rich dude's place."

Helm's estate. "Do you remember how to get there?"

Courtney blew an exasperated sigh into the phone. "Dustin was driving. Hold on." A couple of minutes ticked by, long enough for Kelly to wonder if she was being blown off. Then Courtney came back. "Dustin wants to draw you a map."

"It's that complicated?"

"I don't know. Dustin's just—Dustin. Meet us tonight at the Cascade. It's a bar on the Diagonal Highway. We can have a drink or whatever, and Dustin will give you the map. Come around ten thirty."

◆

Kelly found a parking spot in Louisville's Old Town shopping district and walked a block and a half to Top O' the Morning, a bar and sandwich shop decorated with stained-glass panels picturing shamrocks and leprechauns. Celtic music played on the sound system. Alan Schwartz sat in a booth near the back, shoulders hunched as if he knew they were too wide for his skinny chest.

She slid onto the seat across from him. "Hi, Alan. I'm Kelly."

Alan yawned. "What's up?" He had the smudged look of someone who had just crawled out of bed. He grinned and swigged a draft beer. "Want one?"

"No, thanks."

He raised the empty mug and wiggled it. "Yo, Hannah!"

The server gave Alan a brisk nod and went on taking the order of a couple nearby. "Hannah likes girls." His tone insinuated that straight women fetched him beers at once. Unruly locks curled over his forehead in a way he no doubt thought was sexy. His eyes gleamed with humor, and he gave her the smirk of an intelligent person who'd sworn off serious thought. In ten years, no longer twentysomething, Alan would be the kind of drunk that people pretended not to see.

Kelly put a ten-dollar bill on the table. "Let me buy."

"Hey, thanks."

"You're a lot different than Marcus. How did you guys end up sharing a place?"

"Put an ad in the paper and he answered. He seemed like an okay guy."

"Was he?"

"You know Marky. He takes everything way too seriously. It gets old. The recycling thing was the worst. I have friends over and they throw cans in the trash and trash in the recycling bin, so Marky has a shit fit and tells me to separate out the cans. I had a fucking hangover. I felt like bitch-slapping him."

"Did you?"

"Nah, I just left. Marky separated the cans. He tried to make me feel guilty, but fuck that."

Hannah brought the beer and plucked the ten from the table.

Squinting in the dim barroom light, Alan studied Kelly for the first time. "You're pretty different from Marky, too. How do you know him?"

"Through Odette."

Another smirk. "His Juliet. Yeah, he's gonna save her from her rich old husband. Like she wants to be saved."

"You think she doesn't?"

"Hey, she's your friend. I don't wanna dis her."

"It's okay. I'm interested in what you think."

He downed half the beer in one swig and wiped his mouth on his sleeve. "Why?"

"I want to find out what happened to Marcus."

"You and the cops."

"Well, I'm not them."

"Yeah, I get that." Alan eyed her with bleary suspicion and jabbed a forefinger at her. "But who are you?"

Hannah came back with the change. "Bring another one," he said.

"You haven't finished this one and your shift starts in a few minutes."

"I'll have a beer," Kelly said.

Hannah glared at her. "So you know, the boss is gonna fire him if he gets smashed again."

Kelly felt a twinge of guilt and then decided not to care. It worked for Alan. "So, about Marcus and Odette."

"Hey, why not? I already told the cop. I saw Odette a few times when Marky brought her to the apartment. She whined how her life sucked, she had no freedom, blah, blah, blah. Then bitched how our bathroom's tiny and we don't have fresh fruit. Once she showed off a T-shirt she bought." Alan mimed holding the shirt with exaggerated delicacy as if to say, *Ooh, look at this.* "It cost, like, four bills."

"She likes having nice things."

"I heard them talking. It's not like I was trying to listen, but the walls are paper-thin and sometimes they got loud. She said her husband was gonna divorce her and give her a bunch of money. She wanted Marky to wait."

"What did he say?"

"He thought the old dude was e-e-e-evil." Alan widened his eyes and fluttered his fingers.

When Hannah came back with the second beer, Kelly held out a five-dollar bill. "Keep the change." She slid the mug across the table. "Did you hear anything else?"

"It's not like I was glued to the wall listening. And most of the time they weren't talking. He was in there banging away at her. You wouldn't guess, the little geek is a sexual dynamo. Or maybe you don't need to guess." He leered at her.

"I haven't seen Odette around either," she said. "You think it's possible he and Odette ran off together?"

"Maybe. If she changed her mind about the divorce."

"What happened the last time you saw Marky?"

Alan finished the old mug of beer and took a long gulp of the fresh one. "He was packing for Thanksgiving break. He was gonna drive to Grand Junction next morning."

"When was this?"

"Late Saturday afternoon."

"But he didn't leave."

"I thought he did. I stayed out pretty late. His door was closed when I got back, so I figured he was sleeping. And he was gone when I woke up."

"Could he have still been asleep?"

"No way. Marky gets up ridiculously early. Anyway, I stayed home Sunday watching football and had the TV cranked. I usually keep it low 'cause it bothers him. If he was in there, he would've come out and bitched. Then Monday his mom called asking where he was and that's when I checked his room and found his duffel."

"He wasn't going anywhere Saturday night? Even for a while?"

"He wanted to crash so he could get an early start."

She wondered whether Marcus had kept a secret from his roommate or something happened to change his plans.

"Hey, it's been fun talking and all, but I gotta get ready for work."

"One more thing. Who was the detective who questioned you?" Kelly had a pretty good idea who. She just wanted to confirm her guess.

"Shit, I don't remember. He had nerd glasses and hiking boots." Alan pushed out of the booth and stood, wobbling a little. "They all look the same to me."

The Cascade was a lofty T-shaped building with a clapboard exterior and gabled roofs. It had always reminded Kelly of a photograph of an abandoned mine terminal she'd seen on a postcard once. Floodlights illuminated the area around the building. Farther away, the parking lot was dark except for lamps bordering the access road. She parked under one of them.

She remembered the bouncer from the times she'd gone dancing there, a bodybuilder type with a ferocious grin and unruly hair. The customers were a mix of college students, thirtysomethings who played wild on weekends, and a scattering of dopers and barflies. A sound system blasted hip-hop that vibrated the floor and echoed off a high ceiling where Christmas decorations hung from wires crisscrossed between the rafters—dozens of bright globes, pale angels, and stars coated in glitter dangled amid a mass of tinsel icicles.

She passed the dance floor on the left and walked along a horseshoe bar stretching toward the back. Most of the ground level was open to the roof thirty-five feet above, but a mezzanine jutted over the floor space on the right side, its enclosing wall overlooking the bar.

A mural in acrylic paint covered the wall. Three waterfalls sliced the space into diagonals, and dozens of electric-blue trout and dwarfish miners tumbled over the falls in an ecstatic frozen ride. The artist had drawn inspiration from Max Beckmann and other Expressionists. The mural was crudely done and its style clashed with the architecture of the building, but Kelly couldn't help admiring its energy.

She slipped past the drinkers at the bar and scanned the shadowy area beneath the mezzanine. She couldn't see Courtney among the people crowded around the small tables. Then a woman with platinum hair waved at her. Last spring Courtney's hair had been hennaed, and she'd favored T-shirts and cropped jeans. Tonight she wore a fringed emerald dress overlaid with black lace. A gold pentacle winked on her nostril, and her eyelids were armored with black liner. "Hey," she shouted above the music. "This is Dustin."

Dustin greeted her with a fishhook smile. His oversize Nine Inch Nails T-shirt emphasized the scrawniness of his neck and arms. Another guy at the table floated a stupefied look in her direction. His skin, spotted by an overhead light, had the gloss of basted turkey. A girl clung to his arm.

Courtney said something that got swallowed by the noise.

Kelly leaned closer and caught a whiff of cigarettes and patchouli.

"The mezzanine." Courtney pointed to stairs behind them. She and Dustin walked off without glancing at the other couple.

A staircase slanted up the back wall, enclosed by a solid waist-high balustrade. Anyone going up or down could be seen from below. Empty except for a few pool players, the mezzanine shuddered with aftershocks from the subwoofer.

The hooded lamps above the pool tables flickered in her peripheral vision but steadied when she looked straight at them. The place felt like a refuge from disaster, somewhere to wait for terrible news.

They sat at a table made of recycled planks, the weathered grain embalmed in polyurethane.

"Tell me about the party," Kelly said.

Courtney sniffed. "They weren't exactly thrilled to see us. They did this tight-ass nice-to-meet-you thing and then blew us off."

"Let's take care of business first." Dustin rubbed his thumb against his fingers and stared at Kelly expectantly.

"What? You want money?"

"You want information?" He grinned, displaying teeth too large and square for his narrow face. "Say, fifty bucks?"

"I thought Day was your friend."

"She was a user." Courtney's voice trembled with injury. "Like when she was my roommate? I asked for the rent up front, but she said she worked on commission. She promised to pay when she sold a photo. Then she blew me off and moved in with you."

"She gave you a portrait of yourself."

"So what? Like the landlord gives a shit about my portrait."

In the photograph, Courtney's matchstick body reclined on a fountain's edge, one makeup-laden eye and half a smile peeking from behind her outstretched arm. Day had fretted over the printing and matting. She thought her gift mattered more than money.

Dustin braced his elbows on the table. "We got lots of information. Stuff about her boyfriend and the party. Plus the map. Fifty bucks is no big deal. Not for you. "Make out the check to Dustin Schneider."

Kelly had chosen to buy Alan Schwartz a couple of beers. This was different. She almost walked away, but she couldn't contact Odette without a phone number or address. Her choice was to pay Dustin or forget the whole thing, forget Day.

She scooped her checkbook from her bag, wrote the check, and pushed it across the table. "I'm sure this is once in a lifetime for you, getting paid for what you know."

"Whoa. No need to get bitchy. I wouldn't be doing this except we're broke."

Courtney heaved a sigh as if Kelly were the one making things difficult.

"You're helping us out," Dustin said. "People helping each other—that's a good thing." He unfolded a scrap of paper and slapped it on the table. It was a fragment of a road map. Yellow magic marker traced Highway 119 from Boulder to Nederland and then cut north on Highway 72 and ended at a flamboyant yellow asterisk in the middle of nowhere.

"The house is on the highway?"

"It's back a ways. But the road's paved and all. Right before you turn, there's a weird rock formation. Like a statue of Dracula with his cape spread out."

"What did you want from Day? You wouldn't help her unless you wanted something."

"Just to score some coke," he said. "Someone gave Courtney a number to call, and it was Day that answered."

"Surprise, surprise," Courtney said.

"Who gave you the number?"

"The dude we were sitting with downstairs. And don't bother asking where he got it. He won't remember. Anyway, she wasn't the connection. It was a friend of hers and she answered his phone. But he didn't have any coke."

Cold crept up Kelly's spine. What friend? Tyson?

"Day said there would be coke at this party she was going to," Courtney said. "Like, she knew it wasn't cool, bringing us. She went upstairs with Odette and left us with these Ralph Lauren losers."

"The food was kick-ass," Dustin said. "This huge platter of smoked salmon and a fridge full of Corona. They had a home theater with hundreds of DVDs. We watched *Nightmare on Elm Street.* Then we went home."

"You didn't see Day again?"

"She stayed upstairs with those freaks. Probably munching Odette's carpet while the old dude whacked off." Dustin folded his arms and smirked as if his juvenile crudity would blow Kelly's world apart.

"Oh, please." Courtney eyed him with contempt.

"They were in the bedroom for hours. What you think they were doing?"

"Coke, asshole. They just didn't want to share."

The old dude must have been Stuart Helm. From what Kelly knew of him, she doubted he'd been partying with his wife and Day. So why hole up in the bedroom? And where was Tyson? He claimed to know Helm—why hadn't he taken Day to the party?

❖

Kelly zigzagged between rows of vehicles, the windshields crusted with frost. Behind her the slam of a door exploded like a gunshot. Off to her left, someone shouted, "Yo, bitch, you okay?" Two guys tittered and peered through a car window. One of them rapped on the glass. "You okay? You okay in there?" Louder each time. The other one said something that made both of them laugh, and then they staggered off. Curious, she detoured to the car. It was outside the spill of the lamplight, so she saw only the grotesquely flattened cheek and tangled hair of a woman passed out behind the wheel. The woman had to be deeply unconscious not to feel the icy glass.

Idiot. Kelly's sister had died because of a drunk driver. She started walking toward her Jeep. The woman probably had drinking buddies who would notice her car when they left the Cascade. If not, an employee would investigate after closing time. But if no one bothered, she could freeze to death by morning.

Kelly backtracked to the car. She tried the driver's door and then the other three. Someone about to pass out wouldn't think to lock the doors, but her arm might have pressed the lock switch by accident. Kelly rapped the window and yelled, "Hey!" She rapped several more times, so hard the woman's head must have vibrated from the blows.

No response.

Calling 911 meant waiting for someone to show up. Otherwise they might not find the car. Then she would spend an hour answering questions. After working all day and driving to Louisville and then rushing home for dinner and out again to the Cascade, Kelly needed rest. The bouncer could make the call.

He was still guarding the door, balanced on a stool that looked too fragile to hold his weight. He rolled a tangled lock of hair between his thumb and forefinger while Kelly told him about the woman. "You think something's wrong with her? Besides being drunk on her ass."

"She's totally out of it. She could freeze. I'll show you where she's parked."

"No can do. I'm watching the door."

"Someone has to help her. Want me to call 911?"

"Hold on." The bouncer eased off the stool, turned his muscular back, and muttered into his phone. He faced Kelly again. "Okay, someone's coming down. We're about to close. You'd best go home."

"You need me to show you where the car is."

"We'll find it once the lot clears out."

Kelly sat on a bench in the vestibule and waited. Every time someone opened the door, the cold air blasted her. For the next twenty minutes, tipsy customers shuffled and lurched into the night. She yearned for her warm bed, but she doubted they would help the unconscious woman if she took off. She walked over to the bouncer. "You said someone was coming."

"That's what I was told."

"I'm calling 911."

The bouncer knotted his forehead and sized her up. "I bet she's woke up and took off by now."

"Why don't we go and check?"

He turned his back and had another muttered conversation with his phone. "The manager's coming. Happy?"

Kelly stood next to him as more people crowded through the vestibule, Courtney and Dustin among them.

Dustin veered toward her and winked. "You hustling a date with Animal?"

Animal was the perfect name for the hulking bouncer. He watched the parking lot empty out, headlights cutting on and streaming to the exits. "Where's the car you're talking about?"

It was hidden behind vehicles streaming toward the exit. "There." Kelly pointed. "You can't see it right now."

"You say there's someone passed out in our parking lot."

She turned around. The manager crowded her with broad shoulders and heavy biceps, his moon face almost touching hers. His skin reminded her of lumpy oatmeal. No doubt he was bald beneath the Dodgers cap. She backed up a step. "She's locked inside her car. I knocked on the window and yelled, but she didn't wake up."

The manager took off ahead of Kelly and then stopped to wait. They crossed the parking lot without speaking.

"Here's the car."

The woman's cheek was still plastered against the glass.

The manager pulled a large ring of keys from one pocket and a flashlight from another. He gave the flashlight to Kelly. She held the beam on his keys—two dozen, at least—while he picked through them.

"You have a key to her car?"

"It's an oh-ten Chrysler. I got something that fits."

She began to shiver. "Where did you get all those?"

"I pick 'em up here and there." The manager unlocked the driver's door and yanked it open. A reek of alcohol and air freshener penetrated the cold. "What the fuck. It's Nina." He thrust his hand under her hips and found her keys.

"You know her?"

"She's one of our bartenders, but she's off tonight." He switched on the dome light and pushed her upright. Nina was tiny and cherub-like, with wispy blond hair. He pressed a button to unlock the other doors. "Go 'round to the other side and get her purse." Kelly retrieved a red leather clutch from the foot well. He wrestled Nina from the car and let her slump against him while he hooked his elbow beneath her armpit. Kelly hurried to support her other shoulder. She weighed a hundred pounds at most. They hauled her across the parking lot, her toes dragging the pavement.

Animal rushed outside to meet them. "What's wrong with her?"

"Nothing," the manager said. "She's just shitfaced. Someone her size—four or five shots is gonna knock her on her ass."

Animal scooped Nina into his arms, carried her into the vestibule, and lowered her gently onto the bench. He squatted and chafed her small hands between his big ones.

"She needs a doctor," Kelly said.

"She's breathing just fine," the manager said. "You think she wants to wake up in the hospital with a hangover?"

Kelly began to shiver. "Why come here when she's not working?"

"They let her drink for free and I pretend not to notice."

"Bullshit," Animal said. "She has a sandwich and maybe one beer."

"But how did she get to her car?" Kelly said.

"Probably staggered out the back so we wouldn't see her," the manager said. "I'll take her home and have someone bring her to work tomorrow."

"I'll do it," Animal said. "We're closing in a couple minutes."

"Get back on the stool and do your fucking job."

Kelly imagined curling up in bed, her feet warm, but she was afraid for Nina. Something about the manager. He acted helpful, but his sudden anger, his stubbornness—it felt wrong. Why not let the bouncer take Nina home? Unless the manager had to be certain she didn't end up at the ER. "Why don't you drive Nina home in her car? I'll follow and give you a ride back."

"This is none of your business."

"Yeah, it is." Animal folded his massive arms. "She found Nina."

"You're both a pain in the ass."

The manager drove the Chrysler with Nina in the backseat. Kelly followed in her Jeep, shivering long after the heater began pumping out warmth. He drove with impatience and contempt for other people, the kind of jerk who never got anywhere faster but needed to feel like he was beating everyone else. With the stoplights and traffic on Broadway, she had to stay alert to keep up. He barreled through a red light and left her sitting but got stuck behind a law-abiding driver at the next one, giving her time to catch up. She hung with the Chrysler through another red light and turned left onto Arapahoe. A few minutes later he pulled to the curb without bothering to signal.

Nina lived in a run-down house that had been converted to apartments. They pulled her out of the car and carried her up the porch steps. A light shone on the entrance, four mailboxes nailed to its wide jamb. "Her last name's Ivan," the manager said.

Kelly checked the labels on the mailboxes. "It's number three."

"Upstairs. Just our fucking luck."

She held the screen door open while he dragged Nina inside. Nina's head lolled against her chest, and her eyelids hung partway open, as mechanical as a doll's. No matter how drunk the woman was, she should have reacted to being manhandled. The hallway smelled like a dog kennel. A low-wattage bulb in the ceiling cast feeble light in which objects seemed to half-exist. Kelly gazed up the steep narrow stairs—a hard climb, even with two of them carrying Nina.

The manager laughed, his face hard with mockery. "This is what you get for playing good Samaritan, Kelly."

He knew her name. How? While they hauled Nina up the stairs, Kelly reviewed every moment since she'd found Nina. She hadn't given her name to him or Animal. She was certain.

He propped Nina against a wall while Kelly took the red clutch out of her much larger bag, found the key inside, and unlocked the door. "She doesn't have a phone."

"So? She dropped it in her car or at the Cascade. Either way, she'll get it back."

The apartment consisted of a former bedroom with a kitchenette built into a recess that had probably once been a dressing area. Its desperate neatness seemed like a dam against chaos. The manager dumped Nina onto a bed with a carved mahogany headboard, the satin finish chipped and gouged. Kelly rolled her onto her side and slipped a pillow under her head and then pulled a comforter over her. She laid two fingertips to her wrist. The pulse felt weak.

"She's okay," the manager said. "She just needs to sleep it off."

"You seem pretty sure."

"What am I supposed to do, fucking cry?"

Kelly placed the keys and clutch on a window seat where Nina couldn't miss them. Then she dug a pen and business card from her bag and jotted a note: "I helped bring you home. Please call and let me know you're okay." She slipped the card beneath Nina's keys.

The manager glanced at the card and hissed in disgust. "You done causing trouble?"

The feeling of wrongness clung to her on the drive back to the Cascade. They rode in silence to the outskirts of town. "How do you know my name?"

He held the answer for about ten seconds. "You told me."

"No."

"Then it must've been Animal."

"No." She was certain she hadn't given her name to the bouncer.

"It was Animal. He said a girl named Kelly found a drunk passed out in a car."

He was digging in behind the explanation. No matter how many times she said no, he would say yes. She scoured her memory for an occasion when she might have met him briefly or been noticed by him. Nothing came. Her mind blinked like a light bulb with defective wiring.

"So what's your name? You know mine, I ought to know yours."

"Welch."

"Is that your first or last name?"

"Just Welch."

She signaled for the turn into the Cascade. The building was dark, an inky blackness surrounded by the parking lot spotted with floodlights. "Should I drop you at your car?"

"No, in front." She cut a diagonal across the empty lot and stopped at the entrance. Welch reached for the door latch. She felt the pressure of his gaze. "Do yourself a favor and forget about tonight. Nina got drunk. Don't turn it into something more."

Something more—like what? He got out of the Jeep, shut the door, and strode to the vestibule on short legs. A moment later the building swallowed him, but she kept staring at the entrance as if he might have dropped the answer there.

Kelly opened the curtains on the living room window overlooking her backyard. Beyond the grass white with hoarfrost, a forest of spindly pine stretched up the mountainside. The sky, flat and shining, threatened snow. Not an auspicious day to drive into the mountains following the directions of a stoner in a Nine Inch Nails T-shirt.

The refrigerator hummed, the only sound. Day would have turned on the TV or played music or challenged her to a game of gin rummy. She eyed the TV. On Sunday morning, the talking heads droned politics or shouted religion. Day loved making fun of them, but they depressed Kelly.

The phone chimed, muffled inside her bag. She waited a few seconds before she walked to the dinner table, where her bag sat on a chair, and took out the phone. Dad again. At this hour in Illinois, her parents were probably returning from church, Dad steering along a country road while Mom sat glumly beside him, steeling herself to talk to her estranged daughter. Kelly couldn't face them now. Maybe tonight.

She couldn't face the empty house either. She climbed the stairs and changed into warm clothes for the drive to Nederland. The directions had cost her fifty dollars—she might as well make use of them.

❖

Highway 119 tracked Boulder Creek upstream through bottlenecks and blasted rock, sudden curves and harrowing switchbacks, rising more than three thousand feet in sixteen miles. She swallowed to make her ears pop. Snow was falling, a sloughing of powder from the pale sky. The drone of the engine and the tick-tock of windshield wipers were becoming hypnotic. Music would help, but she didn't want to mess with CDs or radio dials on the twisting road. She passed a waterfall where sightseers flocked in the summer, now shriveled to a glaze of ice over craggy rock.

She kept puzzling over last night, the strangeness of it. How Welch had known her name. She hadn't told Animal. Dustin and Courtney, the only ones who could have told him, left the club before he showed up. He'd insisted on taking Nina home to make sure Kelly didn't take her to the ER instead. She'd needed a doctor—Kelly should have insisted. And Welch seemed confident that Nina wouldn't wake up, no matter how roughly or disrespectfully he handled her—hauling her like a sack of grain, burrowing his hand beneath her butt and pulling out her car keys.

Kelly drew a sharp breath.

How did he know Nina was sitting on her keys? She could have dropped them anywhere, but he went straight to them.

Welch had put her in the car.

As manager, he might take it on himself to remove a drunk from the Cascade, but Nina worked there. He'd left her outside, where she could have frozen to death. And he'd sneaked her out the back. He could have drugged and raped her. Kelly had Detective Peterson's card but nothing to report except a secondhand story the others would deny.

Welch fit Owen's description of the man loading stuff into Kelly's Jeep—short and stocky, wearing a baseball cap—and he knew her name. Peterson might be interested in that coincidence if he were looking for Day half as hard as he was looking for Marcus French.

She drove past a frozen lake. Stray snowflakes whirled above its surface as the sky cleared and sunlight ruffled over Nederland. The town clung like a vine to the slope of the valley. Its root was the interchange where 119 connected with Highway 72. From there it grew into the downtown—a supermarket, a building shaped like a cracker box that housed various stores, and an antique train car converted to a café—and then branched into residential streets and unfurled its tendrils over the slope, where they blossomed into a few dozen luxury homes.

She went north on 72, past the road to Rainbow Lake and a dude ranch closed for the winter, searching for the turnoff to Helm's place. She started looking for a rock formation that resembled Dracula. Supposedly. In Dustin's zoned-out brain, things must morph into monsters all the time. If Dracula had retreated to his coffin, she could always go back to Nederland and ask for directions. The locals might know about Helm's estate even if they had no idea who it belonged to.

The landmark rock loomed on her right, jutting from the pines, vaguely cape-like. A hundred feet beyond it she spotted the turnoff. Nobody had driven to or from Helm's place that morning. Her tires cut black ribbons of asphalt in blank snow. It must have cost a fortune to build a paved road in the mountains.

Leftover snowflakes sifted through a canopy of Douglas fir. The growl of her engine was loud in the silence. She spotted animal tracks. Then an eight-foot gate mounted to two concrete obelisks blocked the road. A bronze plate with raised letters was riveted to the bars:

No Trespassing!
Please Respect Our Space.

A surveillance camera capped with snow peered down from the left obelisk. Beyond the gate, the road continued underneath the trees with no house in sight. Dustin hadn't mentioned the gate. It had probably been open for the party.

She shut off the engine and waited for someone to show up. Minutes passed. Cold crept into the Jeep. The iron bars, the camera, and the warning sign—everything pointed to some kind of illegal activity. Drug dealing? Odette always had plenty of drugs.

Kelly got out of the car and walked closer. An electric fence stretched from both ends of the gate. Insulator spools were attached to metal poles, and through them ran three strands of electrified wire. A determined intruder might crawl beneath the lowest strand and risk getting zapped, but not a casual hiker or hunter. The gate was the same, forbidding but not impossible. Horizontal rails braced its bars in the middle and near the top. An intruder could climb the gate and risk being impaled by the spikes on top.

A Land Rover with oversize tires and an ugly rectangular grille appeared among the trees. The cold stung her face and fogged her breath. By the time the Land Rover halted on the other side of the gate, she was shivering. The vehicle's doors opened like blunt wings. Two men jumped out. She recognized Odette's bodyguard and Animal, the bouncer from the

Cascade. Yount's eyes were hidden behind the sunglasses sitting on his blunt nose, and his mouth looked like a pencil line. His lambskin coat bulged beneath the left arm. He marched up to the gate. "What can we do for you?""

"I want to talk to Odette."

"I don't think she's expecting you."

"Day's gone missing, and I thought maybe—"

"I keep track of who comes and goes. Day hasn't been around for weeks."

"She came to a party here last week. I guess you were off-duty."

Kelly felt his harsh inspection through the sunglasses. Her heart began thumping.

"And you know this how?" he said.

"From the people she came with. They told me there was smoked salmon and Corona, and Day went upstairs with Odette and Stuart and stayed there a long time."

"Stuart? So you're Mr. Helm's friend, too? Then you have to know he doesn't like people showing up uninvited. Why didn't you call before driving up here?"

"The number's unlisted."

"There's a reason for that. Mrs. Helm would have given you the number if she welcomed your calls."

"You bulled your way into my house uninvited. I think you should cut me some slack."

Yount's thin lips crimped in a smile. "All right. What is it you have to say to Mrs. Helm? I'll make sure she gets the message."

"Can't I just talk to her? Call and ask if she'll see me."

"Mrs. Helm isn't feeling well. She's unable to leave the house at present."

"We can talk on the phone."

"She doesn't wish to be disturbed."

"You didn't tell the truth about Day being here. Why should I believe anything you say about Odette?"

"I don't give a fuck if you believe me."

Kelly's face burned against the frigid air. "Will you give her my message?"

"I said I would."

She went back to the Jeep and found the small notebook she used to keep track of gas mileage. She tore out a blank page and scrawled her name and number along with her message: "Day's gone, please get in touch," with *please* underlined. She handed the sheet to Yount through the bars.

Her message would never be delivered. This wasn't security—it was prison.

Yount tucked the notepaper inside his coat, hitching back his arm to show her the holster and butt of his handgun. "We'll be around. In case you're thinking about coming back."

Animal stood beside the Land Rover. Kelly tried to catch his eye, but he fended her off with a scowl and a diffuse stare. She called to him. "I thought you worked at the Cascade."

"She knows you," Yount said without turning to face him.

"Not really. She thinks we're on intimate terms 'cause I talked to her once."

"About what?"

"We had someone passed out in their car. She come and reported it."

Yount nodded. "The responsible thing. Keeping drunk drivers off the road. You're such a good citizen. I want you to promise you won't bother Mrs. Helm."

"I haven't bothered anyone. Stop treating me like a stalker."

"Then don't act like one. If we catch you around here again, you'll be detained and arrested for trespassing. And we absolutely will press charges."

"I've reported Day missing," she said as Yount walked away. "I told the cops all about you invading my home."

Yount let go of the Land Rover's door and turned to face her. "You may regret that. If Mr. Helm is bothered, he'll be forced to take legal action."

"Let him. I can hire a lawyer, too."

They stared at each other through the bars for a harrowing minute. Finally, Kelly retreated to the Jeep. The men watched her maneuver a cramped turn and head down the driveway. The spiked gate receded in her rearview mirror. She clung to the steering wheel, knowing she would tremble if she loosened her grip.

They waited to make sure Kelly was gone before heading back to the house.

It bothered Animal, running into her. Assholes came up to him on the street acting like his personal friend because they knew him from the Cascade. Not that Kelly was an asshole. She'd stuck up for Nina, a stranger who meant nothing to her. And she hadn't called him Animal. He hated the nickname and the way it stuck to him. Yount was an asshole, but at least he addressed him by his last name, Beaumont. Animal appreciated that. Beaumont sounded like the name of someone important, someone competent. A man who might be recruited for full-time employment by Guardians Inc., the premier private security firm on the West Coast.

Animal was driving, so Yount couldn't pretend to be "on task," his favorite way of not listening. The dude crossed his legs like a girl afraid of getting her cherry busted, but he was a mean son of a bitch. Not someone you wanted to mess with.

"You done more thinking about me coming to work for Guardians on a permanent basis?"

"No. Why? Should I have?"

"We talked about it. Like I said, I'd be willing to relocate if that's what it takes."

"I told you there were problems with your records."

That bullshit again. "I never been convicted of anything but DUI."

"You were charged with aggravated assault. There would've been a trial if the man you pounded hadn't left the state."

"He left to save himself from being slammed with a perjury charge. It ain't fair using that against me. I'm innocent until proved guilty."

"That's correct, Beaumont. But it doesn't entitle you to employment."

"You saying I haven't done a good job?"

"Not at all. Any time I need someone to fill in, you're the first one I call. But you can't be permanent without being bonded. There's the problem."

In the early '80s, Animal had worked on a seismograph crew with a dynamiter who'd done time for possession with intent. The dude loved blowing things up—rocks, pine trees, even a cow once—and he was bonded to handle explosives. Which proved that even a maniac could be bonded.

"What's the matter, Beaumont? Aren't you happy working for Tyson?"

Now they were getting to the real reason. Guardians wouldn't take the chance of pissing off a client. "Tyson does right by me. I just feel like it's time for a new direction."

"Can't move up, so you have to move out."

"Something like that."

His dissatisfaction with the job boiled down to Welch, who controlled everything at the Cascade, including access to the boss. Animal spoke to Tyson about twice a month, and then it was "How's it going?" and "Just dandy." Any real communication had to go through Welch. Animal suspected that the asshole had done something nasty to Nina, but he couldn't take the chance of telling Tyson and not being believed. Tyson might even know and not give a shit. Seemed like he cared about coke and pussy and not much else.

Animal had better sense than to share any of this with Yount, who took a dim view of violating the confidentiality of clients.

There was plenty to violate with Odette Helm. She cheated on her old man and everyone knew it. Sometimes she paraded around half naked in front of him and Yount and the housekeeper. In his fantasy he asked Odette if she'd ever done it with an animal. She smiled her magical soft-focus smile, stretched out her hand, and led him upstairs. Then the icy breath of reality brushed the back of his neck. He could guess how that story ended. Odette would turn out to be nothing special. Guardians would never hire him again, even part time. Then some doc-in-a-box would diagnose him with some weird incurable clap her old man had caught from a whore in Southeast Asia. Then his dick would fall off.

The Land Rover emerged in the clearing in front of the house. "Park in the driveway," Yount said. "You'll be using the Rover this afternoon."

"It's a waste of time patrolling. She ain't coming back."

"You're a mind-reader? Come on then, tell me. What she's thinking?"

Animal felt kind of sorry for Kelly. She wanted to find her friend. He doubted that either of the Helms cared enough about anybody to go looking for them. Yount would look, but only if you paid him.

He followed Yount to the back door. "You gonna give Odette the note?"

"Are you questioning my professional integrity?"

"Hell no." At the entry to the kitchen, Animal bent over to take off his wet boots. The old lady housekeeper would be on his ass if he tracked in mud.

"Leave them on, Beaumont. You'll be going back outside." Yount went into the media room, where Odette was watching a movie. The soundtrack music shrieked like the orchestra was being tortured. Animal wandered into the kitchen, plucked a bottle of Evian from the smaller fridge, and escaped to the deck.

He reached over the cedar railing and ruffled his fingers through the treetops. Gazing down the mountainside and across the valley to mountains in the distance—miles and miles of open space—he felt himself expanding, the pressure gone. Then sunshine broke through the clouds and glittered off the snow, so intense that he squinted. He stood there awhile, his mind blank. Inside the house, the music shrieked again when Yount came out of the media room. Reluctantly, Animal turned away from the mountains and went back inside.

Yount ducked into the pantry behind the kitchen and brought out a roll of heavy-duty garbage bags. "Come on downstairs. You have another job before you check the gate."

A flight of corkscrew stairs led to the basement level, which was built into the hillside. Through a row of windows, you could view the shaded ground under the deck and the trunks of trees beyond. He and Yount skirted a treadmill and a row of weight machines.

In a short hallway, Yount unlocked the door to what looked like a storage area. The windowless room had shelves, a narrow cabinet, and a Formica counter along two walls. There was a sink, large plastic trays, and a bunch of equipment. "What's all this?"

"You don't need to know." Yount tossed the roll of garbage bags onto the floor. "Pack everything. Double up on the bags and don't stuff them too full. When you're done, load 'em into that beater of yours." The prick never missed a chance to bad-mouth Animal's 1998 Mustang. The engine ran a little rough, but the Stang carried Animal anywhere he needed to go.

Yount waved toward a shelf that held three cardboard boxes in different colors, each with a label stuck inside a little metal frame. "Give these to your boss."

"Tyson?"

"He's the man you work for, isn't he? Get rid of everything else. Discreetly. Your best bet would be the university dumpsters, a couple bags a night at different spots."

"Some of it looks like it's worth money."

"Yeah, well, you're paid enough you don't have to supplement your income. Now repeat your instructions."

"Give the boxes to Tyson and get rid of the rest discreetly."

"Anything else?"

Animal knew what Yount wanted to hear. "Keep my mouth shut."

Yount nodded. "You're smarter than you look."

Alone in the room, Animal peeked inside one of the boxes. It was stuffed with black-and-white photos arranged like files, one behind the other. He knew whose they were. Day Randall carried that camera of hers everywhere. She hadn't been at the Cascade lately. Nothing strange about that—the boss went through babes like Kleenex—but finding her stuff in Stuart Helm's basement was a little weird. Yount wanted to dump it fast, and Animal's shit detector started blinking its lights and wailing its sirens.

He peeled off two plastic bags, whipped them open, and doubled one inside the other. He had no clue what you called the equipment or how it worked, but Day used it to make photos without a computer—that much he knew. He bagged the big pieces separately. The small items he swept off the shelves or the counter straight into bags. Some of the trays had liquid in them, so he emptied them in the sink first. The cabinet held nothing but plastic clips on zigzags of wire threaded through eyehole screws. He was about to close the cabinet when he noticed that its ceiling tilted. Not by much. The unevenness didn't show unless you compared the distance from the ceiling to the screws on each side and realized the zigzagging wire formed perfect ninety-degree angles with the walls.

Animal almost let it go, but something about the situation felt wrong.

He reached in and pushed the low side of the ceiling. It edged up and the other side edged down. The ceiling was held in place at the middle, probably by a bar attached to the particleboard on the upper side. He stepped back and noted the cabinet's height on the outside. The ceiling was more than an inch beneath the cabinet's top. He pushed on one side, this time hard. It popped up and the opposite side popped down. The edge of an envelope slid into view. He reached between the wires and worked the envelope through the narrow opening.

It was brown, six by nine inches, and sealed. He knew what he should do. Give it to Yount. Hope the prick would be impressed by his cleverness and recommend him to Guardians after all. Instead he slipped the envelope under the waistband of his jeans, put on his parka, and went outside to the Mustang, where he stashed the envelope under the driver's seat.

He made a big deal of getting his car ready for the trash bags, stowing his gym bag in the front-seat foot well, and pushing everything in the trunk into a compact pile. The cold stung his face, but under his clothes sweat dampened his armpits and chest.

Maybe Day Randall had nothing important to hide, but it seemed best to be cautious.

◆

He punched into the Cascade twenty minutes late, but so what? Sundays were slow. The employee lounge was jammed with two couches, four chairs from the club, and a low table loaded with old *Playboy* and *Glamour* magazines. As usual, he banged his shin walking through. He hung his parka on the coat rack.

Nina peeked into the lounge, clutching a bowl of limes to her stomach. "Welch's looking for you." Her morning-glory eyes reminded him of the doll his kid sister used to drag around, but today dark half moons hung beneath those eyes. And he knew why.

"You okay, Nina?" Stupid question.

"I'm fine."

He cleared his throat. "Last night you—"

Panic froze her face before she ducked out the door.

Maybe she remembered some of what happened, but she wouldn't tell Animal, the guy whose job was looking big and mean.

He climbed the kitchen stairs to the offices on the top floor. Welch's door was shut, meaning the manager probably wasn't inside. Animal knocked anyway.

The door to Tyson's office opened and Welch stepped into the hall.

"You were looking for me," Animal said.

"I was just wondering where the fuck you were."

"Yount kept me late. Packing up some shit for the boss."

"What shit?"

"Remember last night, the good Samaritan babe? She was at Helm's place today. Asking about Day."

"She talk to Odette?"

"Yount wouldn't let her in."

"Tell me everything that happened." Welch listened, his pasty face knotted in thought, until Animal came to the part about the photos and darkroom equipment. "Where is it?"

"Right outside."

"Wait here." Welch ducked back into the boss's office and slammed the door.

Animal edged closer. He heard their voices—Welch's shrill and piercing, Tyson's low and resistant—but not the conversation. He caught "rid of it" and "bitch again" from Welch but nothing from Tyson. Everyone acted like Day was dead. Could be she OD'd and they ditched the body instead of calling the cops. Whatever happened, Animal wanted no part of it. Two weeks in jail was enough. He had no intention of going to prison.

He heard footsteps, the door swung open, and Tyson stood there blank-faced. Typical stoner. Beads in his hair like some pathetic deadhead waiting for Jerry Garcia to rise from the grave. "You have Day's photographs."

"Want me to bring 'em inside?"

"Yeah. And tell Yount to go fuck himself."

Animal opened his mouth to say, *Why don't you tell him yourself?* Then he read Tyson's flat stare and recognized danger, the kind of tension he used to feel when he handled nitroglycerine.

"Pay him," Tyson told Welch.

The manager ducked into his office and came back with a wad of cash. "Five hundred bucks." He thrust the money at Animal. "That's for keeping your mouth shut."

It was too much money—way too much or not nearly enough.

❖

After working a sixteen-hour day, Animal drove home and unloaded Day's stuff. It couldn't wait. The apartments in his building opened onto a breezeway where anyone could watch you coming and going. He had more privacy at two in the morning. If some night owl asked what he was hauling inside, he could say he'd bought a bunch of junk at a yard sale.

He had trouble finding room to stash everything in his cramped apartment. He stowed the big equipment by the water heater in the utility closet. The rest he crammed here and there—under the kitchen sink among cleaning supplies, in different drawers, under the bed, with his shiatsu massager and weights. Then he sat at the kitchen table and ripped open the envelope Day had gone to so much trouble to hide.

Inside was a stack of black-and-white photos. The one on top showed a grizzled old man who looked pissed at having his picture taken. The next one showed a woman with spiky hair laughing at something not in the picture, and in the background people stood around at some kind of party. A photo of Kelly, taken somewhere else, captured what Animal knew of her personality. No-nonsense and fearless—maybe a little too fearless—the type who jumps into a lake to rescue someone and ends up drowning herself.

The rest of the photos had been taken somewhere in the mountains. First, Odette knelt on a blanket with a kid who looked about eighteen. It was summer, wildflowers blooming all around. Then the two of them were locking lips. Odette cheated on Helm—no surprise there, her being married to a dude old enough to be her grandpa. Then she dangled a bunch of grapes above the kid's face, her mouth hanging open in a grin and his clamped like a hungry man being tempted with poison fruit.

Next came a photo taken from a distance. Same picnic. Yount stood over Odette and the boyfriend, busting up their party. He must have seen Day running across the wide-open meadow, but he didn't chase her down and grab the camera. Why not? Yount wasn't the kind to let people get away with shit. The Guardians' slogan was "The Ultimate in Protection: Silent, Invisible, and Constant." Her photos flipped him the bird.

The last three were just scenery—the creek that ran through Helm's property, the same creek farther up the mountain, and then the forest floor. Nothing to see but water, pine needles, and pine cones. He understood hiding the picnic photos so Helm wouldn't get hold of them, but why the others? They meant something or she wouldn't have put them in her private stash.

Animal was too worn out to think. He slipped the photos into the envelope. Best to stash them somewhere safe until he knew what he was dealing with.

The lining on the bottom of his couch had torn loose in front. Lying flat on his stomach, he pushed the envelope deep inside the couch until it wedged in the coil springs. He found glue in his junk drawer and glued the lining to the frame, a repair that was overdue anyway.

10

Still in her pajamas, Kelly sat on the sofa with her feet on the coffee table and her computer cradled in her lap. In an hour she would get ready for work. The museum closed on Mondays, but she had to finish the auction program and send it to the printer, mail a few last-minute invitations, and sign for a package from FedEx—one of the donated pieces. Joyce, of course, was taking her usual day off.

Meanwhile, Kelly wanted to find out why Stuart Helm needed guards and an electric fence around his estate.

Her online search turned up several archived articles from *The Los Angeles Times*. Helm owned a private company, Helm of the Orient, which imported rubber building materials and other goods from Southeast Asia. Five years ago, the company almost went bankrupt, but these days it seemed to be thriving. He had a grown son who worked for the company and an ex-wife now remarried. No mention of his marriage to Odette.

A year-old article reported that the DEA had concluded its investigation of Helm of the Orient. Nothing about indictments or who had been under suspicion, Helm or someone else in the company. Nothing definite about the suspects being cleared, either. Drug smuggling would explain why Helm needed armed guards and an electric fence around his property.

She followed a link from the import company's website to the home page of Wildcat Construction, a real-estate development corporation in Denver. Daniel Jorgensen, the nephew of MOR's founder, headed Wildcat's board of directors, which included Helm and Gregory Tyson. Three wealthy men with ties to Boulder, a smallish city. Not so strange to find them on the corporate board of the same company. Another thread connected Tyson and Helm—drugs—but Helm's import company plus Tyson's blood-rimmed nostrils equaled nothing definite.

One thing was definite, though. Day and Marcus had disappeared. The hollow in Kelly's stomach told her they weren't coming back.

Her phone chimed. Joyce. Kelly answered with a sigh. "What is it?"

"Where are you?"

"I'll be there by one."

"I'm worried about the FedEx delivery. Afternoon means any time after twelve o'clock.

"They won't deliver during the lunch hour."

"Just hurry," Joyce said. "And something else has come up. Gee has Day Randall's photographs and negatives."

"How did he get them?"

"I have no idea. But he's offered to donate them to the museum. I want you to go to the Cascade and pick them up."

"Why there?"

Joyce exhaled with an impatient *huh*. "He owns the club and he's there nearly every night. You can go any time after six."

"Fine."

Kelly ended the call and found the Cascade's website. Tyson had built the place seven years ago. A one-time art student at the University of Colorado, he'd created the distinctive mural overlooking the bar. He posed beneath it with his manager, Lawrence Welch, and a group of employees that included Peter Beaumont (aka Animal) but not Nina. All of them grinned as if they wanted nothing more from life than to serve drinks to thirsty customers.

◈

Two guys in parkas pushed ahead of Kelly, flashing driver's licenses as they breezed past Animal. "Get on back here," he said. They slowed and looked at each other before returning to the bouncer's station. "Let's see the ID." Animal studied the licenses with a penlight and handed them back. "Nice job. Someday you'll be good enough to make license plates for the state of Colorado."

"What's that supposed to mean?" one of them said.

"It means you don't get in without valid ID."

"Let's go," the other said. "The place is dead anyway."

Animal was ready for Kelly. "Wait at the bar."

"Have you seen Odette? Is she okay?"

His pale eyes avoided hers. "I'm just a temp. I don't know nothing about the owners." He scowled, more to himself than at her, as if struggling with a problem.

"What?" she asked.

"Nina's here tonight. Could you talk to her?"

"Why don't you?"

"She won't—I don't know, maybe she'll open up to another woman."

"She doesn't even know me."

"Just tell her what happened Saturday night."

Part of her wanted to have the talk. She couldn't forget how Welch reached straight for the car keys hidden under Nina. Another part resisted. She needed to concentrate on what had happened to Day. Besides, she'd left her phone number along with a note. If Nina wanted to talk about that night, she would have called. But if Kelly did this favor for Animal, he might be willing to pass a message to Odette. "Okay."

Animal nodded. "I'll hold off on letting the boss know you're here."

A dozen or so customers sat at the horseshoe bar beneath the gaudy Christmas decorations and Tyson's mural of miners and electric-blue trout tumbling over waterfalls. Cheerful reggae boomed and echoed from overhead speakers. After Kelly chose a stool apart from the other drinkers, Nina came over. Her face was bleak and she moved sluggishly. "What can I get you?"

"Red wine. Beaujolais or something like that."

A familiar voice shouted "Kelly!"

Her ex-boyfriend, out drinking on Monday night. Just her luck.

Ray zigzagged between empty tables, closing in fast. He wore his artist uniform, jeans smudged with dried plaster and an oversize flannel shirt that hid the potbelly on his otherwise skinny frame. Once, his face had seemed sharp and expressive, charged with intelligence and humor. Now it reminded her of a disgruntled imp. "Kelly, how are you?"

She raised her voice above the music. "How's Cara?" She missed Cara, his five-year-old daughter.

"She feels like you've abandoned her."

Kelly stopped herself from telling him to take his emotional blackmail and shove it, but her anger must have shown. He drew on a predictable weapon—the phony guru persona, gentle and wise, who understood her better than she understood herself.

"Kelly! You're still angry about us."

"I'm fine with me. It's you that ticks me off."

He parried with a patronizing nod of approval. "That slashing wit. How I miss it."

Nina set the wine on top of a cocktail napkin. "Six dollars."

"Let me," Ray said.

Kelly slapped down the money an instant ahead of him. "Go sling a pot, Ray."

He opened his mouth for a comeback but settled for a smirk as he drifted away.

"Way to go," Nina said. "If he keeps bothering you, I'll call the bouncer."

"He won't. It'd be funny to see him take on Animal, wouldn't it?"

Nina gave her a twitchy smile.

Not much of an opening, but Kelly took it. She leaned over the bar and lowered her voice so the music covered their conversation. "I'm Kelly. I left you a note?"

Nina pitched a wild glance upward as if she wanted to fly away. "Welch already told me what happened."

"What exactly did he tell you?"

"That I got drunk and passed out. That he drove me home in my car and you followed and gave him a ride back."

"Did you ever find your phone?"

"Yeah. Welch found it in my car." She fiddled with the towel hanging from her apron pocket. "I don't party like that. I came here to have dinner."

"That's what Animal said. He wanted to take you to the ER."

She looked over to the vestibule, where Animal perched on his stool. "He did? Really?"

"It was Welch who insisted on taking you home. You know, it's not too late for you to—"

"Sorry you had to wait." Tyson bent over Kelly's shoulder, so close she smelled his sandalwood cologne and felt tension in his body, a threat of explosion more violent than sexual. His breath ruffled in her ear. "Let's go upstairs. Leave that crap, I'll get you some decent wine." He turned to Nina. "Open a bottle from my stash upstairs. Bring me the usual."

Nina had already turned away.

Her heart thumping, Kelly followed him past the kaleidoscopic screens of the arcade and through a pair of swinging doors. Aromas of fried meat, onions, and salsa stewed in the overheated kitchen. He touched her arm, steering her right, and reached past her to open another door. Kelly doubted he played the gentleman with most women. She represented the museum, so he put on his best behavior for her.

They entered a stairwell like the ones in a million commercial buildings—cinder-block walls, concrete stairs, and pipe railing painted green. Their footsteps echoed as they climbed. She'd never been afraid of Tyson before, but he was no longer the self-indulgent art patron who showed up stoned to board meetings. He owned the bar where Nina had been drugged and probably raped. He might be the rapist.

They passed a landing with doors to the mezzanine and a furnace room. He wouldn't hurt her, not tonight anyway. Joyce had sent her to pick up the photos and Tyson knew that. At the next landing, the stairs ended and emerged into a hallway, its carpet protected by a plastic runner. He sidestepped past her to open his office door and flip a light switch and then stood aside.

She came face-to-face with a demon cloaked in flames. Its sulfurous eyes glinted through a sooty cloud that partly obscured its face. Behind the fangs of its yawning mouth, a chrome-yellow crucifix stuck in its throat. The painting captured the unstable instant when the demon would either swallow the crucifix or choke.

She recognized the painter at once. "Roberto Aguilar."

"You like it?"

"It's . . . intense."

Spotlighted in the darkened office, the demon hovered behind Tyson's desk like a shadow self.

"You want people scared of you?"

He studied her with a faint smile. "Are you scared?"

Her next line was *Should I be?* But she didn't want to go there. She walked over to three rectangular boxes stacked in front of a leather sofa. Day's photographs. "Helm gave these to you?"

"He was going to toss them, but he knew I liked Day's work." Tyson switched on a desk lamp and angled its gooseneck stem toward the sofa. "Go ahead, look at them."

The boxes were fiberboard covered with canvas—expensive. Odette must have paid. Kelly shed her coat and handbag and then removed the lid from the box on top. It was packed with dozens of photographic prints. She pulled out a handful. Leftovers from one of Day's few commercial gigs.

He sat beside her. "Jesus. It's like having Diane Arbus do your wedding."

The newlyweds had asked for unconventional pictures, but they hadn't been pleased with the results. Day's images stripped away the prettiness of the ceremony. A bridesmaid pouted down at her bouquet. Another one smirked. The bride was stubby in her satin gown, its elaborately beaded train puddling behind her. The groom looked like a businessman worried about being late to his next appointment. Some of the shots were slightly off-kilter, underscoring their strangeness.

"They refused to pay," Kelly said.

"I bet."

"Day had their deposit at least."

She unstacked the boxes and opened the other two. The negatives were stored in the bottom box, the brown envelopes labeled by date. "These are better off at the museum. The archives are temperature- and humidity-controlled."

"That's why I want you to have them."

She replaced the wedding prints and grabbed another handful, this time from the bottom box. Close-ups of Tyson. As usual, Day's camera discovered something new and unexpected in each shot. The Cupid's bow of his upper lip, the planes of his cheekbones and forehead, the high peaks of his eyebrows were all exaggerated in a subtle way that made him attractive from one angle, repulsive from another. Then she recognized the window behind him. Day had taken the photographs in her room while the two were in bed together.

Kelly's cheeks warmed. "Wouldn't you like to keep these?"

He glanced at the image on top and then stuffed the photographs into the box as if afraid of seeing more. "So. What did you find out about Day?"

"I talked to her friend Courtney. Day took Courtney and her boyfriend to a party at Helm's place."

Tyson nodded as if her news confirmed what he already knew. "Did Day say anything to her about blowing town?"

"You knew Day brought friends to the party."

"Yeah. So?"

"You could've mentioned it. Given me a description of them. You asked me to find anyone who might have talked to her recently."

He shrugged. "They left before I got there."

"Who told you they were at the party? Helm?"

"He just mentioned that Day showed up with people who weren't invited. He was pissed about it."

"Did he also mention that I tried to see Odette? Your bouncer was there helping to intimidate me."

"No shit?" Tyson studied her with hooded eyes. "So Animal's moonlighting with the Guardians. I had no idea."

Nina came in carrying a tray of drinks. She laid paper cocktail napkins on the desk and served a large shot of whiskey, a glass of water without ice, and a glass of red wine.

"Thanks," Kelly said.

Avoiding her eyes, Nina hurried out.

Tyson downed the whiskey in one gulp and brought the wine to Kelly. "This okay?"

She sipped and nodded. It tasted richer and cleaner than bar wine, something he apparently kept for special occasions. There were no tables near the sofa, so she set the glass on the floor. He sat closer to her than before, and she again felt his tension pushing against her, almost a physical force. She had to stop herself from scooting away.

Kelly decided to talk about what had happened to Nina and gauge his reaction. "I met Courtney and Dustin here at this bar. I had no idea you owned it until Joyce ordered me to come out here and pick up the photos."

"She had to order you? I'm crushed."

"You seem pretty uncrushable."

He looked away. "Nobody's uncrushable."

Kelly drew a sharp breath before going on. "You should fire that manager of yours. I suppose he told you about Nina."

"No. What about her?"

"I found her passed out in her car. It was freezing cold—"

"You know Nina?"

"Not before finding her. She wouldn't wake up. She needed a doctor, but Welch wouldn't—"

"I'll look into it."

"She's afraid to talk about it. I don't think she remembers—"

"I'll look into it." His scowl warned her to stop. "Where does Courtney live?"

"She can't tell you anything. She's angry at Day."

"I want to talk to her anyway. What's her last name again?"

"Lamb. Day used her number and address on the museum's contact form. It's still on file. I can send it to you. But I need you to do something for me, too. Get your friend Helm to let me talk to Odette."

"Don't go back there, Kelly."

"What it is with Helm anyway? Why does he need body-guards and a locked gate?"

"You're not hearing me. Stay away."

"The police want to question Odette."

"You called the cops." His voice was empty—no accusation, not even coldness—just detachment that felt absolute. "You shouldn't have done that."

"Why not? Day's missing. I filed a report."

In the lamplight, his face became a mask, his eyes extin-guished. The demon floated behind him. The distant bass of the subwoofer echoed her heart, beating hard and too close to her throat.

"This was a mistake," he said. "You need to go."

Kelly made her voice brave. "Odette's boyfriend is missing, too. For over a week."

Tyson looked through her as if she were already gone.

She opened her mouth to say more and found she had no breath. She stood from the sofa, took a step, and knocked over the wine glass. Red liquid spread over the oak floor. It would leave a stain, but Tyson seemed not to notice. He continued to stare at something far away as she snatched up her things and fled.

When she reached the bouncer's station, Animal said, "Whoa, Kelly."

She turned reluctantly.

He studied her for a moment, his face unreadable. "I'm supposed to carry some shit to your car. Drive up to the door. I'll bring it out."

She hurried to the Jeep, her skin feverish in the cold. Soon the shivering would start. She cranked the heat and then swung the Jeep around the lot and pulled up alongside the building. Animal wasn't back yet. Whatever had happened to Marcus, Helm had some part in it. He would find out who talked to the police. Beneath the anger, Tyson was afraid.

Animal emerged from the Cascade carrying two of the three boxes. She got out and opened the cargo door. "Did you talk to Nina?" he asked.

"Until Tyson interrupted us. You said you'd wait to call him."

"I did." Animal stowed the boxes. "He must've come down on his own. Or Welch told him you were here."

Welch emerged from the Cascade carrying the third box. She registered his furious face and got into the Jeep. Tyson hadn't wasted time asking him about Nina. He passed the box to Animal and waited for the bouncer to finish and go inside.

Then he stooped to the driver's window, so close his breath fogged the glass. Kelly thought about driving away, but she was too entangled in this thing to ignore any part of it. She lowered the window.

"Bitch." He loaded the word with venom. "Come 'round here again and I'll cut your fucking tits off."

11

The next day, Animal's shift started at five, but Welch called and ordered him to get his ass to the Cascade in an hour. He missed his workout at the gym. When he tromped upstairs to find Welch and the boss, they were holed up in the boss's office. He could have knocked, but instead he went down to the bar.

Nina had a stack of cards listing the day's specials and was sticking them into plastic stands to put on the tables. There were dark blotches under her eyes. Makeup and tears.

"What's wrong, Nina?" Another stupid question. He couldn't seem to stop.

"Nothing. Just—the boss said to call him when Welch came in, so I did. Then Welch gave me shit for doing what I was told. He's got a black eye. I think him and the boss had a fight." She sniffled. "God, I hate these people."

"I hate 'em, too." Animal forced a grin. "Let's quit."

She gave a flicker of a smile. "I have to pay for Christmas presents."

"There's other jobs." Maybe Nina could never forget what happened, but she sure as hell wouldn't forget as long as she worked at the Cascade.

"I make good tips here. And I like the people I work with." Her gaze brushed his face, soft as kitten fur. "I mean, as opposed to the people I work for."

Animal cleared his throat and steeled himself. "Would you like to go out sometime?"

"Sure." She jumped at it like she'd wanted him to ask.

Tyson chose that moment to pop through the swinging door from the kitchen. Welch followed, with a bloody handkerchief against his eye. "He tripped on the stairs," Tyson said. "Take him to the doctor."

"What doctor?"

"I don't give a fuck."

Animal turned back to Nina. He loved her eyes, morning-glory blue and so soft, never mind the tears. "Talk to you later."

❖

He drove fast. He didn't want Welch to drip blood on his car seat. The hankie kept getting soaked, and every time Welch refolded it, Animal saw the gash that had severed his left eyebrow. It was almost an inch long, separating two lips of fatty tissue bleeding hard. "Motherfucking Gee," Welch said. "You never know what the fuck he's gonna do. I'm talking to him about Nina and out of nowhere he slams his fucking fist in my face."

"What about her?"

"How she passed out in her car."

"Why'd he punch you?"

"The dude's nuts."

"Nina wasn't drunk," Animal said. "You know that."

"Fucking Gee doped her."

Animal pictured Tyson's body covering Nina's and gripped the steering wheel hard. "What makes you so sure? You help him?"

"I know how fucking crazy he is. Look what he did to me."

Maybe you deserved it. "The boss gets plenty of babes without drugging them." *You, on the other hand . . .*

Welch glared with his undamaged eye. "What part of crazy don't you understand?"

Animal drove along a narrow driveway to a parking area behind the clinic. Whoever had hurt Nina—the boss or Welch or some customer at the Cascade—Animal meant to hunt him down and beat his face to a pulp.

The doc-in-a-box handled walk-ins, but Animal figured it wouldn't be that busy on a weekday. He was wrong. Sick people packed the waiting room. An hour passed before a nurse called Welch's name, and forty-five minutes later he was still in there. How long could a few stitches take?

Animal shifted in the hard plastic chair. Sick of last month's *Newsweek*, he checked out the eight other people in the room. They eyed him with expressions ranging from curious to angry to downright scared. He felt like baring his teeth and growling.

He tossed the magazine onto the table and checked his phone again. Nina hadn't answered the text he sent twenty minutes ago, asking what days she had off. *Hopefully same as me,* he sent now. *I can always call in sick.* He added a grinning emoticon and then scowled at the ugly carpet. He felt like ripping it off the floor.

Finally, Welch walked out with a patch of gauze taped over his eye and a prescription in hand. "Let's go. We gotta stop at the drugstore."

"What for?"

Welch grinned, a gruesome sight with his bruised cheek and patched eye. "Vicodin."

"You scored Vicodin for *that*?"

"It fucking hurts."

Animal drove to the drugstore, went in and got the script filled. He read the label stapled to the bag—thirty Vicodin, no refills—and noted the doctor's name in case he ever needed painkillers. When he got back to the car, Welch snatched the bag, twisted the lid off the pharmacy bottle, and swallowed two pills dry. Then he handed Animal a piece of paper with an address written on it. "These people could be holding something Gee wants. Go check it out."

"What am I looking for?"

"Some black-and-white photos. Day could've given them to these kids, and they could've passed them off to Kelly. Have a talk with them and find out."

Animal's shit detector went off. "Photos of what?"

"Never mind what. Anything you find, bring it to me." Welch tossed him a roll of hundreds. "Here's some cash to smooth the way."

Black and white—like the photos hidden in Day's cabinet. Animal wished he'd never laid eyes on them.

⬥

His target lived in a rabbit warren of apartments, two cracker boxes from the '80s shebanged together with an add-on. Her place was downstairs facing the street, one of the nicer spots if you had to live there. She answered the door in a shriveled lace dress that hung on her bony frame like cobwebs. Pot smoke and barbed-wire guitar noise belched from the apartment.

"Hi, Courtney."

She gradually brought him into focus. "Animal?"

You had a high-profile job like his, every piece of trash in town knew your name. "Day left a package with you."

"Huh?"

"A package. You still got it? Or you gave it to Kelly?"

"What are you talking about?" She kept glancing into the screeching maw of the apartment.

"Who's in there, Courtney?"

"Just my roommate."

"Go on, invite 'em to join us," Animal said, full of bonhomie. *Bonhomie* was a word he'd learned while improving his vocabulary in jail back in Heber, Utah. It meant "nice guy" in French. And he would be nice, if possible.

She turned around and hollered, "Dustin!" over the din of the music.

The roommate pulled himself off the couch and came at them, a puny kid with attitude. He halted in mid-swagger when he saw Animal. "What's up?"

"That bitch Kelly ratted us out."

"For what? We didn't do nothing."

"Oh, yeah?" Animal said. "So how come Courtney's talking like you did?"

"What's it to you anyway? You're not the cops. You got no right." Dustin was yap-yapping like a Pomeranian or a Chihuahua, a vicious little ankle-chewer.

Animal controlled his temper. "Did you give the photos to Kelly?"

"What photos?" Courtney said. "Dustin gave her directions, that's all."

"Directions to where?"

"None of your fucking business," Dustin said.

Animal bulled his way into the apartment. Both of them backed off as if he had a force field around him. He went to their CD player and turned it off. With the music gone, other sounds became loud—cables and power cord popping loose as he plucked the metal box from the shelf, floorboards groaning as he shifted his weight and pivoted. He raised the player above his head and paused, giving them a last chance.

Courtney's eyes opened wide, the pupils like bull's-eyes on two little targets. "What do you want from us?"

"Answers."

"Okay."

Animal put the unit back on the shelf. "Go sit on the couch."

"You're paying for that," Dustin said.

Animal picked up the CD player and slammed it to the floor. When it crashed, Courtney and Dustin bounced an inch off the couch. "Something else you want me to pay for?"

They glared at him. Slack-jawed, Courtney shook her head.

He went to shut the front door. He was taking a chance, considering that someone who heard the noise might come knocking. But he figured people partied day and night in these crappy apartments and the parties got out of hand on a regular basis. He came back to the couch and loomed over the goths. "What did you give Kelly?"

"Directions to a place in the mountains," Courtney said. "She paid us fifty dollars. Did she complain or something? If she did, she's a fucking liar. It's not like we forced her to pay us."

"Shut the fuck up, Courtney."

"Why? We didn't do anything."

"Whose place?" Animal said.

"I don't know. Some rich people. A friend of ours was invited to a party there. We gave her a ride."

"Day Randall," Animal said.

"Why are you hassling us if you already know?"

"Day gave you some photos."

"She never gave us shit." Courtney tossed her white hair. "She used us the way she used everyone."

"She say anything about photos?"

"She was a photographer," Dustin said. "What else would she talk about?"

"That a yes or a no, smartass?"

Dustin smirked.

"She never said anything about photos," Courtney said.

"So if I tear up your place I won't be finding any?"

"Please. Whatever you're looking for has nothing to do with us."

Courtney scrunched her face, ready to cry, but that wasn't what convinced Animal. It was the fifty bucks that they made Kelly pay for directions to Helm's place. Just the kind of half-ass shakedown those two would pull. If they'd sold her Day's photos, too, they would have said so. He could skip searching their apartment—if they had any photos, they didn't know it.

Animal dug in his pocket and scooped out the cash Welch had given him on the way over. He peeled two hundreds from the roll and dropped them in Courtney's lap. "Here's for your CD player. I'll have a look in your car." He held out his hand. "The keys."

"Kiss my ass," Dustin said in his pipsqueak voice.

Animal sighed. He reached down and grabbed Dustin by his skinny ankles. He could curl 160 pounds—more than the kid weighed—so it wasn't much of a workout yanking Dustin off the couch and hoisting him upside down. His torso and head thumped the floor hard, but he wasn't hurt enough to give up the fight. He flailed and shrieked like a chicken.

"Stop it," Courtney said. "I'll get them."

Animal lowered Dustin until his upper body rested on the floor, but he kept holding his ankles while Courtney fetched the keys. Then he let Dustin drop and quick-stepped back, guessing the kid would try to kick him. And he did make a feeble swipe.

"Where's your car?"

"It's parked on the street," she said. "The green Chevy."

"I'm calling the cops," Dustin said from the floor.

"Do that." Animal grinned. "Someone a lot worse than me will come looking for you."

He found the Chevy down the block from the apartment. He emptied the glove box onto the floor, groped under the bucket seats, and peered into the crevices between the seats and the console. He checked the console compartment. In the back, he thrust his hand between the bottom and top seat cushions and groped every hidden inch. Day probably couldn't have hidden anything in the trunk without cooperation from Courtney and Dustin, but Animal searched it anyway. He spent five more minutes going through a bunch of dirty clothes they hadn't taken to the laundromat yet and lifting the trunk's bottom mat to check underneath. When he was finished, he felt certain Day hadn't confided in Courtney and Dustin or hidden any photos in their car.

He went back into the apartment. The living room was empty, so he tossed the keys onto the couch along with an-other hundred-dollar bill.

❧

Driving back to the club, Animal began to see the picture more clearly. Forget Welch's bullshit, it was Yount who wanted the photos. Which meant Helm. The photos threatened Helm big time and probably got Day killed. And Animal had copies of them. He was in deep shit if Welch or Yount found out. Unless . . .

Helm might pay big money to get them back, enough money for Animal to start a new life somewhere. With Nina.

He basked in the fantasy for about ten seconds before reality smacked him in the face. He and Nina hadn't even gone out. He would be killed for taking the photos and to keep him from talking.

The Cascade was dead. A dozen customers sat scattered along the bar, and Nina was slicing limes into little chunks. She had on fresh makeup.

"Hi," she said, her voice softer than usual.

"You get my text?" Animal asked.

Her smile caught him by surprise. It was downright seductive. He felt the beginning of a hard-on and was glad the bar shielded him.

"I got Monday off," she said.

"Me, too. We can eat a steak dinner, maybe see a movie."

"Okay. I'll text you my address and phone."

"How about I pick you up at seven?"

He floated through the shift. Business stayed slow, so he spent minutes at a time watching Nina tend bar and sweep up the silver icicles that kept drifting from the ceiling. It had been years since he'd taken a woman on a date where he'd asked ahead of time. He'd hooked up with lots of women, but it wasn't the same. Animal felt as skittish as a high school kid. He thought about suggesting they have a drink after work—kind of a pre-date—but it seemed best not to rush things. Besides, he needed to see those photos again.

He said good night to Nina and punched out a few minutes early. When he got home he grabbed a beer from the fridge, retrieved the photos from their hiding place in the couch, and set them on the kitchen table. The ceiling light was dim, so he brought a lamp from his bedroom. He stacked the photos in three groups: pictures of the picnic, pictures of the empty land behind Helm's house, and pictures of people.

He began with the picnic photos, taken in the summer. He guessed they'd come first. Odette mugged for the camera, pretending to have fun. The weird shine in her eyes reminded him of something. He kept staring until he remembered. Somewhere online he'd watched a clip from a video taken by a pair of psycho killers. The video was evidence at their trial and showed their victim, a woman tied up in a chair, her eyes bright with terror. She knew what was coming. Odette wasn't nearly that scared, but she was waiting for something bad to happen.

When Yount showed up, Day had moved off and snapped the photo of him standing over Odette and her baby-faced boyfriend. Yount was doing what Guardians did—protecting his client's interests. The wife was cheating. The husband would be told. The kid looked pissed, too dumb to realize he was a problem to be disposed of.

Animal moved on to the pictures of the land behind Helm's property. Now they made sense. The boyfriend was buried out there, and Day had found the grave. Animal picked up the photo of the forest floor. The ground was sunken, not so deep that you noticed until you studied it up close, and clods of dirt were sprinkled here and there among the pine needles, cones, and twigs. The other photos gave directions. Follow the creek up the mountainside until you come to—what? He scanned the second photo of the creek until his attention rested on a spruce in the foreground. There was a mark on the trunk, a faint cross scraped into the bark. Hard to see. You had to be looking.

He shuffled through the pictures of Kelly and the two strangers. Somehow or other these people were connected. He suspected that Kelly knew the grizzled old man and the woman with spiky hair, but he couldn't risk asking her. She might go running to the cops.

He was dead if Helm found out he had these photos. The cops wouldn't save his ass. They were more likely to bust him and twist the evidence to make him look guilty, like they'd done after the bar fight in Heber. And it would've worked if their star witness hadn't blown town. Even if the Boulder cops believed him, Yount or another Guardian would snuff him while Helm's lawyers worked their legal voodoo and made the charges disappear.

The smart move was to burn the photos. Animal took out a frying pan and set it on the stove. He tossed the photos in the pan and rifled in the junk drawer until he found matches. Standing over the photos, match in hand, he stopped. He couldn't burn them. If things turned nasty with Yount or Tyson, they were the only bargaining chip he had.

The couch no longer seemed like a safe hiding place. Animal put the photos in the envelope and sealed it inside a zip-lock baggie. He removed the grill on the bottom of his fridge and slipped the baggie far back under the refrigeration coils, taking care not to disturb the dust in front.

12

On Wednesday evening Kelly stripped the sheets from her bed and carried them to the laundry room. Stuffing them into the washer, she remembered Day's sheets. *Might as well throw them in, too.* She hurried through the kitchen and down the hall. At the closed door she halted. She hadn't entered the room since she discovered Day gone. Shoulders tense, she reached for the doorknob, drew a long breath, and went in.

A window let in sterile winter light. Except for the Amish quilt, the room seemed anonymous, unoccupied. Nothing left of Day but the smell of petroleum distillate, a chemical ghost that awakened Kelly's dread. She folded the quilt and draped it over a chair. The blankets underneath were spread neatly without the edges tucked in. She pulled them off. No sheets or mattress pad. Day—or someone—had taken them. But why?

The smell was stronger now.

Kelly wrestled the mattress off the box spring and tipped it onto its side. A large stain darkened the bottom. A faint line left by the cleaning fluid outlined the stain. She let the mattress fall against the wall, where it blocked most of the window. She switched on the ceiling light.

The stain looked like blood. Maybe Day's period had come while she slept and she'd turned the mattress to hide the damage. No, the stain was too large. Blood had soaked the bottom sheet and pad before seeping into the mattress and spreading over an area two feet wide and three feet long. Someone had bled to death in that bed.

She went to find Detective Peterson's card.

◆

Forty minutes later he was drinking tea at her dinner table, squared-jawed and disheveled in his scholarly glasses, his parka draped over the back of the chair as if he'd dropped by for a friendly visit. *If only.* He was a cop, Kelly reminded herself, no matter how sexy his green eyes were.

He brought the cup to his mouth and blew on the tea before sipping. "Tastes good." But his faint grimace told her Cash preferred black coffee to Earl Grey. He set the teacup down. "I'll cut the stained fabric from the mattress and take it to be analyzed. With your permission. But the chemical probably makes it useless as evidence."

"Do you still think Day just left town?"

His gaze settled on her with a touch of exasperation. "We're investigating. Is there anything else you can tell me?"

"Have you talked to Yount yet?"

"We haven't been able to contact him or his employer."

Kelly laughed, an angry *humph*. "Drive out to Helm's estate. Yount will come to the gate."

"You said you'd never been there."

"I went last Sunday."

"By yourself?"

"At that point you weren't looking for Day, only Marcus. I thought Odette might know where she was. But Yount wouldn't let me see her. He flashed his gun and threatened legal action if I came back."

"He pulled the gun?"

"No. Just made sure I saw it under his jacket."

Cash studied her, his eyes narrow and grim like the set of his mouth. "Go over everything, starting from when you realized Day was missing. Don't leave anything out."

Kelly described the strange smell in the house when she'd gotten home from the airport, her spotless Jeep. She went over Day's relationship with Gregory Tyson and how he'd asked for help in finding Day—things she'd covered when she made the missing-person report. She repeated Courtney's story about the party at Helm's place and gave more details of her confrontation with Yount.

Cash scribbled in a small notebook. "Day had a key to the house, right?"

"Of course. She lived here."

"And where's that key now?"

Her face warmed with embarrassment. Worried about her car keys, she'd forgotten about Day's house key. Anyone could have it. A stranger could walk into the house while she slept.

"Is there somewhere you can stay tonight?" Cash asked. "With a friend?"

Only Annie Laible. Kelly would feel awkward showing up at her doorstep with a suitcase. She shook her head.

"Then stay at a hotel until the locks are replaced. The guy who was seen loading your vehicle probably took the key."

"The guy could've been the manager of the Cascade, Welch. He matches the description, short and stocky. And he was wearing a Dodgers cap the night I talked to the goth kids." She remembered his huge ring of keys and shuddered.

"Welch. Is that his first or last name?"

"Last. His first name is Lawrence." Kelly hesitated. What had happened to Nina, the bartender, had nothing to do with the missing-person cases, but it still bothered her. "Another thing. I found a woman passed out in her car in the Cascade's parking lot."

"When?" He snapped the question like a whip.

"The same night. It was cold, so I told Welch. The bouncer and I wanted to take her to the hospital, but Welch said she just needed to sleep it off."

"The vote's two to one, but this Welch guy makes the call."

"He was in charge. He drove her car home. I followed in my car and gave him a ride back."

Cash shook his head in disgust. "You're lucky you didn't end up in a ditch somewhere."

"What?"

"Come on, Kelly. You're not stupid. This Welch could've killed you."

"The bouncer knew where I was going."

"So you trust your life to a sleazebag bar manager and a muscle head who tosses drunks for a living."

"I trusted the bouncer."

"Really? Why?"

She knew that Animal cared about Nina but couldn't explain how, not in a way that Cash would understand. "I—just did."

"Well, that makes total sense. What's his name?"

Kelly unclenched her teeth. Her worst error in judgment had been thinking this jerk was sexy. "It's on the Cascade's website, but I don't remember it. They call him Animal."

"No wonder you trusted him."

She decided not to mention that Animal also worked for Helm. She'd taken more than enough sarcasm and scolding.

"What brought you to the website?" Cash asked.

"To find out who owned the place."

"I thought everyone in town knew that. The bartender—what's her name?"

"Nina. She lives somewhere on Arapahoe."

"There's no point in talking to Nina if she doesn't want to make a complaint. I take it she doesn't."

"Then why are you writing this down?"

"Things change." He gave her another narrow-eyed inspection. "Tyson felt comfortable asking you to help him find Day."

"That was the first time I talked with him anywhere but the museum."

"Oh? Where did the two of you talk?"

"The Dushanbe Teahouse."

"What about next time? The teahouse again?"

His questions felt like an assault. "What makes you think there was a next time?"

"You said *first* time, not *only* time."

"I went to the Cascade to pick up some photos Tyson donated to the museum. They were Day's."

"Where'd he get them?"

"From Helm. They were stored out there before she disappeared."

"Out there?" he said. "You mean Helm's house? What did you and Tyson talk about?"

"He asked what I'd found out, and I told him about Courtney. And about Nina."

"How did Tyson react?"

"He was . . . upset. And he must've said something to Welch, because Welch threatened me."

"Threatened you. Give me his exact words."

Kelly fought her embarrassment. "He said he'd cut my tits off if I ever came back."

"Nice guy." Cash kept writing. "Anything else?"

"I think Welch carried Nina to her car after she passed out. She was sitting on the keys and he knew right where to look."

He put away his notebook and pen and stood. "Let me have a look at the mattress."

After inspecting the stain, he jogged out to his car and returned with a paper bag. He cut out the stained fabric with a pocketknife and sealed the evidence in the bag. "Don't touch anything, and stay out of the room."

Cash backtracked to the kitchen for his parka while she waited at the front door, glad to see him go.

He came up to her and paused. His face softened and his gaze lingered on her. "Look, I'm sorry I ripped into you like that. But these are nasty people we're dealing with. Do me a favor and stay somewhere else until your locks are changed."

13

Cash wanted to think the silence between him and his partner meant they were comfortable with each other, but Bridget made him edgy. She appeared calm enough, hunched in the car seat, iPad on her knees, but she hummed with mental energy. He admired her intelligence—he just couldn't connect on a personal level.

Little things put him off, like her hair, dyed an unnatural black and streaked platinum at the temples. But he knew that judging her appearance was totally out of line. She might hate his ten-dollar haircut as much as he hated that dramatic do of hers.

He caught sight of ice ahead and slowed down. He needed to keep his mind on the road. The surface was dry except for patches of ice where runoff had pooled and frozen.

"Marcus's mother called again," Bridget said. "Poor lady, she's starting to realize he's not coming home."

Cash had no answer to that sad truth. "You found out more about Helm?"

"Just what you'd expect, shady investments and offshore accounts. We'll need a warrant to find out more."

"What about his marriage?"

Bridget's laugh grated on him like sandpaper. "Which one? He's been married three times."

"Tell me about all of them."

"Number one, Marjorie Arnette, divorced from Helm in 1997. She died of cancer in 2010. Helm has a son by that marriage, vice president of the company. Number two, Cindy Dryer, married in 1997 and divorced in 2005. Number three, Odette Champion, married in 2009. It's the usual pattern. Helm was married to Marjorie for twenty-three years, and then he dumped her for Cindy, who was fifteen years old at the time." Bridget offered the information without glancing at her iPad or anywhere else to double-check the dates, but no doubt she had them right.

"Where'd they get married, Utah?"

"You got it. Same thing with Odette. He married her at fifteen."

"He's a pedophile."

"And rich enough to get away with it."

Their eyes met in a moment of shared outrage.

He drove past a sparkling lake and descended into Nederland, one of his favorite mountain towns. A bakery there made perfect cinnamon rolls with plenty of spice and not too much sugar. He spotted the street where the bakery was located and controlled the urge to turn. They could stop on the way back. He tried to remember how late the place was open.

"What's your thing with Tyson?" Bridget asked. "He and Helm have business dealings, but that doesn't prove he's involved in the rest of it."

"He is. Scumbag."

She treated him to another harsh laugh. "It's good you're not prejudiced against the man."

Cash told her about the woman who'd been drugged at the Cascade last year. "It's not our jurisdiction, but she came to the Boulder station. It was me who took her complaint. I went along with a county deputy to interview Tyson, who wasn't exactly cooperative. He and the manager talked to us once. Then it was 'Speak to my attorney.'" He could have added that Tyson wore his hair in a ponytail and reeked of woodsy cologne, but it seemed safer to avoid the subject of hairstyles. "A couple days later I get called in. The chief orders me to leave Tyson alone unless we've got hard evidence. Turns out Tyson has suck."

Bridget grimaced. "It's all about doing business as opposed to doing right."

"It pissed me off, so I ran a background check on Tyson. Turns out he has an older brother, Renald, serving life for first-degree murder. Renald tortured and killed a dealer who ripped him off. It was brutal. I talked to the detective who worked the case back in Nashville. He said there was evidence placing Greg at the scene, just not enough to charge him."

"You think Greg helped his brother do the murder."

"I don't know. He was in high school then. A good student. But according to friends, he worshiped his big brother. Followed him around like a puppy."

"If he was there, let's hope it scared him straight."

"Let's hope." Cash told her about Nina.

"So who drugged her?" Bridget said.

"I'm thinking Tyson or the manager, Lawrence Welch."

"We should talk to her."

"You should. She's more likely to listen to you. But we'd better take Kelly's statement first. I have to call her and arrange a time. I didn't want to push it yesterday. She was kind of upset."

Thanks to him.

He worried about Kelly. People like her, naïve people who live in their safe little worlds, have no clue what could happen to them. She wore almost no makeup. Her skin was too pale—not the outdoorsy type who loved hiking, camping, and skiing. In other words, not his type. But her sadness and earnestness lingered like perfume. No smugness there. Not the type who thought she was hot shit because she did Pilates and her bedroom had feng shui.

After yesterday, he was pretty sure she hated the sight of him. He had no business getting personal with her anyway, not while he was working this case.

"Kelly's holding something back," he said. "She works with Tyson all the time and talks like she hardly knows the guy."

"I doubt she's dating him, Cash."

"Who says she is?" He bristled at the amusement in his partner's voice. She grokked his attraction to Kelly with some female sense he couldn't fathom.

Bridget touched her iPad to access the GPS. "Helm's driveway is coming up on the right."

"Stay!" Yount said like a Nazi giving orders to his guard dog.

Animal got out of the Land Rover anyway and stood by the door. Yount tramped toward the gate, leaving ugly footprints in the pristine snow. *Pristine* was another word Animal had learned while improving his vocabulary in the Heber jail.

Nothing stayed pristine with people around.

Yount halted a few yards from the gate. Behind the bars stood a man and a woman. At first glance they looked like tourists who'd lost their way to Winter Park and stopped to ask directions. The gal's hair was black with white streaks, kind of like a skunk sitting on her head. The dude had on a parka, geek glasses, and expensive mountaineering boots. He could have been a lawyer or a college professor except for the straight-arrow stare and the aggressive set of his shoulders. Dudley Do-Right. Big surprise, he whipped out a badge.

"Can we help you, officer?" Yount said in an unhelpful tone.

"We're here to speak with Odette Helm," Do-Right said.

"For what purpose?"

"Police investigation."

"Of what?"

"Are you Mrs. Helm? Then tell her we're here."

"She's in California with her husband."

Skunk Lady stayed in the background, taking everything in. Animal glared when she inspected him, and her face kept its neutral expression. He felt like flipping her the bird.

"We need to know where they are in California," Do-Right said.

"Do you have a warrant?" Yount said.

"A warrant for an address? Are they in hiding?"

"Mr. and Mrs. Helm value their privacy, and my job is protecting it. If you care to leave your card, Mrs. Helm will contact you if she wants to talk."

Do-Right passed a business card to Yount through the gate bars. "Your employer is involved in the disappearance of Marcus French and Day Randall."

"Never heard of them."

Do-Right's smile mirrored the thin smile Animal had seen many times on Yount's face. "There's a witness who's seen Mrs. Helm with both of them."

"And who would that be?"

"I'll share that information with Mrs. Helm."

"You'll have to speak to Mr. Helm's attorney." Yount made a clipped turn like a soldier and marched back to the Land Rover. He scowled at Animal. "I told you to stay in the vehicle."

Tired of taking shit, Animal waited until Yount slid behind the wheel before getting back in. "Looks like Kelly went to the cops."

"Don't overtax your brain, Beaumont. It might explode."

In the Land Rover's side mirror, the cops watched them from behind the gate. The iron bars looked like jail. Cops locked up—what you call poetic justice. Animal waited until they were out of sight. "So what are we gonna do?"

"Nothing. I'll report to Mr. Helm."

He couldn't go on telling himself Guardians was a legit company. He'd bought the shit about needing to be bonded, but the truth was, Yount found him lacking. And Yount was right. Animal might get carried away in a fight and kill someone, but he couldn't coldly push a button on a target. Yount could. The evil son of a bitch would do his own mother if the price was right.

A few minutes later they pulled up to the house. Yount leaped from the Land Rover and bounded toward the utility entrance. Instead of coming to heel as usual, Animal lingered outside. The sting of the wintry air kept his thinking clear. He spotted critter tracks in the snow—coyote, most likely—and imagined heading into the mountains. Instead, he took off his boots and went inside.

Carol, the housekeeper, brandished a coffeepot. "Want some coffee?"

Yount was nowhere to be seen, so Animal took a seat at the kitchen table.

Carol filled a mug and set the steaming coffee in front of him. She was tiny and wizened, her hands knotty like tree branches. She reminded him of a troll in a fairy tale. He wondered why she was treating him so nice. Usually she ignored or scolded him.

"You're almost done working here, is that right?" she said.

"Just a couple more days."

She leaned close to his face. "Mrs. Helm wants to speak to you. Take your coffee and go downstairs. Now, while Mr. Yount's in his office."

Animal carried the mug down the corkscrew stairs and found Odette waiting among the weight machines. Her chestnut hair tumbled in loose waves over her breasts, her nipples hard under a tight sweater. He was careful not to stare. "You wanted me?"

"Let's go outside."

Animal set the mug on an abductor machine and followed Odette into the area beneath the deck. He felt hyped, as if his bloodstream were flooded with caffeine after just one swallow of coffee. They stood behind folded outdoor furniture that had been stacked against the building and covered with a tarp. He was pretty sure they couldn't be seen through the basement windows.

Odette nibbled her lower lip and studied him with cautious pussycat eyes. "I need your help, Animal."

Did she have to call him that? Why couldn't she call him Beaumont like Yount?

"You went to the gate," she said. "Was it someone to see me?"

"Yeah. Cops."

She took a quick breath like someone poked with a needle. "What did they want?"

"They were asking questions about Day and some dude named Marcus. Seems like they're missing." He watched her face for a ripple of surprise, but she just stopped gnawing her lip.

"What did Yount tell them?"

"That you was in California with your old man."

"The other day—did someone come?"

"Yeah, Kelly. She's looking for Day, too."

"All Day's stuff is gone."

"You mean the photos? Tyson's got them."

She took his hand and pressed a scrap of paper into his palm. Her eyes pleaded with him. "Here's Kelly's number. Will you call her for me?"

A voice in Animal's head shouted *Run*, but he stuffed the paper into his pocket.

"Tell her I'll be taking a walk every day after lunch and she should wait out back where the creek goes under the fence. Tell her one o'clock so we don't run into the noon patrol." Her voice wavered between fear and contempt for the men who guarded her. "Tell her I promise to go there every day."

"For how long?"

"Until I can't. Or until it doesn't matter anymore."

Animal nodded and walked away before she could beg anymore. He'd be risking his ass. For all he knew, Odette was setting up him and Kelly both. A couple of threats and a slap in the face and she'd probably do whatever Yount said. Nothing about her signaled a lie, but he'd been wrong before. Safest to throw the paper in the garbage and forget the whole thing.

Except Kelly wanted to talk to Odette and he owed Kelly a favor. He'd be risking her ass, too.

His parents were losers, but he'd respected his granddad. "Do what's right," the old man had told him, "even when it costs you." Good advice but hard to follow, especially when right and wrong looked pretty much the same.

Kelly rinsed her underthings in the hotel sink and draped them over the shower rod. She'd forgotten to pack an extra bra when she moved to the hotel last night. Tired from working all day, she chose hand laundry over driving to Ash Mountain Estates. She could go tomorrow, but she might as well wait until Monday afternoon, when the locksmith would come and she could move back in.

She settled into the mound of pillows on the bed, picked up *The Goldfinch*, and turned on the reading lamp. At least she'd remembered to bring a book. But the page blurred as she pictured Day sprawled on the bloody mattress. Shot? Stabbed? Her neighbor Owen would have heard gunfire—unless the shooter used a silencer, which meant he'd come there to kill Day. Had she seen Welch assaulting a woman? Kelly doubted that Nina had been the first.

Her phone was chiming. She picked it up, glad for any distraction.

"Kelly?"

She recognized the rumbling voice. "Hi, Animal."

"Odette wants to talk. She's gonna wait behind her house where the crick runs under the fence."

The regional pronunciation of *creek* still sounded odd to Kelly. "Where is that?"

"Way in back. A couple hundred yards past Helm's driveway, there's a dirt trail on your right. It'll take you to a clearing in the trees. No one can see your car from the road. Be sure to turn it around so you can leave fast if you need to."

"Someone might be chasing me?"

"Not if you time things right. The Guardians patrol the back meadow between noon and 12:40, so don't come out in the open until after that. Follow the fence up the mountain and around the turn and you'll come to the crick. If Odette's not there, don't wait around. You have to get back down the mountain before the next patrol at one thirty."

"How long will it take to hike up there?"

"Twenty, twenty-five minutes. Which means you got ten or fifteen minutes to talk."

She doubted he was intentionally sending her into a trap, not with his painstaking directions and advice, but the trap might be there. "Do you trust Odette?"

Animal laughed. "Hell no. But I don't think she's setting us up. She wants to talk to you."

"Tell her I'll be there tomorrow."

"I can't tell her shit. She ain't allowed to talk to anyone but the housekeeper. We had to sneak outside to talk."

"Thanks for doing this, An—" She felt awkward calling him that. "What's your real name, anyway?"

"Beaumont."

"Thanks, Beaumont. Stay safe."

She quailed at the thought of sneaking past armed guards, possibly into a trap. She could ask Cash to come along, but he'd probably sideline her and go by himself. Confronted by an abrasive cop, Odette would panic and run and never trust Kelly again.

If she went, she had to go alone.

Kelly almost missed the dirt trail, an unmarked hole in the trees. She drove through scrub pine to a ramshackle shed and turned the Jeep around.

She tramped uphill over pine needles glazed with ice. The white sky sloughed snow, a whirl of flakes that stung her face. She reached the meadow divided by an electrified fence, the boundary of Helm's property. There was no patrol in sight. She checked the time on her phone—12:38.

She emerged from the trees and began hiking along the fence. "No Trespassing" signs were nailed to every tenth fence post. Stalks of milkweed and tufts of bleached grass poked through the snow. The pines darkened into shadows on the mountainside. The stippled gray of aspen trunks and the dun and pinks of rocks paled into a ghost landscape. She felt gone, already gone. She pictured Yount in his lambskin coat, the bulge under his arm, and recognized the feeling as fear. But she could handle it now.

Her boots left conspicuous tracks in the snow. The guards might notice them on their next patrol. After she was out of there, she hoped.

Up ahead, the fence entered a pine forest where she would be less exposed. She bent into the wind and slogged uphill until she reached the shelter of the trees. She was breathing hard and sweating beneath layers of clothes, her pant legs fretted with ice from dragging through the snow. She walked through the pines, keeping the fence in sight. The wire ran through ceramic insulators nailed to tree trunks or attached to posts anchored in the ground by concrete. It had to short-circuit sometimes and couldn't be watched day and night. If you were sneaking onto Helm's property, here would be the place.

The fence turned a corner and stretched sideways along the mountain. Water burbled. She caught sight of a gully where a half-frozen creek flowed between rocks and under the fence.

On the other side, Odette sat cross-legged on a waterproof ground cover, the kind campers spread under their tents. She spotted Kelly and scrambled to her feet. "You came." She sniffled and wiped her nose on the sleeve of her jacket. "It's freezing out here." As usual, she was beautiful, chestnut curls cascading beneath her angora cap, a Pre-Raphaelite girl who'd somehow ended up in a universe of swirling snow.

"You couldn't call me?"

"That asshole Yount took my phone. Him or one of his clones is watching me every second."

"How did you get away from them?"

"I told Stuart I'd kill myself if I couldn't at least go for walks."

"And he believed you?"

"He had to." Odette lifted her chin, a defiant child. "After they killed Marcus, I took a bunch of pills."

"So Marcus was murdered."

"Surprised?" she said with a trace of scorn.

"No, it's just—" Hearing the news was like touching the electrified wire of the fence. It shocked no matter what. "Who killed him? Yount?"

"I don't know. I wasn't there. He died all alone." Odette held her brave pose, her voice grainy with tears. "It's my fault. He called to say good-bye before he left for Thanksgiving. I was crying because Stuart—" She pulled a tissue from her glove and dabbed her eyes, smudging her violet eye makeup. The winter light bleached her skin and made the smudges as stark as bruises. "Just the usual stupid shit. I should have kept my mouth shut."

"So Marcus got angry and drove up here."

"He wanted me to leave with him. He didn't understand."

"Didn't understand what?"

"He knew about Stuart."

"Knew what?"

"He thought being a good person would protect him. He was so good."

"Knew what?"

Odette shook her head. "I warned him, 'You don't threaten Stuart.' And Day—I warned her, too. I told her she was gonna end up dead like Marcus. She thought Gee would protect her."

"But he didn't," Kelly said.

"I don't know. Maybe he tried. Anyway, he was there."

"What?"

"At your house. When they killed Day."

Cold penetrated Kelly's body as if the wind could blow right through her. Tyson's whole routine—asking for help to find Day, claiming he was worried—had been a lie. "How do you know?"

"I listened to Stuart on the phone, talking to Yount. Saying he'd pay Welch to haul away Day's stuff." Odette's mouth twitched in a contemptuous smile. "That's how come I know Gee was there. Welch is like his Igor."

An image broke the surface of Kelly's mind: her friend cornered in the guest room, eyes wide, terrified. She pushed it back under. "Day knew about Stuart, too?"

"She knew where the clones buried Marcus."

"Clones?"

"Yount's crew. They work for this company, Guardians. They dress the same and act the same."

"They don't work for Stuart?"

"God, you're slow. Stuart has a contract with Guardians. He tells them, 'Kill Marcus,' so they do. He tells them, 'Go bury Marcus,' so they do. Day found out where they buried him. She was gonna tell the cops unless Stuart gave me a divorce and the money he promised. Shit, it was like begging to be killed. I tried to stop her."

"What money?"

"The settlement. Stuart's gonna divorce me when I'm twenty-four. I get five hundred grand. One-fifty goes to pay my dad's debt to Stuart, but the rest is mine. All we had to do was wait. I told Marcus that."

"Come with me," Kelly said. "You can tell the rest to the cops."

Somehow Odette's face turned a shade whiter. "I'll be dead if I do that."

"You might be anyway."

"I'll take my chances."

"Then why are we having this meeting? So you can cry on someone's shoulder?"

"God, can't you work it out? I tell you shit and *you* go to the cops. They bust Yount and throw his ass in prison."

Despite the melodramatic posing, Odette looked out for herself. She wanted to punish the underling, stay married to Helm another few years, and collect her severance pay at twenty-four, too old for her ex-husband but luscious enough for plenty of other rich old guys. She would marry one of them and find another fool like Marcus French to keep her entertained.

"Fine," Kelly said. "Where's Marcus buried?"

"Somewhere up this crick."

The half-frozen creek disappeared into a canopy of pines, branches heavy with needles, meshed in shadow. "Up there?"

"Yeah. Somewhere."

"Day never gave you directions?"

"She couldn't. We were having a party. Stuart was there. She said they carried the body, so she must've found tracks."

"You're talking about the party where she brought Courtney and Dustin?"

"Who?" Odette frowned, baffled for a moment. "Oh. Goth girl and her boyfriend. Day brought them without asking us. Stuart said she needed a lesson in manners."

"She needed a ride."

"She must've wanted to get here early and do her blackmail thing before Gee came."

"What happened?"

"She showed Stuart the photos."

"Photos of what?"

"Where Marcus is buried." Odette sniffled and dabbed her nose with the tissue. "God, it's cold."

"What did Stuart say?"

"That she was fucking dead. She told him there were copies hidden in different places, so nothing better happen to her. Like that's gonna stop him."

"You saw these photos."

"Yeah. Day gave me copies, but Yount took them."

He must have searched the house the night he murdered Day. Kelly pictured him rifling through her bedroom drawers and shuddered. "Do you remember them?"

"Not really. They were pictures of trees. Like landmarks. If I hiked up the stream I might recognize something." Odette flung a glance over her shoulder. "The patrol's coming."

Kelly checked her phone. "It's only 1:10."

"I don't know, they're early. Remember to stay in the trees."

"I followed the fence coming up. Animal told me to."

"Shit." The violet smudges magnified the terror in Odette's eyes. "If they see your footprints, I'm screwed."

Kelly's heart stuttered. "They patrol along the fence?"

"No, but they have binoculars." Odette stepped off the plastic ground cover and began folding it, moving briskly to align the corners. "Stay in the trees going down."

Helm's fence cut straight through the meadow. Staying in the trees meant circling far out of her way and maybe getting lost. The cold claimed Kelly's whole body now. Her parka and layers of clothing seemed to hold it in rather than keep it out. People froze to death in the mountains.

"It's no big deal," Odette said. "Just keep walking downhill until you come to the road."

"Sure. Miles from my car."

"Please, just do it."

"What difference does it make now? My footprints are already there. And it's snowing pretty hard. Maybe they won't see me."

"Do what you want, then." Odette stuffed the folded ground cover into its matching nylon bag. "No one should care about me. The people who care about me get killed."

Kelly turned her back on Odette's self-pity and retraced her footsteps to the edge of the trees, where she paused. She had to decide—fence or tree line. Her toes were numb. The cold scared her less than Stuart's Guardians, but they were on the other side of the fence. Even if they spotted her through the falling snow, she could reach the Jeep and escape before they caught up.

Probably.

She was already walking. Her decisive part chose the fence while the other part agonized. She moved briskly downhill. Ten more minutes and she'd be hidden in the trees below. She had to call Cash. Marcus's grave would be within hiking distance; Day had gone on foot to take her blackmail photos. The cops would find it.

They would search Kelly's house, too. The murder scene. The image of Day's terrified face surfaced again. She surged ahead, desperate to outrun it. She couldn't live in that house anymore. Her mind flew into the net of mundane problems that came with selling—dealing with a realtor, finding somewhere else to live, negotiating a new mortgage.

She heard the muffled growl of an engine. Across the meadow, a Land Rover crawled uphill, blurred by the snow but not hard to see, which meant the patrol could see her. She dropped to her knees and stretched flat on her stomach. Her heart thudded against the ground. The wind chilled her backside. She imagined a Guardian in a lambskin coat scanning the meadow with high-power binoculars. She released a breath and drew in another and wondered why snow smelled so much like iron. Her breath steamed the air, a ghostlike flag. But she had to breathe. She lifted her head. The Land Rover reached the top of the meadow and turned. It was moving toward the fence.

Better to wait a few more seconds. See if the Land Rover made another turn before reaching the fence. They might not have spotted her. Her heart wanted to smash through her chest and flee without her.

She bolted.

She scuttled on her knees and elbows toward the trees below. About fifty yards away. Half a football field. Her muscles knotted themselves with the effort. Steam billowed from her mouth. Crazy to think they wouldn't see her puffing along the fence like a cartoon train. She stumbled to her feet and ran. She understood how a scared rabbit felt.

The Land Rover's engine roared in triumph. When she reached the trees, she looked back. It barreled toward her. The fence would stop the Guardians, but they saw where she was running. Going south to Boulder, she would drive past the turnoff to Helm's house. They knew that. They would go down to the road and wait.

The snow was patchy beneath the trees, but the glazed pine needles on the ground held traces of her footprints. She followed them back to the Jeep. She brushed the snow from her clothes and got in. With a shaky hand she scooped the car keys from her pocket and started the engine. Her teeth chattered and she cranked the heat. It would take a while for the Jeep to warm up, but the whirring fan and whooshing air comforted her.

She came to the road and went north. Over and over she checked the rearview mirror. Nothing. No Guardians followed. But the patrol had started early. Either Animal had gotten the times wrong or Yount had known ahead of time about her rendezvous with Odette. No one could have told him except Animal or Odette. It made no sense for Odette to set Kelly up. Animal worked for Yount and could have seized the chance to score points with the boss, but he'd given her such painstaking instructions on the phone. Was he that good an actor? Kelly couldn't believe she'd misjudged him so completely.

Kelly peered between the curtains of the curtains of the fleabag motel room where she was holed up overnight. A snowplow rumbled through the parking lot. So much snow blanketed the vehicles that she couldn't recognize the Jeep, but she remembered where it was parked. The sky, dusky silver, brightened by the minute. Security lamps faded toward nothingness. She felt like the lamps, as if dawn would make her vanish.

She left the window and found a phone book in a drawer. Cash's number was in her phone, but her phone was gone. It had fallen from her pocket while she crawled through the snow to escape Helm's men. So she used the motel-room phone. She didn't usually worry about germs, but the beige hand piece looked so filthy that she wiped it with a soapy washcloth and dried it with a hand towel before making the call.

A woman answered. She asked Kelly's name in a business-like voice and told her to state her business with Detective Peterson.

"It's about the Marcus French case. He knows me."

The woman put her on hold, not for long. "Detective Peterson is unavailable. Leave your number and he'll get back to you."

"I'll just call later."

The Guardians would be waiting at Kelly's house, but probably not at the museum. MOR was closed Mondays. Ordinarily she had the day off, but this week she needed to work on the fundraiser. She could reach MOR by nine o'clock if she started for Boulder now, but an almost sleepless night had left her exhausted. She climbed back into bed. Just a few more minutes.

She was drifting toward emptiness, a pleasant haze, when three sharp raps on the window made her sit up. She hurried to the curtains. Animal stood outside holding two Styrofoam cups in a cardboard frame. He grinned. For a crazy moment she thought he was bringing her coffee, but he turned and ambled along the sidewalk fronting the motel rooms. He entered one of them. Kelly retreated to the phone and tried again to reach Cash.

❖

Animal handed a cup of coffee to the Guardian. "Room 4." The dude's scowl and pursed lips puckered his face like an anus. He gave a whole new meaning to butt-ugly. "She see you?"

Animal sat on the motel bed and pried the lid off his coffee. "Nah, she's asleep."

"Then she's an idiot. Let's take her now."

"And if she screams? We'd best stick to the plan."

Butt-Ugly stirred creamer into his coffee, the powdered kind made from chemicals you couldn't pronounce. "Then get out there and spike her tire."

"There's a guy plowing the lot."

"She could wake up any time. Go out to the road and—"

"I know what to do," Animal said. "I just don't wanna do it with that guy perched up on a snowplow watching."

"I'm in charge, Beaumont. Get the fuck out there."

Animal re-capped his coffee, heaved himself to his feet, and went outside. He trudged across the plowed lot and down the driveway, breathing in the crisp air. Sky and mountains glittered like crystal. This Guardian shit was ruining a beautiful day.

He wondered how Yount had found out about Kelly. Not from Odette. When she got back from her walk in the meadow, Yount had grabbed her arm, twisted it until she howled, and then pushed her into his office. Animal sat at the kitchen table with Butt-Ugly, listening to her scream and beg. No way was she faking that. Two other Guardians were already chasing after Kelly—in the wrong direction. Yount figured she'd scurried back to Boulder, but she outsmarted him by heading the other way. By the time he worked it out, she had a head start and the snow was coming down hard. Still, he sent Butt-Ugly and Animal after her.

They checked the parking lots of every cafe, motel, and bar along the road—not easy through the swirling snow. Butt-Ugly spotted her Jeep in front of the cheap motel outside Estes Park. He phoned in for instructions, and they had the pleasure of bunking in a musty room with sheets that stank of bleach.

Near the Jeep, Animal dug out his pocketknife and thumbed it open. When he glanced at the snowplow, the driver was facing away from him. He ducked beside one of the Jeep's front tires and touched the knife tip to the sidewall. Kelly was probably watching. He knew damned well that Butt-Ugly was.

Whether he spiked the tire or not, Animal would catch shit from someone, so he made his own choice.

Back in the motel room, he drank the lukewarm coffee. Butt-Ugly was watching a cop movie with lots of squealing tires and gunfire. On the screwed-up TV, white faces became bright red and black faces purple, so everyone in the movie looked drunk or pissed off. Animal stared out the window. With the curtains open, he had a full view of the parking lot. Four college kids were sweeping snow off their SUV. Their skis were propped against a nearby snowbank, waiting to be loaded. Two of them lobbed snowballs and joked while the other two worked. Animal daydreamed about skiing, the trees flying past.

Then the patrol car pulled into the lot.

Butt-Ugly made a noise that was half groan, half snarl. "What the fuck!"

"Hold on," Animal said. "They could be here for anything."

"We're not waiting around to find out."

They reached the Land Rover in twenty seconds. Animal swept the front windshield while Butt-Ugly started the engine. They pulled onto the road just as Kelly opened the door to the cop.

16

They called it an interview room, but it felt more like an interrogation chamber—hard chairs, a metal table, drab institutional walls, a greasy window opening into a corridor. Kelly sat across the table from Cash and his partner, Detective Farrigan, a thirtysomething woman with a tight mouth and dramatic platinum streaks in her dark hair.

Kelly expected Cash to be angry, but she hoped he might be impressed, too. She'd done something brave, furnished information that solved their case. Even a glimmer of admiration in those green eyes would have made things easier.

He leaned over the table and jabbed her with questions, drawing answers like blood. How well did she know Animal? When did she learn he worked for Helm? What kind of pills had Odette taken in her suicide attempt? Had Kelly searched her own house for Day's photographs of the grave?

Her voice wavered or stumbled each time she looked at his grim face. He made her repeat the story and harried her over every detail she omitted, added, or changed. Meanwhile, Farrigan typed steadily on a laptop. They weren't recording the interview.

"You're treating me like I did something wrong," Kelly said.

"You didn't," Cash said. "Only something stupid."

Farrigan cautioned him with a stare and gave Kelly a thin smile. Like a glimmer of sunshine on a stormy day, it counted for a lot. "We just want to get things right. Do you need a break?"

"I need to use the restroom."

"Okay. I'll show you." Leaving Cash in the interview room, Farrigan took Kelly down the corridor and around a corner and opened the door to a single-toilet restroom.

For a horrible moment Kelly thought the detective meant to come inside with her, but Farrigan waited in the hall. An air freshener filled the bathroom with a nauseating flowery scent. The mirror over the sink reflected Kelly at her worst. She needed a comb and lipstick. She usually skipped makeup, but today her face was dead-fish white. Her eyes had a feverish gleam. A lock of hair stuck out sideways from her head despite her attempts to wet it down while the state cop stood awkwardly in the motel room. He'd escorted her all the way to Boulder and watched from his car as she entered the police station, where Cash and Farrigan were waiting.

Kelly took her time peeing and washing her hands and then splashed water on her face and patted it dry with a stiff paper towel. She dreaded going back out there.

She'd told them everything. Almost. She left out the detail that Animal was one of her pursuers. He'd rapped on her window to warn her, so she owed him something. And she hadn't said anything about Tyson's being present when Day was killed. She told herself it was scruples. He shouldn't be accused of murder based on Odette's assumption that Welch followed him everywhere. If Tyson had been involved in the killing, the police would find out. But the omission stuck in Kelly's throat like a half-swallowed pill.

Farrigan was still there when she came out.

"How much longer?" Kelly asked.

"We're almost done with yesterday. We also need to get your statement regarding Nina Ivan."

Cash waited in the corridor with a Styrofoam cup. He handed it to Kelly. "Sorry, we don't have tea." The coffee in the cup was black with a greenish oily film.

"Do you have cream or something?"

"Give it here," Farrigan said. "You want sugar, too?"

"Just cream, thanks."

Kelly stared at Cash's boots, lightweight boots designed for hiking, and pictured him trudging up the stream above Helm's estate, searching for Marcus's grave. He wouldn't have a clue where to go except for her. She deserved a thank-you for that anyway, but she wasn't holding her breath. She started back into the claustrophobic interview room.

"You could've been killed," he said.

"I know that."

"Why didn't you contact me when Peter Beaumont called you?"

"Odette wouldn't talk to you. Or to Detective Farrigan, nice as she is."

"You think she's nice?" He sounded surprised.

"Nicer than you anyway."

Cash let out his breath in an exasperated gust. "We could've covered you. You could've worn a wire and given us something solid to take to the judge."

"So my statement's no good and you're torturing me just for fun."

"Your statement helps, but a recording would be a lot harder to argue against. Just so you know, this is no fun for me, and it's not torture. Torture is what they did to your friend before they killed her."

Shocked, she looked up at him. Hard eyes, mouth tugged downward in a frown. He meant for the comment to hurt. Kelly refused to give him the satisfaction of knowing it had. "Animal called out of the blue. He made it seem urgent, like if I waited one extra day Odette might not be there."

"I know you talked to Alan Schwartz. You interfered with a police investigation."

"For talking to Marcus's roommate? Really? Tell me something. If Marcus hadn't gone missing, would you be looking for Day? At all? You think she's just another loser the world is better off without."

He stared back at Kelly with his pretty green eyes, as surprised by her outburst as she was.

Farrigan returned with the coffee. It was barely lukewarm and the creamer gave it a flat taste. Kelly smiled her thanks.

"Have you changed the locks to your house?" he asked in a subdued tone.

Then she remembered. "The locksmith's coming. What time is it?"

He checked his wristwatch. "Just after one."

"I have to go."

She started for the interview room to get her coat, and Cash stepped in front of the doorway. "We're not done here. You'll have to reschedule."

"I lost my phone."

Farrigan offered hers. Kelly found the locksmith's number online and called to reschedule. The soonest he could get to her was Wednesday at three.

"Move your valuables somewhere safe," Cash said. "I'll send someone with you to the house."

"Thanks. I've got that covered." Her laptop and a few pieces of jewelry were locked in her room safe at the Boulder Marriott. She doubted Yount cared about anything but the blackmail photos, but she needed the computer and felt possessive of the jewelry. "Are you going to fingerprint Day's room?"

"Yes, but I don't think there's much to find. Someone did a thorough cleanup. The stain on the mattress is blood, but the lab can't determine the type." Cash held out his hand. "Your key."

When she gave it to him, her fingers brushed his callused palm and their eyes met. She pulled her gaze away. "When can I have it back?"

"Sometime tomorrow. I'll bring it to you."

"I'll be at the museum."

"We need your fingerprints for comparison," Farrigan said. "And an object with Day's prints."

"She gave me some photographs. They're on the desk in my office."

Kelly imagined Day tied to the bed. They must have hurt her badly. Made her bleed. Even after she broke down and told where the photographs were, Yount would never be satisfied. He would suspect her of holding back. He couldn't make certain he had all the photos until he'd inflicted as much pain as she could bear.

Tyson shared the guilt even if he wasn't there. She was protecting him because she wanted to believe he cared about Day and because Joyce would blame her for involving the museum, even indirectly, in a murder case. That made Kelly a fool and a coward.

She startled at a touch on her arm.

"You all right?" Farrigan asked.

"There's something else."

"What?" Cash pounced as if he'd known all along that she was holding back.

"Something Odette said. She thought Gregory Tyson might have been there the night Day was killed. She didn't have any evidence. But since Welch was there—"

The detectives exchanged looks.

"Not much we can do with that," Farrigan said.

Cash nodded. "But we can go after him with Nina. If she's willing to make a complaint."

"She didn't want to talk about what happened," Kelly said.

"Try again."

"You want me—"

"She's more likely to listen to you," Farrigan said.

"You like playing cop," Cash said. "Here's your chance."

It was midafternoon before the detectives finished with Kelly. She spent a tedious hour buying a new phone and waiting while her stored data downloaded. Before leaving the store, she checked her voice mail. She listened to two messages from Joyce demanding to know where she was. Then another voice echoed the question.

"Where are you? Someone broke into your roommate's car. Which you promised to have towed, by the way. Her junk's all over the place." Owen's voice lifted toward hysteria. "Look, I don't want to call the cops. Will you please come home and clean it up? You still live here, don't you?"

Not for long, thankfully.

When she reached Ash Mountain Estates, the sunset was fading from the mountaintops, the sky overhead already dark.

She passed houses ablaze with Christmas lights and turned onto her street. Boxes and piles of stuff were strewn around Day's Corolla. Kelly pulled into her driveway, grabbed the flashlight from the glove box, and hurried to the curb.

The Corolla had been locked, but that wouldn't stop Yount.

A sleeping bag lay open on the sidewalk. A ripped-open pillow spewed clumps of foam. Just about everything had been pulled from the car—tangled piles of clothes, photography magazines, takeout menus from restaurants in California, spiral notebooks, a baseball mitt. Scraps of paper fluttered across the snow, some of them onto Owen's property. Paperbacks had been dumped from two cardboard boxes. She picked up a dog-eared copy of *A Separate Reality*.

"I hope you don't plan to leave this trash overnight."

Startled, she dropped the book. Owen stood on the sidewalk several feet away, wearing unlaced running shoes and a parka over his pajamas.

"When did this happen?"

"Sometime last night. I've been trying to reach you all day."

"I've been kind of busy."

"You should pile everything back in this junker and have it towed."

"So you didn't see anyone out here?"

Owen sniffled. "I told you, no."

"Well, this was a break-in. You'll have to talk to the cops."

"Don't give them my name." He shrank back as if Kelly had attacked.

"I wouldn't worry. It's not like you have anything to hide."

"That's not the point. You ever read *The Trial?*"

The last thing she needed was paranoia from Owen. She had enough of her own. "Make you a deal. Try harder to remember and I'll forget to mention you to the cops."

"I'm not holding out on you, Kelly. I didn't see who broke into the car."

"What about the night Day left? Anything, even the tiniest detail—"

"The lights were on."

"What lights?"

"In your house. Before I saw the guy in the baseball cap, I noticed lights."

"How long before?"

"Two hours, maybe. It's not like I was timing it. Look, I'm freezing." Owen scuffled away in his loose shoes.

She opened the driver's door and found the trunk release. When she raised the trunk's hood, a reek of sweat and mildew ballooned in her face, but only the spare tire was inside. She closed the trunk and aimed the flashlight into the car's interior. The floor in back was littered with trash from meals eaten in the car—Hardee's bags and burger wrappers, cellophane bags that once held pine nuts or pretzels, paper cups, 7-Up and Dr. Pepper cans, wrappers from Milky Way bars and Reese's peanut butter cups.

Kelly spotted something with a perforated edge.

She climbed into the car and, reaching between the front seats, plucked a strip of film negatives from the refuse. She turned on the dome light and studied the dark images—five shots of Odette and Marcus sitting somewhere outside. Kelly wrapped the film in a tissue and slipped it into her coat pocket. She sifted through the wrappers and cans and groped beneath the seats but found nothing else.

On her way to the Jeep, she turned and shone the flashlight on the Corolla a final time. Its once-sky-blue paint had bleached to a milky color. The undercarriage was pocked and eaten by rust. Day had driven up and down the West Coast, through Death Valley and over the Continental Divide in the old car. Kelly doubled back and picked up *A Separate Reality.* She put the paperback in the glove box with the flashlight and then she called Cash.

His Outback pulled into the driveway forty minutes later. He lowered the window and frowned. "You shouldn't have come here alone."

She told him about the message from Owen. "He sounded upset, so I drove straight out. Then I called you."

"You should've called us first."

"I wasn't alone. Technically. There's Owen. You can bet he's peeking right now from his window."

His face tightened. "It's not a game, Kelly." He got out of the car and went to inspect the clutter around the Corolla. "Did you move anything?"

"The negatives I told you about. And a book I want to keep."

"Let's see them." She brought the paperback from the Jeep. Cash thumbed the pages and smiled. "The path of the warrior."

"You read this?"

"In high school."

"You don't seem like the Castaneda type."

"Which shows how little you know about me." He gave the book back to her. "By the way, you're wrong. I care about Day. I care about anyone who gets victimized." He reeled off the statement as if he'd been waiting for the chance to make it, so Kelly just nodded.

She took out the strip of film negatives and held it by the edges, steadying her hand against her other arm. He examined the frames with a compact halogen flashlight. "These mean anything to you?" he asked.

Kelly shook her head. "They're pictures of Odette and Marcus. Maybe you'll see something important after you develop them. Day wouldn't throw this on the floor of her car. One of Yount's men must've found it and then dropped it."

"You'd think guys like that would be more careful." Cash took the film and sealed it inside an envelope. "You sure it was Yount? Tyson could've killed your friend."

"Why? Because Odette thought he might have been here that night? I know he and Helm are in business together, but he cared about Day."

"Christ, Kelly. A guy resembling the Cascade's manager is seen at your house the night she disappears. The Cascade's owner probes you for information. And the Cascade's bouncer happens to be working for Helm."

"Animal?"

"Don't act surprised. You had to know. You just chose not to share the information." Cash gave her a smile that made her want to hide. "Anything else you haven't told me?"

She let out her breath. "He warned me." She told him how Animal had knocked on the window of the motel.

"He likes you. Why is that?"

"Because I helped Nina."

"Which reminds me, when I come to your museum tomorrow, be ready to leave with me. I'm taking you to her place."

"I doubt your presence will reassure her." Kelly trailed him to his car. "Why can't I go to the Cascade after work?"

"I don't want you anywhere near the Cascade. And Bridget and I both think Nina's more likely to listen if you approach her somewhere she feels safe."

"So I just show up at her door?"

"Call ahead if you want."

"I'm going to be busy tomorrow. I missed work today."

He slid behind the wheel of the Outback. "You have time for lunch, don't you?" He backed the car into the street and stopped. After a few moments he lowered the window. "You need to be careful."

"I know."

"Don't go anywhere except work. And call if you think someone's following you. I'd assign someone to watch you, but we don't have the resources."

She felt the weight of his gaze and hated feeling afraid. "I promise to be careful."

17

Sunlight bleached the computer screen. Kelly angled the monitor away from the light and scooted her chair to one side. Problem solved—except she had to twist her neck and type with the keyboard in her lap. She was composing a last-minute e-mail to remind MOR's members of the fundraiser. It seemed pointless. Those who intended to come would remember and the rest wouldn't care.

"Why are you sitting like that?" Joyce leaned on the door sill, watching Kelly with an amused smirk. "You look like a pretzel."

"Because there aren't any blinds on my window."

"We've been through that. The windows have to be stark. Putting anything on them would—"

"Compromise the integrity of the architect's vision. I know. But right now I'm more worried about the integrity of my vision."

"There's a police officer waiting outside. He's asking questions about the museum's security. He implied you could be in some kind of danger. Is that why you missed work yesterday? You told me you drove to Estes Park and got stuck in the snow."

"I did." Kelly put on her coat and picked up her bag.

"If I'm in danger, too, I deserve to know."

"You aren't."

Joyce kept blocking the doorway. "He asked questions about Gee and Day. What have you told him? If you've maligned the museum's reputation—"

"Since we're talking about this, it would be better if someone else picked up the donations from Annie and Leonard. Especially with Leonard living out in the country."

"I told you, there's no one else I trust to handle the artwork properly."

"If they come after me again, it could be damaged."

"Come after you?" Joyce gave a weak laugh. "How melodramatic. And who are they?"

"Detective Peterson didn't tell you?"

"He wouldn't answer my questions, but he expected me to answer his."

"He can be annoying that way." Kelly squeezed past her and walked out.

She found Cash in the Magic and Realism exhibit, studying a painting—Salvador Parra's *Finch with Cat*, one of her favorites.

"I don't get it," he said. "There's no magic, and there's sure as hell no realism."

"My boss isn't happy with you."

"Yeah, I have that effect sometimes." He handed her the key to her house. "We're done with Day's room, but I don't want you going back until the locksmith changes the locks. And call me first so I can meet you there."

They walked through the Native American galleries. "Okay, this stuff I get," he said. "Pottery, rugs—you use them every day."

"But their makers went to the trouble of making them beautiful."

"I like beautiful things. That painting back there isn't beautiful. It's just weird."

"How can you read Casteneda and not appreciate a painting like this one?"

Cash laughed. "I never did drugs. Maybe that's my problem." At least *Finch with Cat* hadn't spoiled his mood. His eyes were soft and reflective. "We got lucky. There's a partial fingerprint on the negative strip from Day's car. It matches Lawrence Welch's. He probably found a bunch of negatives and dropped the one strip while looking through them."

"Just like I thought."

He acknowledged the point with a lopsided smile. "It's proof that Odette and Marcus knew each other. We have a warrant on Odette, too. If we can find her. Helm's lawyer claims she flew to California yesterday."

"What about Welch?"

"We'll bring him in for questioning."

An elderly couple strolled into the gallery. Charlie, one of the guards, trailed after them and halted in surprise when he noticed Kelly. He eyed her and the detective. They fell silent until they were halfway down the stairs to the lobby.

"Welch was arrested for rape twice in his twenties." Cash kept his voice low. "Charges were dropped, same reason both times. The victim backed out."

"You think he threatened them?"

"There's a lot of reasons why rape victims don't come forward. The big one is they want to get on with their lives."

She caught the note of scorn, faint and dry. "And you have a right to pass judgment?"

"I'm not judging the victims. I just hate their self-delusion and the way it plays into the rapist's hands."

"You expect victims to be heroes?"

"Yeah. They have to be. Otherwise the rapist stays on the street and more women become victims."

They passed through the lobby and stopped near the front entrance.

"Look, I'll be straight with you," Cash said. "We can't charge Welch with the rape. We need physical evidence from a rape kit, and it's too late for that."

"Then why put Nina through this?"

"We already have Welch with the fingerprint on the negative. With her statement we can get a warrant to search the Cascade and bring Tyson in for questioning."

"Is Tyson a suspect in the rape?"

"He owns the bar where it happened. And he was allegedly at your house the night Day disappeared."

"So this isn't really about Nina."

"The point is she won't have to testify in court and Welch will go to prison."

Kelly turned toward the elevators. "I'm parked in the garage."

He stepped in front of her. "I'm driving."

"No. Nina won't talk to me if she sees you."

He frowned and started to say something but thought better of it. "I'm parked out front. I'll wait for you."

"What if she's not home?"

His gaze shifted to Marta, who watched them curiously from the front desk. "Give her a call before you knock."

"I don't know her number."

"I'll text you."

"Fine." She took the stairs instead of the elevator. She needed the extra time to calm down. Cash intended to use Nina. His noble reasons didn't change that basic fact. Kelly remembered the panic on her face the night they talked at the Cascade—fear of Welch and, even worse, terror at acknowledging what he'd done to her. What if Nina needed the amnesia of Welch's drug?

Kelly drove the Jeep out of the underground garage and around the corner to the front of the museum, where Cash waited in his Outback. She followed him through town, trying to fasten her mind to the task of driving. Her stomach roiled. She couldn't make Nina report the rape, only give her the choice. And if Nina refused, Cash might not shrug his shoulders and say, "Oh well." He or Detective Farrigan might try their kind of persuasion, something they no doubt considered to be gentle.

Cash drove past the house on Arapahoe and parked about fifty feet down the block. Kelly pulled to the curb. A few moments later her phone beeped, announcing his text. She called the number and waited through half a dozen rings. She got ready to leave a message.

"Hello?" Nina sounded breathless and a little forlorn.

"Hi, Nina. It's Kelly. Can we talk?"

"About what?"

"That night."

A long silence followed. "Beau put you up to this."

"Kind of." It wasn't a complete lie. Animal had asked her to talk with Nina the night she picked up the photographs.

"Well, you don't have to."

"I want to."

More silence, precarious.

"Please," Kelly said.

"I'll meet you at Angkor. You know where it is?"

"I'm parked outside your apartment if you want a ride."

Nina choked out a laugh. "You were pretty sure I'd say yes."

"No. But if you did, I wanted to be there before you changed your mind."

"I'll be down in ten minutes." Nina hung up.

Kelly took a breath and called Cash to report the new plan. "Good thing I drove my own car. What if she was waiting outside the restaurant and saw me get out of yours?"

"You made the right move. Is that what you want to hear?"

She couldn't help enjoying his irritation. "It's a nice change."

"Before you gloat too much, let's see if you get anywhere with Nina."

❖

Angkor was located in a strip mall, wedged between a yarn store and a shoe repair shop. Kelly spotted Cash's Outback, but he wasn't in the car. He'd gone into the restaurant. He could ruin everything if he did blatant surveillance and Nina noticed. Angkor's waiting area was crammed with chairs. A computerized register sat behind a cabinet displaying aspirin, antacids, and breath mints. The bottles and rolls of tablets had the undisturbed look of museum exhibits. Beyond an archway decorated with scarlet fringe, a narrow room extended toward the back, tables along one wall and booths along the other. Peacock-blue brocaded curtains enclosed the booths, shielding the diners from view.

"I was hoping for a booth," Nina said.

"We can wait if you want."

"No, that's okay."

The hostess, a college girl in platform shoes, led them to a booth and held a curtain open. The booth was vacant after all. After Nina sat, the hostess dropped the curtain on that side and winked at Kelly as if they shared a secret. They did. Both of them knew Cash had flashed his badge and arranged to lurk in the next booth.

The hostess spread menus in front of them, and a minute later a server showed up to take their order.

"Let me get this," Kelly said.

"Well, you better. It was your idea." Nina tried for a sprightly tone, but it came out brittle. The light from a wall sconce shadowed the tension in her mouth and around her eyes.

"Are you feeling okay?"

She fingered the fork on her place mat. "There's no reason to talk about what happened. It's over with and I've moved on."

"Have you seen a doctor?"

"Why should I?"

"You could have a disease."

The murmur of conversations from other tables welled in the silence. Nina stared at the fork as if it held the power to transport her somewhere else.

Kelly tried to forget about Cash spying in the next booth. "I think you know that somebody drugged you that night. How did you feel the next morning?"

"Just fine." Nina lifted her chin and glared defiantly.

"Welch probably raped you." She repeated what Cash had told her about the charges against Welch and how they were dropped. "He probably threatened those women. Has he threatened you?"

Nina's glare turned furious. "You told the cops."

"I met a detective when I reported Day missing. And yes, I told him—"

"Day's missing?"

"Since Thanksgiving. You knew her?"

"She was at the Cascade with Gee a couple times. I like her. She treats everybody like they matter. Even me." Her smile twitched and died in a moment. "I figured Gee was just over her. He never stays with anyone for long."

"Welch will hurt someone else if you don't stop him."

"You mean well and everything, but you don't have a clue. Welch doesn't need to threaten me. I know what happens if I rat to the cops."

"So he gets to keep on drugging and raping women."

"I can't help that. It's not wrong to take care of myself. Who else will? Sorry, but I've got my own life." By now Nina was gripping the fork in both hands, squeezing out its nonexistent magic.

"You're just going to keep working at the Cascade?"

"Until I find something else that pays as good."

"What if Welch rapes you again?"

"Why would he?" She finally looked straight at Kelly, her chin high and defiant. "Anyway, I got someone to protect me now."

"Animal."

"Beau won't let anyone hurt me."

"Does he know what Welch did?"

"No. And don't you go telling him."

"He's smart," Kelly said. "He'll figure it out if he hasn't already."

They heard the server coming and fell silent while she tied back the curtain and served their tea and food. Kelly got a curry dish she couldn't remember ordering. When the server was gone, she said, "Is that the only reason you're going out with him—for protection?"

"It's not your business why I do anything."

"Welch dumped you in your car and left you to freeze to death."

With a sigh, Nina set down the fork. With food on the table, its magic had fled. "He knew Beau would find me after the lot cleared out. He doesn't want any embarrassing dead bodies at the Cascade."

"What makes you think that's a problem for him? He can bury you up in the mountains, the way he buried Day and Marcus."

"Buried? What are you talking about? Who's Marcus and how do you know all this anyway? From the cops?"

Kelly was pitched forward, her voice louder than she meant it to be, so she let herself relax against the back of the booth. "Welch might kill you anyway, just to be sure. And Animal might not be able to save you. He's big and strong, but he can be killed, too."

"Fuck you." Nina twisted her mouth as if the swearword tasted bad. She pushed aside the peacock-blue curtain and struggled to her feet.

Kelly hurried after her. "Let me drive you home."

"I don't want a ride from you."

"It's three or four miles back to your place. And it's cold."

When they reached the lobby, where the hostess waited behind the cash register, Nina bolted out the door. Kelly paid for the untouched food, and by the time she signed the credit card receipt and hurried outside, Nina was nowhere in sight.

"Nice try." Cash caught up and offered her a consoling smile. "I couldn't have got that far with her."

"She's scared." Kelly peered down the busy street. "I have to find her."

"Call me if you can't."

"That's all she needs, to be picked up by the cops. It'll do wonders for her paranoia."

"Why should she be afraid of the cops, Kelly? Ask yourself that."

Kelly opened her mouth to say that not everyone who distrusted the cops was a criminal. But every second she stood there, Nina was walking farther away. The argument would have to wait. She left Cash standing in the parking lot of the run-down strip mall. She drove a couple of blocks before spotting Nina plodding along the sidewalk. She pulled to the curb and lowered the window. "Please get in."

Nina's face and hands were blistery red after a few minutes in the raw wind. Scowling, she trudged across the curb and got into the Jeep. She huddled in the seat, hands tucked up her coat sleeves. Neither of them spoke during the drive back to the apartment, and as soon as the Jeep stopped, Nina hopped out and slammed the door behind her.

18

"I thought you were in L.A. another week," Gee said.

"I was, but Yount tells me everything's going to shit out here." Stuart lounged on the leather sofa in Gee's office. In his sixties, Stuart could run a marathon in under four hours. His body and face seemed to harden instead of soften with age, a kind of petrifaction set off by his deep suntan and shock of white hair.

"Did Yount mention he caused most of the shit himself?"

Stuart squeezed out a smile. "He gave me the negatives today. They were in her car the whole time. Why wasn't it searched that night?"

"We were kinda busy."

"But not very productive."

Gee felt a wrongness in his body and a desperation that flared from out of nowhere. He needed a hit of coke. "I don't know what Yount told you, but that's on him. And we've got other shit to worry about. Welch is back to his old habits."

"Terrible." Stuart shook his head, a civilized man appalled at the state of the world. "But it's not my problem, it's yours."

"Sooner or later it's gonna bring the cops. You really think Welch can keep his mouth shut?"

"Can you?"

"Why are you here, Stuart?"

"Day." Stuart made a show of looking wistful. "I enjoyed having her around. She was game for anything and kept Odette amused. She made foolish choices. Bringing those punk kids to our party, taking up with you. Blackmailing me. But I could never bring myself to hold it against her."

"You just wanted her dead."

"I didn't want it. It was necessary."

"Well, she's dead and you got the fucking negatives."

"But not the photos. God knows how many sets she made. The little bitch taunted me. She said I'd never find them all and her friends would turn them over to the cops if she went missing."

"But nobody has."

"It's been two weeks. The people holding them might not know she's missing yet. There's something else—Yount found negatives of shots I never saw before. They weren't among the ones she used to blackmail me. They're compromising, for him in particular."

"It's not my problem, it's his." Gee enjoyed throwing Stuart's words back at him and watching as anger turned the old man's face to stone.

"It's very much your problem. A couple days ago, Kelly and Odette had a meeting in the meadow behind the house. They'll search the land behind my property. It's government land, so I can't stop them, only slow them down." Stuart jabbed a knobby finger at him. "We could've been done with this if you let Yount do his job."

"Yount's a fucking sadist."

He raised his eyebrows and crimped his mouth as if saying, *It is what it is*. "The fact remains—this problem must be taken care of. The cops have no evidence yet. Only Kelly Durrell's story. The story has to change or she has to go."

"What the fuck? You're talking about wasting her? You think they won't work it out?"

"Hopefully it won't come to that. A lot depends on you. Your charm. Convince her to change her story and help us track down the photos."

His charm. That was a joke. "Kelly's not like Day. She's got family."

"Her parents are hundreds of miles away. Yount knows how to stage these things. He's done it before."

"With people like Day, who don't count."

"You'd be surprised. He's taken care of small-time politicians who were causing trouble and women whose husbands couldn't afford a divorce. Of course, it has to convince the cops, and that's where Yount excels. He used to be a cop, you know."

"Leave her alone."

Stuart eyed him curiously. "You're not in love again?"

"I'm sick of people dying." Every cell in Gee's body screamed for coke. He couldn't draw air into his lungs without a conscious effort.

"You look like shit. Yount tells me you've been sucking a lot of powder."

Another stab in the back from Welch. Gee wished he'd pounded the troll's face to pulp. "I won't do it."

"Then Yount will. Go ahead and take a vacation. The cops can't make you a suspect if you're in the Caribbean."

Gee's brother used to poke at tied-up dogs with sticks. They barked and growled at first, but by the end they crouched and whimpered, helpless. Stuart was the same. A power freak.

"What happens if Yount gets popped?" Gee said.

"He won't. He'll be gone. When this is over, I'm asking Guardians for another crew."

"After all you've been through together."

"There's an alternative. I sell my house and move back to the coast and pretend I never knew you."

"Go ahead, break my fucking heart."

"I'll do it, Gee. In a heartbeat."

"You can kiss my connections good-bye. How you gonna move your shit without them?"

"It will hurt me financially." Stuart spoke more to himself than to Gee. "But I'd rather take the bite than go to prison."

Two-thirds of his income came from his various dealings with Stuart. He couldn't afford to lose that. Yount had no doubt tracked down his connections, and they could be persuaded to buy direct from the source. "Okay, I'll have a talk with Kelly."

"Take her first. Then have a talk." Stuart rose from the sofa and ambled to the door. He paused with his hand on the knob. "Yount had better talk with her, too. I can't trust you anymore." He closed the door behind him gently.

Gee clutched the edge of his desk and waited a long minute before laying out two fat lines of coke. The instant the drug hit his nose, the rush punched into his brain and warm aftershocks spread through his body. He could breathe again. He turned his full attention to his rage.

Stuart gave the word and people died—nice and clean, no consequences. Crazy old asshole. Gee knew all about psychos like him, thanks to his brother Renny. He knew the cost of standing up to them. And the cost of lying down.

◈

Whether Gee was sixteen, Renny had shown him how to do business.

He remembered the kids skateboarding in the darkening street, their raucous shouts joined to the chorus of starlings settling to roost. The scent of lilacs wafted from somewhere, too sweet. Gee hung back on the porch steps. Renny swaggered to the door, his thumb hooked in the front pocket of his jeans. No one answered the bell. He stepped to the window, cut the screen with his jackknife, and sent Gee inside to unlock the door.

Dougie was taking a shower. Light from the bathroom shone on Renny's rapt smile. Gee heard the shower curtain rip, hooks popping off the rod, and a croaked "What—" Thumps and scuffling. Then a louder thump and a scream.

They dragged Dougie into a bedroom and hogtied him with twine. He was a small dude with a hairless chest and not much pubic hair. He curled on the dirty carpet, wet hair pasted to his face, bleeding from his mouth and panting like a dog.

"The shit I tasted was rock," Renny said. "The shit you delivered was stepped on."

"The suppliers—"

Renny slammed his fist into Dougie's face. "I bought from you, not them. Ain't my fault you trusted a bunch of fucking spics."

"Basement," Dougie jabbered. "Third shelf up. Cinder block."

"Check it out, Gee."

Gee found the basement door where he expected it to be. Same with the light switch. As if the floor plan of Dougie's house had been burned into his brain at birth. As if he never had a choice. The shelves held the usual clutter—a busted toaster oven, a couple of bowling trophies, a glass jar of pennies. The money was stashed in the cavity of a cinder block. Not enough. Gee brought the pennies, too.

The bedroom stank of urine. "Nine hundred seventy." Gee tossed the roll of bills to Renny. "Plus change." He shook the jar of pennies and placed it on the floor. Doing things like that—provocative things—made him less afraid of his brother.

Renny grabbed a sock from the floor and stuffed it in Dougie's mouth. Shadows warped his smile into something monstrous. "You owe me seven large. I want my money, bitch. You gonna give me my money?" When he struck the first match, Gee looked away. A scream gargled in Dougie's throat. The bedroom carpet was green and littered with tiny pebbles and burned-out matches. The useless details stuck to Gee's memory like lint. He wanted to bolt, but Renny would be waiting at home and their parents wouldn't protect him. Dad thought weaklings deserved what they got, and Mom was just a slave.

"Where should I burn the cocksucker now? I'm thinking his balls."

Gee tasted vomit. "He'd probably like it, the faggot."

The hogtied body thumped like a landed fish. Dougie made urgent whimpering noises. He had more to say. Renny yanked the sock from his mouth.

"Cl-cl-closet." Dougie's gaze jerked upward. "Sh-sh-shoe box."

Gee pulled shoe boxes from the top shelf of the closet. In two of them he found Dougie's real stash. Hundred-dollar bills and fifties and twenties, sorted into piles and rubber-banded. He showed his brother the money and began counting out loud. "Two hundred, three, four, five, six . . ." The diversion worked. Renny came and stood over him while he counted the money. Nine thousand two hundred and thirty dollars.

"Asshole could've just paid me."

Gee hoped that it would end there, that his brother would be satisfied with a three thousand-dollar profit and let Dougie keep his life. But Renny strangled Dougie with a belt from the closet and then tossed Gee the car keys. "There's a can of gas in the trunk. Bring it."

The firefighters showed up fast. Their station, it turned out, was two blocks away. Dougie's body was mostly unburned, and the cops lifted a partial fingerprint from the belt. It wasn't a certain match, but a neighbor ID'd their car and Dougie's friends testified to Renny's psycho reputation.

Gee never rolled over. He was handcuffed to a table for hours. He begged for the toilet, but the two ugly cops just laughed. They laughed more after he pissed himself. They claimed a witness had seen his face and showed him a drawing that looked like him. But Gee wasn't stupid. It had been too dark for anyone to make him. The cops yammered on and on about their solid case and how he would be so popular in the slammer that his asshole would be looser than his mama's pussy. Now and then they changed tactics and called him a good boy, a straight-A student, and promised him that Renny was going down so he'd best cut a deal while he could. Through it all, Gee kept the guilt and horror locked inside. And finally they had to let him go. They had nothing.

Renny was confident that he would walk free, too. Gee had been in the courtroom when the jury came back. Had seen his brother's face when the foreman spoke the word *guilty*—the rapt smile, like the moment he'd sailed into the bathroom to take Dougie down.

19

The next morning started out hectic. With the fundraiser only three days away, Kelly was scrambling to find a replacement for the cellist in the string quartet, who needed emergency gallbladder surgery. Her ex-boyfriend had contacts at the university's music department, so she gritted her teeth and called him. She expected snark from Ray, but instead he gave her a few phone numbers and promised to show up at the fundraiser. Not that he would.

"Cara really does miss you," he said.

Kelly missed the little girl, too, but before she could say so, he ended the call.

By the time she found a substitute cellist, it was after one o'clock. Since Joyce insisted that no one else could handle the artwork donated by board members, Kelly had to squeeze another errand into her schedule. Annie wouldn't take long, but Leonard lived several miles east of town. She had to drive out there and somehow make it back to her house by three o'clock for the appointment with the locksmith.

Unless Yount's men grabbed her along the way. She set her phone on the passenger seat, within easy reach.

She parked in front of Annie's restored Queen Anne house. She peered up and down the quiet street lined with cars. There was nothing suspicious. No black Land Rover. Annie's veranda was forlorn and shadowed in December, its tapered posts like bleached bones. Teak rocking chairs creaked. Silver wind chimes jangled mournfully. She rang the bell and waited, rang and waited some more. She rapped the bronze knocker.

Annie's number had been transferred to Kelly's new phone along with her other contacts. She called and got no answer and left a hurried message. There wasn't time to wait, not if she wanted to keep her appointment.

She tramped to the side of the house and looked through a window. The downstairs served as a gallery for Annie's art. Through the sheer curtain, she spotted a crate on the floor. She backtracked to the door and tried the knob. It turned. She stepped into a large reception area. "Annie?" She wandered toward the stairs. Annie could be upstairs showering or sleeping, but more likely she'd stepped out for a few minutes and left the door unlocked.

Kelly touched a raw gash in the banister. How had that happened? Annie babied the old house.

The crate was pushed against a display case that Annie had bought secondhand from a jewelry store going out of business. Inside were earrings and pendants made of glass in vivid colors and whimsical shapes. Misshapen unicorns were her specialty. People loved them. Although she sold two or three expensive pieces a year, she made most of her living with the trinkets.

The crate seemed ready for pickup, but there was no label or note. Reluctant to take it without checking the contents, Kelly brought the tire iron from her Jeep and pried off the lid. Inside transparent bubble wrap was the piece Annie had donated, a sensuous sculpture of blown glass ribboned with deep oranges and blues. She hammered the lid back in place with the flat end of the tire iron and carried the crate to the Jeep. Once she had it stowed in the cargo area and secured with bungee cords, she returned to the house for her things. She sent a text to Annie: *Got the sculpture, sorry to miss you. Thanks for your generosity. See you Saturday night!*

◆

Leonard Proud lived in a 1930s bungalow in Niwot, a small town on the plain east of Boulder. As she walked to the door, a teenage boy emerged from the house. A mutt with terrier blood and sulfur-colored fur bounded past him and wandered through the yard, nosing milkweed stalks and dormant grass.

The teenager's eyes avoided hers. "I'm to load my pa's collage into your car."

Kelly returned to the Jeep and opened the cargo door.

"It's huge," he said. "It's not gonna fit in there."

"Help me fold down the backseat."

"Won't be enough. You gotta move that crate."

He helped her carry the crate to the passenger seat in front. She wrestled with the bungee cords, and by the time she got the crate strapped to the seat, Proud and his son were sliding the collage into the Jeep's cargo area. The collage was wrapped in a blanket and tied with twine.

"You should have packed it better," Kelly said. "It could be damaged."

"Costs money. I'm a janitor, not a professor."

"All right. I'll be careful with it."

"You do that." He was wearing a flannel shirt, no coat. A bitter wind lifted his straggly hair, but he seemed comfortable. "Tell your friend the photographer I say hello."

"Day? She's gone. You didn't know?"

"How would I? I don't come 'round that sorry museum except for board meetings. Where'd she go?"

Kelly's throat tightened. Telling him was somehow like finding Day missing all over again. "I don't know. She left while I was in Illinois and didn't—"

"Come in."

The orange shag carpet in his living room was circa 1970 and so loose in spots that someone could trip on the slack. The dog lay on a couch covered with a Hudson Bay blanket with broad blue and yellow stripes. The teenager was nowhere in sight. Her nostrils shrank from the odor of simmering beef stock.

"I'm boiling bones for soup. Sit down. I'll be right back." Proud disappeared through a doorway.

She eyed a chair with collapsed springs and chose the sofa instead. The yellow dog crawled closer and rested his head in her lap, so she stroked his rough fur and scratched the hollow behind his jaw. His tail thumped the seat cushion. A dog would be good company. Too bad she wasn't home enough to take care of one. She noticed that her palm was black with dirt. The animal must have rolled in the mud. She was rummaging in her bag for a tissue when Proud returned with a large envelope.

"Your friend mailed this to me."

She took the envelope and spilled the contents from the torn end: an eight-by-ten close-up of Proud trying not to smile, a smaller envelope marked "For Kelly," and a handwritten note.

Hey, nice meeting you. Heres your photo thats not going in the newsletter. I still want to see your work sometime if Im still around. But if Im not please give this to Kelly. Your the best. Day

Kelly opened the envelope addressed to her, pulled out several photos and looked through them. Her heartbeat spiked. She knew that fence and creek from her rendezvous with Odette. She understood at once the sunken patch of earth.

"Something wrong?" Proud asked.

"I have to go." She fought the tremor in her voice. "Thanks for these."

"Your friend's a real person. One of the few."

Was.

Was real.

The wind slapped at her face as she walked to the Jeep. Her head seemed to float, buoyed by the chemistry of excitement and fear. She called Cash. The call went to voice mail, so she left a message. "I'm heading home to meet the locksmith. I might be a few minutes late. I just got something from Day. Some photos that you need to see. There's one—I think it's where Marcus is buried." She gripped the steering wheel to calm herself for the drive back to Boulder and then across town to Ash Mountain Estates.

She was ten minutes late. As usual on weekdays, the development seemed deserted except for a few cars at the Community Center. The stay-at-home moms and sometimes Owen hung out there, exchanging cookie recipes and bitching about eyesores like Day's Corolla. No crime-scene tape decorated her house. The police had either taken it down or skipped it altogether. Skipped it, she hoped. Otherwise, someone on the Community Board would show up with questions. There would be questions soon enough when the realtor's sign went up, and a letter reminding her of the covenant she'd signed.

She pulled up behind the locksmith's van in her driveway. Cash hadn't shown up yet. She fumbled the phone from her bag, called him, and left another message. "I'm at my house. Get here as soon as you can."

She raised the garage door and got out of the Jeep. She hated to keep the locksmith waiting any longer. The van's windshield and driver's window reflected the winter sky, but she flashed an apologetic smile and waved at him to follow her into the house. She hurried through the laundry room into the kitchen and dropped her bag and Day's photos on the counter.

A smell flooded her nose and mouth, metallic, choking.

She looked a long way down.

The man crumpled on her kitchen floor was soaked in blood from the wet hole in his chest. His body seemed shrunken, discarded. A few feet away, his metal toolbox lay on its side.

"Don't." Tyson stood at the entrance to the front hallway. He held a gun.

She stared at the barrel, dark and hollow and shining with oil. She leaned on the kitchen counter, lightheaded.

"Don't move," he said. "I'm here to save you."

"What?" The door behind her was open. She could duck into the laundry room before he pulled the trigger. Maybe.

"Just—don't." He took careful steps across the kitchen, edging around the body.

Cash was supposed to be there. She should have waited outside, locked in her car, but she was running late. In a hurry. Stupid. He might still show up. She had to keep talking. "Why did you shoot him?"

"Yeah. Sorry." Tyson's mouth twitched. "Wrong place, wrong time."

"I talked to Odette. She said you were there when Day was killed. Were you?"

"Down on the floor. On your stomach."

"Please." Her voice was ghostlike.

He took a handful of twine from his jacket. "Just do it, Day."

"Kelly." She knelt slowly. "I'm Kelly."

Tyson seized her shoulder and pushed her onto the floor. Her face burned against the cool tile. Her heart thumped in her teeth. He straddled her legs, sat on her thighs, and jammed the gun against her spine. "Hands behind your back."

She placed her hands on her lower back. Her legs ached beneath his weight. After setting the pistol on the floor, he looped twine around her wrists in a figure-eight pattern and then wrapped it around itself between her hands and knotted it. The twine cut into her skin. "It hurts."

"Not for long. He was taking something out of his boot. She strained to see over her shoulder. "Don't move," he said. "I could fuck up and kill you." A needle stung the inside of her arm. A rush of heat liquefied her body and flushed away every thought. Nothing hurt and she stopped caring. Then she was gone.

.

The forensics crew filed across Kelly's front yard, a parade of shadows until they reached the light at the front door. Every part of her house was lighted, including the garage. Cash and Bridget and Detective Harry Sorensen stood near her Cherokee, the presence of which proved she'd made it home. "She went inside while the killer was still there," Cash said. "He was most likely waiting for her. He jumped her and took her away in the locksmith's van."

"Or killers. Could've been more than one." Bridget's face scrunched in a frown, her default expression while concentrating. "I doubt they walked from town, which means they parked somewhere nearby. They drove the van to their vehicle."

"One guy would have to abandon the van there," Harry said. "More than one, they could've ditched it anywhere. We'll put out a BOLO and canvass the area."

Bridget watched him shamble through the garage and into the house. "Is he okay?"

Harry and his partner had drawn the murder, and since it dovetailed with Cash and Bridget's investigation they were working together. Harry's long face and jowls had gotten him tagged with the nickname Deputy Dawg.

"He's smarter than he looks," Cash said.

"That's not saying a lot."

Cash imagined Kelly hogtied in the trunk of a car, duct tape slapped over her mouth, fighting for breath. Desperation seized him. "If I'd gotten here on time—"

"Where were you anyway?"

"Driving back from Denver. I was trying to get the paperwork squared away so we can search the land behind Helm's house."

"It's public land. What's taking so long?"

"Take a wild guess. They've probably dug up Marcus French and burned him by now." He needed to dial down his anger, much of it aimed at himself. He couldn't help Kelly like this, but his usual detachment seemed out of reach. "I should have called you and had you come out here. Or at least called Kelly to let her know I was running late. But I was on the phone with someone from the BLM. I didn't get her message until I was almost here."

"What time did you arrive?"

"Three twenty-three. Enough time for the killer to get out of the neighborhood. She had photos showing where Marcus was buried."

"Yeah. You said. Her message, backed by Proud's testimony, should be good in court."

"Unless Helm's lawyers get it thrown out." Cash waved his arm impatiently. "Why are we talking like she's already dead? The assailant could have killed her right here."

Bridget nodded. "He wanted her alive. But that's not reassuring. If he thinks she has information—"

"I know." He couldn't let himself think about that scenario.

A light winked in the corner of his vision. It came from a second-floor window of the house next door. Cash turned in time to glimpse a silhouette behind half-open blinds. "Up there." He pointed. "The night Day went missing, the guy in that house saw a man loading stuff into Kelly's Jeep."

Bridget eyed the window. "He has an unobstructed view of the driveway."

"And he likes to peep. He was looking at us just now."

"So let's talk to him."

"I'll do it. You go and see what they've found in the house."

Cash trudged through the snow to the neighbor's front door and rang the bell. He heard soft scurrying, like a mouse inside a wall. He waited a moment and rang again, leaning on the button. Finally the door opened an inch or two and the neighbor peered out. Cash dangled his badge. "Detective Cash Peterson, Boulder Police. I need to ask you some questions."

"What's going on?"

"There's been a killing."

The neighbor swung the door open. He was pixie-like—short and slender with a fine-boned face, huge eyes, and a mass of dirty blond curls. "Kelly's dead?"

"No. But the killing took place in her house."

"Was it a contract hit?"

"I doubt that very much. Can I come in?"

"You're the police. I don't have to let you in."

"No you don't. I could get a warrant and drive you to the station."

The little man stepped back far enough for Cash to squeeze past him. The living room was crammed with expensive electronics and a few pieces of cheap furniture. "Who got killed? The locksmith?"

"What's your name?"

"Why do you need to know?"

Cash leaned over him. "Are you hiding from the police?"

The nutcase cringed, his mouth working as if he were chewing something nasty. "Owen Olison."

"What did you see, Mr. Olison?"

"Nothing, really. Just the van and the locksmith."

"Describe the van."

Olison's eyes rolled up as if he were viewing an image stamped on the insides of his lids. "It was a white GM cargo van, three or four years old. *Rocky Mountain Locksmith* was stenciled on the side with a dark green logo of a mountain range that morphed into a key shape."

Cash held his notebook in his palm and scribbled fast. "And the locksmith?"

Olison's eyes rolled back to normal. "He was thin and about six feet tall, wearing a leather jacket and jeans."

"What color was the jacket?"

"Black or maybe dark brown."

"Hair color?"

"He was wearing a hat, I think."

"You're not sure?"

"I only saw him for a second or two." Olison paid more attention to inanimate objects than to people, probably because he felt less threatened by objects. Anyway, his description of the locksmith didn't match the dead man in Kelly's kitchen. He'd seen the killer.

"What was the guy doing?"

"Just walking to his van. He pulled into the garage."

Cash tapped the pen against the notebook. "Why would he do that?"

"I don't know. To bring his tools closer?"

"Could you identify him if you saw him again?"

"I doubt it."

"The man you saw wasn't the locksmith. He murdered the locksmith and kidnapped Kelly. Suppose I come back with some photographs and you take a look."

Olison's trapped gaze bounced around the room. "If I have to."

"You can help us catch him before he hurts someone else." Cash thanked Olison and headed back to the crime scene. Bridget would scare up a recent photo of Gregory Tyson. Even a tentative ID by Olison would give them enough cause to question Tyson and search his residence as well as the Cascade. But Cash wasn't hopeful. Olison was going out of his way not to cooperate.

❖

The parking lot glowed in the pinkish sunset. Animal counted eight cars. The club was dead even for dinnertime on a Thursday. Helm had left a stench that clung to the Cascade thirty hours later.

He'd shown up with two Guardians in leather coats. Their heads swiveled like terminators, scanning for the army of ninjas crouched behind the bar. Not long ago Animal had dreamed of being one of them, but clearly his head had been up his foolish ass. One Guardian had waited at the bar while the other one went upstairs with Helm. A few minutes later Helm came back down and they took off. The old man's face had been unreadable. And ugly, with eyes like a rattlesnake's.

The floodlights in the parking lot switched on, cutting off the sunset. Animal made the unmarked sedan even before it stopped near the Cascade's entrance and Dudley Do-Right emerged from the passenger side. His partner, the gal with skunk streaks in her hair, slid out of the driver's seat. Animal called upstairs to warn Tyson. "We got cops."

"I heard. I already called Baldacci. Stall them."

"Will do."

The detective strode across the vestibule in his expensive hiking boots. "I thought you worked for Helm."

"Not really."

"You were guarding his house."

"The regular guard was sick. I was filling in."

He pulled out his shiny badge. "Let's see your ID."

Grinning, Animal took out his wallet and displayed his license.

"What's funny, Mr. Beaumont?"

"I say the same thing a hundred times a night."

The detective nodded, acknowledging the joke. "How long have you worked here?"

"I'll be inside, Cash." Skunk Lady waltzed past them and made a beeline to the bar. She hopped onto a bar stool in front of Nina.

"What's she doing?"

Cash the Cop smiled mildly. "You're open for business, aren't you? She wants a Coke. You were telling me how long you've been employed at the Cascade."

"I ain't answering questions without my lawyer."

"Good idea!" Cash laid on the sarcasm. "You need one. Kelly Durrell was kidnapped a few hours ago. The perpetrator killed a man to take her. I happen to know she received a phone call from you last Saturday at 9:24 p.m. What did you say to her?"

Animal's attention drifted to the gaming arcade, where images moved inside the bright screens like caged ghosts. Right now Kelly was most likely screaming answers to Yount's questions and begging to tell him more about all the ways Animal had helped her. He could try trading the photos for his life, but Yount would just take them and kill him anyway. He needed to get his ass out of Colorado, but he couldn't leave Nina. She was in danger because of him. He doubted she'd pack up and come with him, not after one date and a few sweet kisses.

"Mr. Beaumont? I have enough evidence to bring you in for questioning. Unless you want to cooperate." The detective studied him the way you study a bug under a magnifying glass. The focused sun rays heat up the bug until it smokes and burns, a tiny insignificant flame. Animal refused to be that bug.

"I got nothing to do with kidnapping Kelly."

"Then answer my question." Cash the Cop actually seemed to believe him.

"Odette wanted to talk. There's a stream runs under the fence behind Helm's house. She said she'd wait there for Kelly."

"What did Odette want to talk about?"

"She never said."

"Why didn't she call Kelly herself?"

"Old man wouldn't let her."

"Why not?"

"Oh, I don't know. Maybe because he's a fucking douche?"

"Then help me bring him down."

Animal shook his head. "I'm not part of that shit."

"You work for the douche."

"Not anymore."

"A black Jaguar was seen near Kelly's house around the time she was kidnapped. Your boss drives a black Jag."

This cop was blowing it out his ass. If he knew the Jag was Tyson's, he'd be upstairs cuffing him.

"You should be talking to Helm, not me," Animal said.

Cash cocked his eyebrow like a teacher surprised to get the right answer from a slow student. "You think Helm kidnapped Kelly? Why?"

Animal felt praised by that eyebrow. "It just makes sense. She knows Odette. She was nosing around his property. And Yount—" Unless he was careful he would give away too much and end up at the police station. He didn't trust the cops or Tyson or anyone else to protect Nina.

Inside the Cascade, Skunk Lady leaned over the bar and wagged her finger while Nina shook her head, mouth clamped like a kid refusing to take medicine. She was too honest. It made her helpless.

Animal jumped off his stool and headed for the bar with Cash glued to his tail. On the way he called Tyson and said he couldn't card customers with the cops hassling him. Not that there were many customers tonight.

"Jingo can cover for you. Baldacci's on his way." Tyson sounded miles away, and not because of the phone. Animal hated working for a cokehead.

Nina was swabbing the bar with a grayish rag, the same spot over and over.

"Hey, Nina. You okay?"

"Yeah, Beau." But her face was pale and tense, her eyes raw with an emotion he couldn't nail down.

"I'd like a Coors. In a bottle."

She shot him a grateful look and reached into the cooler.

"Nina was telling me about the night Kelly found her," Skunk Lady said.

Nina uncapped the bottle and plunked the frosty Coors on the bar. "How could I? I don't remember."

Cash gave Animal a cop stare, the kind that nails you. "How come you didn't help her, Beau?

Kelly had blabbed about Nina, too. It figured. "I couldn't leave my station, so I called Welch." He turned to Nina. It hurt to look at her bleak face and admit he hadn't protected her. "Me and Kelly thought you should be going to the hospital, but Welch said to take you home." He couldn't say *I'm sorry*, not in front of the cops.

"The manager, Lawrence Welch," Cash said. "Is he around?"

"Nope." When Animal had clocked in yesterday, Welch was gone.

"Do you know where he is?"

"No idea." On vacation, according to Tyson. The sorry little freak had no life outside the Cascade, but suddenly he was on vacation.

A customer came up to the bar and waved his empty glass. Nina trotted over to him. She would take her time mixing that drink. She looked so breakable in her twirly skirt, her thighs no bigger than Animal's arms. He imagined that freak Welch running a hand along her leg and realized his fists were clenched. Both cops were watching. He let out his breath and relaxed his hands.

Skunk Lady turned on the bar stool and leaned back, her elbows braced on the bar. "Is he into drugging women?"

"Welch?" Animal measured out a smile. "I never saw him show an interest."

"An interest in what?"

"Anyone. I mean in a sexual kind of way." It was the truth. Welch never advertised his freak show.

"Tell us more about Helm." Cash had edged back, so Animal had to twist around to see him.

"Not much to tell. He's a private kind of guy."

"How come he needs guards?"

"You'd have to ask him."

"I don't suppose he's been in the Cascade lately?" Skunk Lady asked.

They were tag-teaming him, upping the pressure, and he had to make a judgment call. The cops could have the place under surveillance and already know about Helm's visit, but if they didn't, he would divulge a valuable piece of information and piss off Tyson. "The Cascade's kind of low-rent for Helm."

"Is that a no?"

"I guess."

Cash treated Animal to another cop stare. "You guess."

Animal took a drink of beer and wiped his mouth on his sleeve. "I ain't around every hour of the night and day."

The boss's shyster, Baldacci, finally bustled into the Cascade. He started talking before he reached the bar. "Cash. What brings you out here? This isn't your jurisdiction."

"The crime took place in our jurisdiction. Murder and kidnapping."

"Then you have a warrant." Baldacci marched up to the detective with his hand already out. He was five-six and probably wore lifts in his shiny loafers, and his baldness made his name a joke. But he took immediate charge of the situation. Animal had to give him credit.

"We don't need a warrant to interview good citizens like these two."

"Well, the interview's over."

"We have enough to bring Mr. Beaumont in."

"Why?" Animal said. "I already answered your questions."

"We need a written statement about the phone call you made to Kelly."

"Does it have to be tonight?" He cast an anxious glance at Nina as she counted out the customer's change.

And Cash the Cop noticed. He eyed her in a speculative way that Animal didn't like. "It can wait if you answer a couple more questions. What happened to Day Randall?"

"Camera Girl? How would I know? I ain't seen her in a while."

"How long a while?"

"Before Thanksgiving. She was a customer off and on. Then this one night we had live music and I noticed her and the boss dancing." Slow dancing to some mournful tune, Animal remembered, their bodies glommed together.

"When was this?"

"Like I said, before Thanksgiving. I don't remember the date."

Cash studied Animal's face as if Day's photographs were there for anyone to see. He turned to Nina, who had come back. "What about you? Do you know where Day is?"

Wide-eyed, she clutched the damp grayish rag she used for wiping the bar. Animal stepped between her and the cop. "You got no reason to bother her."

Skunk Lady snorted.

"I know you two aren't criminals," Cash said, "but it might not be enough to keep you out of prison. If you know any-thing—"

"Enough," Baldacci said. "Interview's over. Mr. Tyson told me to send you two home. I'll arrange a time for the police to take your statement."

Nina dropped the rag and headed for the gate at the end of the bar. Animal hurried after her. He ignored Cash, who called after him, "Be seeing you, Mr. Beaumont."

Animal and Nina clocked out and went to the overheated employees lounge. He held her coat while she shrugged it on.

What had happened the night Kelly found her was a silence between them, thanks to the cops, a silence so heavy that they might stop hearing each other through it. "I'm sorry."

She looked over her shoulder. "For what?"

"Not helping you."

She turned to face him, her eyes soft with hurt. She reached up and brushed her cool fingers across his cheek. "You didn't know."

"I should've taken you to the hospital."

"I'm glad you didn't. I don't wanna deal with those people. That cop. She kept at me and at me. She just wouldn't . . ." Her voice trailed into silence as they shared the pain of what happened. They couldn't even say it out loud. Rape. She was raped. "Do you still like me, Beau?"

Animal stroked her silky hair, feeling clumsy. He'd never in his life touched anyone with that kind of tenderness. Rage pushed into his throat, making it hoarse. "I'll kill him."

Nina shook her head. "It's not him I'm scared of."

"Stay with me tonight."

She gave him a smile, sweet but crimped with anxiety. "Thanks, but the Super 8 might be smarter."

"I ain't coming on to you, I swear. I'll sleep on the couch."

Her smile changed subtly. "Uh-uh. I won't evict you from your own bed. If anyone sleeps on the couch, it's me."

By the time the cops left, Gee was shaking apart. He took the keys to the Box from his desk drawer. He'd added the Box after construction, using a builder with no connections to Stuart. Only three people knew it existed: the builder, Gee, and Welch. Its purpose was to hold inventory that wasn't sold immediately.

Gee entered a storage closet on the top floor and squeezed past rolls of leftover carpet, crates of roofing tiles, and other junk that might come in handy someday for repairs. The stuff gave the closet an excuse for being there and concealed the sliding door behind it. A dummy smoke alarm swung upward on a pivot to reveal a lock. Gee inserted the first key and unbolted the door from the ceiling beam. He pushed the hidden door inward an inch and slid it sideways into its pocket.

Halfway down a flight of claustrophobic stairs, he stopped to retrieve his dope from a cache beneath one of the steps. He continued downstairs and through a passage and unlocked a door with the second key. He switched on the overhead fluorescent, illuminating a room that was ten by fifteen feet. In the center were a camcorder on a tripod and two spotlights and a diffuser on stands. The lights and the camera pointed down at the mattress where Kelly sprawled.

Several hours had passed since the knockout shot. He readied a hypo of ketamine and morphine, enough to keep her down for several more hours, and slipped the needle into her forearm vein. He turned her onto her side to keep her from choking if she threw up.

Items for her comfort were stowed in the passage between the hidden stairs and the Box: bottled water, energy bars, a plug-in kettle and a box of teabags, a suitcase packed with her toiletries and clothes, and a hospital toilet. He carried everything into the Box and assembled the toilet. Even with ventilation, the smell would be nasty. Better if she stayed unconscious as much as possible.

Yount knew where Kelly was. Tonight, with the cops at Stuart's gate, he'd be too busy to plan an incursion, but tomorrow . . . Tomorrow would be a busy day.

Gee returned to his office, careful to lock the concealed door behind him, and shot up enough morphine to put him to sleep. The drug kicked in while he staggered to the bathroom. As he bent over the toilet, nausea squeezed his stomach, but nothing came up. He hadn't eaten since yesterday. He reeled to the sofa and sprawled, gone before his cheek touched the leather cushion.

❖

Blue sky filled the window above the sofa. Gee stumbled to the desk and checked his phone. Quarter after eleven. He'd slept later than he'd meant to. He snorted two fat lines of coke off the metal casing of his laptop. Renny would love this shit. Pure rock. Within seconds he achieved liftoff. Not an ecstatic rush—he never got that anymore—but a coming together, a fierce concentration. His hands steadied, his screeching nerves settled into an electric hum. The sludge of fear and doubt drained from his mind, and triumph became possible.

He called Animal and told him to come to work right away. In the background he heard the chirpy voice of his bartender. "Bring Nina."

"Don't have to. She's got her car."

So Animal had scored. When Nina first started working at the Cascade, Gee had flirted with her and gotten nowhere. At another time he would have wondered how Animal had done it, but he had one more call to make.

Yount answered on the first ring. "Gee."

"Nice to hear your voice. It always surprises me, a shark that talks."

"You're high."

"So?"

"I don't like doing business with junkies."

"Get over it." Gee unlocked a desk drawer and took the photos from their envelope. "I have what you want."

"Kelly Durrell."

"Something she was carrying." He stroked the glossy surface of the one on top. Day could transform anything into art, even a patch of dirt in the forest.

"More photos. How many copies did your girlfriend make?"

Far away, Gee heard himself laughing.

"It's not funny, asshole."

But it was. Yount and his Guardians scurrying like clowns. Welch had found the negatives among the trash in Day's car, but there could be more prints, more bombs rigged to explode. Stuart would tiptoe through that minefield for the rest of his evil life. Gee cackled a few more seconds before getting control of himself.

"Who was holding them?" Yount said.

"No idea." Gee had tossed the outer envelope addressed to Leonard Proud. He liked the old Indian too much to get him killed.

"I suspect it was someone connected to the museum where Kelly works."

"Oh yeah? Why would you suspect that?"

"We spoke with Annie Laible this morning. You know her."

"Spoke with her, huh? She still alive?"

Yount's silence gave him the answer. Poor frumpy Annie with her glass sculptures that declared her slavish devotion to Dale Chihuly. Gee liked her, too. "You can have the photos," he said. "After that we're done."

"Not good enough. I want Kelly."

Gee lifted his empty hand and studied its tremor. "I'm keeping her for now."

"Really? What's your strategy, Gee? You can't turn her loose. Remember the dead body in her house? The police are hunting for the killer. You're too careless not to get caught and too weak not to cut a deal. I can't let that happen."

Yount thought he controlled the world.

"You'll come after me anyway. Why make it easy?"

"I should've killed you that night."

A vortex formed at the center of his mind, the beginning of disintegration. Already. "How come you didn't?"

"Mr. Helm still believed in the partnership. That's changed. You can't survive on your own. Even your friend Welch sees it."

"He's not my friend."

"Associate, then. Former associate."

Of course Welch went scurrying to Yount with his prize negatives. He was Stuart's troll now. Nothing left but the end-game.

"Bring it on," Gee said.

He changed his shirt before heading downstairs. He found Animal and Nina sitting together in the employees lounge. The bouncer looked different. His shoulder-length hair was brushed into a glossy mane, and the blue of his T-shirt deepened his eyes. Most of all, the wildness was gone from those eyes. Then Nina smiled at her man and Gee understood. It was more than a hookup. That changed things.

"Animal, can we talk alone?"

On her way out, Nina gave Animal one of those meaningful looks that happen only between partners or close friends. She expected something, probably something that screwed up Gee's plans.

Gee waited until she was out of earshot. "Welch quit."

"I kinda figured. Ain't seen him around."

"I want you to manage the club."

"Me? I can't keep books or any of that."

"Neither could Welch. I have a bookkeeper. The manager's job is more hands-on. Hiring people, scheduling their shifts, making sure they show up. Doing inventory and ordering supplies. And you choose the bands when we have live music. It pays five grand a month."

"I don't have experience," Animal said, but his voice quickened. He liked the money.

"You're smart, you can learn. The big thing is, you know the Cascade. And you go the extra mile, like driving Welch to the doctor."

Animal seemed to be waiting for more.

"What?" Gee said.

"I don't like doing shit without knowing why. You want me to manage the club, I want to know what I'm getting into. And no more illegal shit."

Gee almost laughed at the absurdity. Animal stood there with his arms folded, his T-shirt showing every bulge and ripple of his massive pecs and biceps. He was muscle. The whole idea of being muscle was doing things without question. "What illegal shit?"

"Shaking down those kids."

"What kids?"

"Justin and Courtney."

"Oh, yeah, Day's punk friends." Helm had wanted them checked out because they drove Day to the party where she blackmailed him, but nobody said anything about shaking them down. "Did you hurt them?"

"Not really. But I committed home invasion, assault, and destruction of property. Just to search their car for some photos Welch thought might be there."

"Were they?"

Animal shook his head. "What's the deal with the photos?"

"Ask Helm."

Animal drew a sharp breath as if he'd meant to keep asking but something changed his mind. "What you're saying is you want me to guard this place."

"Just for a couple nights. Until me and Welch reach an understanding."

"I don't know."

"Both of us will sleep here. There's a couch in my office that's big enough for you. I'll keep watch from closing time until six o'clock, then you take over until we open at noon."

"And if he shows?"

"Scare him off. You'll have a gun."

"I ain't shooting nobody."

"Of course not. We're talking about a warning shot."

Animal's blunt face tensed with thought. "Okay, I'll be your manager. But I don't want Nina mixed up in this."

"You're in charge of scheduling. Send her home early and cover the bar yourself."

"Who's gonna be the bouncer?"

"You, until I hire someone. After Nina goes home, Jingo can take the door. He's big enough, and he doesn't ask questions."

"Maybe he should."

❖

Nina set a cherry Coke on a paper coaster in front of him. Just the right amount of ice. Like always. Looking back over the past months, Animal realized that Nina had been trying to get his attention long before he noticed her. He would never forget last night, Nina like a baby finch with her mouth wide around his cock and her fingertips feathery on his thigh. It was hard for Animal to be gentle, but she made it worthwhile.

"Well?" she said. "Did you tell him?"

"The boss fired Welch and promoted me to manager. Sixty grand a year."

He figured she'd at least be glad to have Welch gone, but she looked at him with sorrowful eyes. "Oh, Beau."

"Nothing's changed. We'll save money faster, and in a couple days you can quit just like we planned."

Last night he and Nina had made long-range plans. As soon as he found other work, they would quit the Cascade and move in together. She would get a job waitressing at a nice family restaurant. They'd scrimp and save enough to move to Eugene, Oregon, where her family lived. A year from next summer, they'd get married by the ocean, barefoot in the sand, the way she always dreamed.

"In six months we can save ten grand," he said. "We can get married this year."

"Don't let him get you in trouble, Beau." She plucked a rag from the dishwater and began wiping the bar as if she wanted to wipe the Cascade out of existence.

He finished his cherry Coke and chewed the ice. He needed to tell her he was staying overnight to guard the club. Delaying would just make her madder, but the words stuck in his throat.

She kept darting suspicious glances at him. Finally she said, "What aren't you telling me?"

Last night had changed things. Nina had a claim on him now. And he wanted it. Wanted to marry her on a beach stinking of seaweed and live in a cramped apartment, working some dead-end job to support her and their kids while she pecked the hell out of him with her little beak.

"We're not busy tonight," he said. "You can leave early and go back to my place."

"How will you get home?"

"I'll sleep here. There's a couch in the boss's office."

She stopped wiping and gave him another sorrowful look. "What's going on, Beau?"

Animal couldn't tell her about the photos. Couldn't explain that even if they walked out now and never set foot in the Cascade again, Yount might come after him.

"You're scared," she said.

"Yeah. For you. Honest to God, Nina, I'd die to protect you."

"Then tell me what's going on." She gripped his forearm. Her fingers reached only halfway around, and he imagined how easily they could be broken.

"Nothing you don't already know. The cops want Welch and Helm, so the boss cut them loose and they're pissed. He's camping out here till they're busted."

"Let's go. Now. You want to protect me, that's how you do it."

One night together and she knew how to twist him up. "We're broke. We gotta hang on at least until payday."

"We could walk out that door right now. Don't tell me we couldn't." She let go of his arm and stalked off before he could answer. Just as well. Nothing he said would make any difference.

22

A circle of light floated in darkness like an angel's lost halo. Somewhere stuffy and overheated, but she felt chilled. Her head ached in a symphony—temples throbbing, brasses echoing inside her skull, violins shrieking in her left eye. Whatever Tyson had shot into her arm caused a Wagnerian hangover. She rolled onto her side and released a stink of sweat and musk.

Her hand touched carpet. She sat up and reeled with dizziness. The room lurched and stretched like an image in a funhouse mirror. Eventually her vision steadied and she looked around. She sat on a mattress on the floor. The room was windowless and dark except for a spotlight aimed at the ceiling. The floating halo. A camcorder and two photographer's lights with diffusers loomed over her.

Kelly climbed to her feet and moved slowly to the only door. Bolted. She flipped a light switch and a fluorescent bulb illuminated the room. In the corner was a portable toilet with a tubular metal frame, a plastic seat, and a pan underneath. A roll of toilet paper and a bottle of hand sanitizer sat on the floor nearby. How thoughtful. She did need to pee. Unless the pan got emptied every hour or two, which seemed unlikely, the toilet was going to stink, but she had no choice.

Afterward she unpacked a grocery sack near the toilet. She tore a bottle of water from its plastic collar, unscrewed the cap, and took a long swallow. Then she walked alongside a metal table that stretched the rest of the length of the wall. It displayed dildos and other sex toys, packs of condoms, a bottle of Ultra Pleasure Personal Lubricant, manacles attached by lengths of chain to a padded leather collar, a laptop, a wireless printer.

She picked up a scuffed leather camera case. Her shaky fingers pried it open.

A 35 mm Pentax.

The camera trembled in her hands.

Day's bed was stained with blood, but her Pentax was here. Terrible things had happened in this room, too. The sex paraphernalia, the camcorder and photography lights, the mattress covered with a hot-pink satin sheet mottled with stains—it fit together. Tyson must have brought Nina here after drugging here. And others. Who knew how many others?

Kelly was gasping as if she'd run a mile. Her forehead throbbed. She sank into a chair in front of the laptop and clicked the mouse. The Window's desktop loaded onto the screen. No password. Tyson had left her a way to give a virtual scream for help. Was he really that coked up and crazy? But when she opened the browser, a message popped on the screen.

The computer wasn't connected to the Internet. No wireless? She ran the diagnostic. A network was available, and the system should have connected to it. Tyson must have changed the settings so you had to enter the password. She tried *TheCascade* and just *Cascade,* but neither got her online. She didn't know him well enough to guess what other passwords he might use.

He'd left the laptop for her to find. There was something he wanted her to see. Probably videos of the victims.

She searched until she found the folder. Named simply "Stuff," it held eight video files. Kelly hesitated. She felt scared and helpless enough without this, but she had to make sure. She clicked on a video. Nina sprawled on the pink sheet, naked and unconscious. Welch strutted into the frame, naked except for a condom on his erect penis. He knelt between her legs and moved them around, posing her like a doll, and then crawled on top of her and started pumping.

Kelly fast-forwarded through the rest. She sped through several more videos. All featured an unconscious woman— sometimes just lying on the mattress, sometimes being raped by Welch. She saw three victims, including Nina, but no sign of Tyson. She doubted he was behind the camera. She heard nothing on the soundtrack except flesh slapping against flesh and Welch's grunting. Tyson would make some kind of noise.

He hadn't participated, but he knew.

Tyson had left the evidence for her to find. He hadn't bothered hiding it because she wouldn't be leaving the room alive, not after what she'd seen. His drug hadn't knocked her out completely. She remembered the dead locksmith sprawled beside her and being dragged through the snow and locked in the trunk of a car. She didn't remember being tied up, but there were purple welts on her wrists.

She imagined Cash standing over her body in his cold detective role. "Ligature marks," he would say to Detective Farrigan. "She was bound before she was killed." A coroner would dissect her body and look for evidence of sexual assault.

A motor kicked on nearby, followed by rumbling and whooshing. A furnace. And sneaking beneath those sounds, footsteps approached the door. Tyson knocked. As if she could keep him out.

Kelly stood and almost toppled into a swell of dizziness and sparkling blackness. Head throbbing, she leaned on the table. "Come in."

He entered almost bashfully. His skin was the color of parchment, cheeks hollow, eyes glossed. He palmed a syringe in his right hand. "How you doing?"

"How do you think?"

"I had to do this."

"Had to." Her laughter caught in her throat.

"Yount was gonna kill you, so I moved you somewhere safe." He stepped toward her and stopped. "Don't look at me that way. I don't deserve it."

"You killed the locksmith."

He sighed beneath the unfair burden of her anger. "The dude showed up out of nowhere. Look, you'll be out of here in twenty-four hours. Sooner if the cops get Yount before I do. Stuart's gone, but they might catch him before he leaves the country. What do you know about him?"

She backed away. "Where did you get Day's camera?"

Tyson inched closer. A mixture of funk and cologne flooded her nostrils. "What is it you know, Kelly? It could be something I can use."

"Use how?" She barely heard herself whisper.

"To take him down. What else?"

"He's in California, you said."

"Tell me," he said, his voice suddenly hard. He wanted to find out whether the cops would arrest Helm based on what she knew. He was mixed up with Helm in a dozen evil ways, including Day's murder, and Helm would give him up. He couldn't let that happen.

"You're going to kill me."

"If I wanted you dead, you'd be dead by now. What did Odette tell you?"

"You're just keeping me alive until you find out what I know."

"Then you'd better know something." He stroked her cheek, but his face stayed rigid.

"Yount killed her boyfriend."

"And?"

"He killed Day because she found out. But you're the one with her camera. Where did you get it?"

Tyson blinked at the Pentax as if it had popped up from out of nowhere. "From Yount. His sick idea of a souvenir. I want you to have it. Listen. When I let you go, you're gonna tell the cops that Yount grabbed you. You stole the camera from him."

Kelly nodded.

"Give me your word."

"I promise. Yount deserves to be punished. He killed Day."

The glossy eyes tracked her face. He believed her. Maybe. "Another twenty-four hours and I'll let you go. I'll give you a shot. You'll sleep through it."

"No."

"Why not?"

So easy to kill her with an overdose of something. Safer than letting her go. "It gives me a crushing headache."

"You won't feel it when you're asleep." He uncapped the needle.

"I want to be awake."

"Hold still and it won't hurt."

He outweighed her by fifty pounds and she could hardly stand. She hurled herself at him anyway, seized the hand with the syringe with both her hands, and squeezed with all her strength. Liquid squirted from the needle, and a thrill of triumph raced through her before he backhanded her face. She collapsed to her knees, stunned, cupping her cheek as if to keep something precious from spilling. The needle stung her arm.

23

Gee dragged her onto the mattress and arranged her arms and legs. She hadn't gotten the full dose and he considered giving her more, but he worried about an overdose. She wasn't used to the shit. He hated shooting her full of dope, but he couldn't risk her pounding the walls. A customer might hear. Or Animal.

Her lips were chapped. She needed to drink more water.

He watched her breathe awhile, her breasts swelling and falling. They were small but elegantly shaped. He traced his forefinger around one. It had been years since he thought of making art, but now he felt moved. He found a pen on the table but no paper, so he sketched on the plasterboard wall. As he drew, he forgot the gulf between himself and the world. There was only her, the instrument in his hand, and the image forming beneath it. A woman unconscious, compelling his desire. She would hate him, no matter how much he sacrificed to keep her breathing, but someday she might think of his drawing and understand.

Gee used to believe he was an artist. He'd majored in art at the University of Colorado, and for that he needed money, so he began earning the only way he knew—the way Renny had taught him. At first he peddled lids to other students. When his supplier realized that he was experienced and trustworthy, he began fronting him kilos of weed. Gee made new contacts and became a middleman, turning several kilos at once. Lower risks, higher profits. He had so much cash lying around that he bought a laundromat to launder it and laughed at the irony. As the dealing required more and more of his time and energy, he lost the desire to make art. He just wanted to balance the books. Then he met Stuart.

He brokered deals between Stuart and his contacts. He seldom took possession of the product, and the transactions stayed clean and profitable. He knew Yount did some nasty violence, but it hadn't touched him until Day decided to save Stuart's worthless twat of a wife.

Tenderhearted Day. Stupid Day.

They'd gone for a drive in the mountains. Gee still hoped he could save her. Slumped morosely in the leather seat of his Jag, she denied everything. "I never gave the photos to anyone. I lied to protect myself."

"Not smart, Day."

They drove without speaking for a stretch of minutes that felt like hours. Day crossed her legs so her shoe touched the polished burl veneer of the Jag's dash. She wanted him to give her shit. Anything to change the subject.

"I hate Steely Dan," she said. "All the songs sound the same."

Gee shut down the music. "What did you take pictures of?"

"Trees. Dead wildflowers."

"Don't fuck with me, Day."

The Jag swept through a long curve and his gaze leaned into her profile. His groin tightened, and he wrenched his attention back to the road. Amazing how she could hold him. She wasn't beautiful or pretty or even sexy in the usual sense. Her nose looked like a parrot's beak. Her eyes and hair were a nondescript brown, her freckles too pale and widespread to be cute. Worst of all, she was flat-chested. Welch had tits as big as hers.

"How come you're doing Yount's job for him?" she said with a contempt that made him angry and sick.

"Lucky for you I am." He pulled into the dirt clearing of an overlook and stopped. "Let's get out for a minute."

Day fiddled with the strap on her camera case. Now she was afraid of him.

They walked to the edge. Hundreds of feet below, autumn pastureland mottled with sunshine stretched to mountains that crowded the horizon. The distance seemed unreal. Gee was dead to so much space. Long ago, tripping out of his brain on acid, he'd stood on a high place and understood that everything he beheld was a bubble. If he so much as breathed, the bubble would burst and he would fall into the darkness of outer space. He hadn't touched psychedelics in years, but the moment was still powerful. He'd almost gone over that edge.

"So is this where you push me off the cliff?" She gave him that strange look of hers, as if seeing him for the first time.

Day was unlike anyone else he'd known. She didn't take pictures—she gathered them like rocks or seashells to be shaped and polished in her darkroom. Her eye registered what no one else saw. She looked at Gee as if he were a mountain range or a seacoast where she ranged at will and collected her treasure. Even at her most helpless, hands bound and camera out of reach, she gave him that exploring look. He'd fucked her senseless, crammed her with uppers and downers until she was paralyzed. It made no difference. The moment she became conscious, that look broke the surface like a dolphin breeching into a new element.

He could have kept driving until they were gone from Colorado. He could have hidden her. Instead he turned around and brought her back to town, where death was waiting.

◈

Yount stripped the bed and covered the mattress with plastic sheeting. "Nice quilt. Looks Amish." He and Welch bound Day's wrists and ankles with bungee cord and tied them to the legs of the bed frame. Within minutes her hands and feet darkened. Welch stuffed a dishrag in her mouth. She saw the boning knife in Yount's hand and began to writhe. "Gee. Lie on top of her. Hold her down."

Gee watched from the doorway. Terror crawled over his skin. "We don't have to do this."

"Welch," Yount said.

The troll laid his thick torso across Day's thighs, immobilizing her while Yount made precise cuts—strips of skin almost identical in size, parallel across her stomach. Blood welled from the raw flesh and washed her hips and pooled on the plastic sheeting. Yount dropped the sad ribbons of skin between her legs.

The Guardian loved his work as much as Renny had and raised it to a higher art. Renny lacked the control to execute such a systematic flaying. Day was choking on the dishrag. Gee hoped she would die, but Yount told Welch to get off her.

Her chest heaved. Her throat gurgled as she labored for air. Blood streamed off the plastic onto the mattress, and Gee wondered why Yount had bothered with the protective sheet.

"Take the fucking rag out of her mouth," Gee said.

Yount shot him a contemptuous look. "Good idea. I think she wants to talk."

Gasping, Day told them to look for an envelope taped behind the toilet tank in the downstairs bathroom. Welch fetched the envelope like the dog he was. Yount took out several photos and examined them. "Where are the negatives?"

"Hidden . . . at . . . Stuart's." Each word sucked away her breath.

"Where at Stuart's?"

"Kitchen."

"Where in the kitchen?"

"Behind the . . . bottom drawer by the . . . fridge."

Yount slipped the prints back into the envelope. He touched the boning knife that was lying on her stomach—a reminder that she was nothing but the thing holding his instrument, a lump of meat to be worked. She shuddered and he smiled faintly. "If you're lying I'll take all your skin. The pain you feel now, imagine it covering every inch of you." He clamped her jaw between his thumb and forefinger, forcing her mouth open, and stuffed the rag in. Then he called one of the Guardians at the house and told him where to search.

They waited.

Day looked at Gee, her eyes dark with shock and rebuke.

"You're not gonna get the truth this way." Gee hated his voice, meek like a stooge. "She'll say anything. That's what people do when they're tortured."

Yount glared. "Get the fuck out."

Gee stayed put. Neither of them would back down with Welch watching, so their standoff continued until Gee's head crackled and he felt faint. Yount's goon came back on the phone.

Yount listened for a minute and said, "Why am I not surprised?" He put away the phone and picked up the boning knife. "Give a nod when you're ready to tell the truth."

Day nodded frantically, but Yount started to work with the knife. Soon she was choking on her screams. The red of her blood showed through the translucent plastic.

Gee couldn't take any more. He retreated to the dinner table and snorted coke until his face was numb and bitterness flooded his mouth. He'd betrayed Day. It was on him to save her.

Outside, the air burned cold against his face. The neighborhood was dark except for light from Kelly's house and a second-floor window next door. A night-owl neighbor. The last thing they needed. But the night was as silent as Day's blood. Yount's Land Rover was parked behind Gee's Jag in the driveway, so close their bumpers almost kissed. *"Kiss my ass," said the classy sedan.* He heard himself laugh at the joke, a strange titter that belonged to someone else. He leaned over a fender into the Jag's trunk, lifted the floor panel, and found what he needed stashed in the wheel well.

Gee sat behind the wheel with the dome light on. He had to work fast. He uncapped the needle, jabbed it through the rubber cap on the bottle, and drew back the plunger until the syringe filled. He withdrew the needle with trembling hands. They had to be steady when the time came. A skin pop would calm his nerves. Gee stared at the needle, wanting it. Just a taste. Too much and he would nod off in the driver's seat while Day was skinned alive. He capped the needle.

He pulled up his jeans leg and slipped the syringe into the shaft of his boot, under his sock, needle upward. He took his

.22 from the glove box and checked the magazine. Fully loaded. He dropped the revolver into his coat pocket where it would be noticed. Yount would expect the gun but not the hypo.

Coming into the foyer, he heard Welch say, "Looks like you was right."

"I plan for every contingency," Yount said.

Gee forced himself to walk. At the doorway to her bedroom he hesitated, as if crossing the threshold would commit him to action, like Caesar crossing the Rubicon.

Welch slouched in an upholstered chair in the corner. Day's head lolled. She looked unconscious. Yount perched beside her on the bed. Her blood had stained his expensive wool slacks.

Gee snorted. "How you gonna explain the blood to the dry cleaner?"

"I always burn my clothes after."

"Ready to try it my way?"

Yount's eyes glittered with contempt. "What way is that?"

"A stick works better with a carrot in front of it."

"And you're the carrot." Yount made a noise more like a growl than a laugh. "You wanna stick your carrot in her, Gee?"

The troll snuffled.

Gee felt the gun's weight in his pocket and imagined Welch's head exploding like a melon. His own death would almost be worth it. "Come out here and talk to me."

Yount studied him for what felt like minutes before standing and coming to the doorway. He brought the boning knife with him.

Gee stepped back into the hall and Yount followed, crowding in close. The Guardian was four inches shorter, and closeness gave him the advantage. The knife could be in Gee's belly before his long arms could block.

"Let me talk to her," Gee said. "Alone."

"I don't think so."

"Sometimes pain makes people forget. I can give her a reason to remember."

"A promise we won't kill her? I doubt she'll believe that, even from you."

"I'll promise her to protect Kelly. And I'll mean it."

"Why would Kelly need protection?"

"Everyone needs protection from you."

Yount gave another throaty laugh. "You think you're up to that?"

"We're on the same side."

Yount reached into Gee's pocket and took the gun. "You shouldn't carry a weapon loose. You might shoot yourself in the dick. Ten minutes. And the door stays open."

"Okay. But you and Welch have to back off. It won't work if she sees you."

Gee circled the bed and sat on the other side, where his legs were concealed from them. He drew shallow breaths, trying not to smell the copper of Day's blood. The raw flesh of her belly glistened. He tried to swallow, but his mouth was dry. He took off his coat and covered her. Bending over, he yanked off a boot and palmed the syringe before pulling off the other boot. He thumbed the cap from the syringe and lay beside Day, propping himself on one elbow with his forearm over her upper arm. His other hand held the needle ready.

In the hallway, Yount whispered something and Welch snuffled again. They thought Gee was going to fuck her, half dead as she was. He lowered his head and nuzzled her neck.

"Day?"

"Gee." Her voice barely rose from her throat.

"I'm sorry."

She said nothing. An apology from him wasn't worth the effort.

He kissed her shoulder, giving Yount and Welch the show they expected. "Are there more photos? They won't let you go until they have everything."

"Then . . . kill . . . me."

She knew.

Gee touched his lips to her nipple. He shifted his weight so his arm pressed against hers and the veins in her wrist bulged. He slipped the needle in. He whispered, "I love you," and plunged the morphine into her blood. With a growl, Yount rushed the bed. Gee jumped back, pointing the empty syringe like a weapon. It looked pathetic against the gun Yount aimed at him. Gee's own .22. His heart pounded in his ears.

Yount's face was empty with rage, empty like the gun barrel with death waiting behind it. He wouldn't shoot—not here, where the shot would wake neighbors and bring the cops—but Gee almost pissed himself.

He began talking fast. "If she had any more prints squirreled away, she'd give them up first. Before the negatives. Especially if they were hidden somewhere else. She knew you'd keep her alive until you had them."

"She didn't give up the negatives," Yount said.

"They're here somewhere. We'll find them."

"We'd better." He held the gun on Gee for endless seconds before lowering it slowly. "I'll see what Mr. Helm wants to do about you."

"Yeah, you do that."

It took hours to search the house, pack Day and her stuff into the vehicles, and scour the bedroom. At first Gee rode the crest of his triumph, boosted by line after line of coke.

But after a while, the high no longer lifted him. He drifted on a sluggish river, watching his life happen, knowing he could never come ashore again. From a distance, he watched Gregory Tyson caress Day's face before wrapping her in plastic. He watched the pathetic asshole gaze into her eyes as if expecting consciousness to break their dead surface like a dolphin. But none of it belonged to him. Grief was a passing landscape on his journey downstream.

He would leave it behind as he left everything, untouched.

Animal perched on the bouncer's stool, waiting for closing time. With Nina safe at his place, there was nothing to look at but the parking lot. The Cascade's floodlights turned the snow a weird Popsicle blue, like something from an acid trip. Maybe the boss always saw the world like that. Tyson was a cokehead and a little nuts, but he had no reason to kidnap Kelly. He wasn't Stuart's dog anymore. And he didn't own the only black Jag in Colorado.

In the next hour, two customers left and none came in. Jingo was drinking beer, hiding the glass under the bar between swallows, as if Animal gave a shit. He thought about going inside to talk, just to relieve the boredom, but the cook's jailhouse attitude made him jumpy. Jingo kept his wagons circled even when he laughed.

Animal's phone played its generic tune. He took it out, expecting Tyson, but it was Nina. Before he said a word, her quivery voice filled his ear. "Beau, they broke into your apartment. Stuart's men."

His heartbeat spiked. "Where are you?"

"I got out. I saw them drive in the parking lot and ran down the back stairs. They were at your door when I left."

"They see you?"

"I don't think so." She sounded less than sure. One of them might have followed.

"Where are you now?"

"Driving out of Louieville."

"You know where San Francisco Pizza is?"

"In the mall."

"How close to it are you?"

"About fifteen minutes."

"Go there and wait. I'll come get you."

"I can't eat anything, Beau."

"Order a pizza. We'll take it with us." The restaurant would be crowded on a Friday night. She would be safer with people around her. "Listen. Park near the building, not in the parking garage."

"Okay, Beau."

"I'll get there fast as I can."

Animal told Jingo he'd be back in a couple of hours, and the cook treated him to a surly ask-me-if-I-give-a-fuck smirk. With luck Animal could drop Nina at a hotel and return before the boss knew he was gone. He wouldn't waste time asking permission.

He reached the mall in twenty-five minutes, cussing at traffic. Snowflakes cooled his face as he rushed to the nearest entrance. Nina's old Chevy was nowhere in sight, but the mall was huge, with lots on three sides. He pushed through crowds of shoppers, past a fat Christmas tree winking with colored lights. "Santa Claus is Coming to Town" drifted from above, bells jingling with fake merriment.

Walking fast, sweating, Animal fumbled with the zipper on his parka and yanked it open. He scanned the tables through San Francisco Pizza's glass wall. No Nina. She might be in back. With the place jammed, you had to take the first empty table. A dozen people lined up at the podium where a girl took names for the waiting list. Nina should have gotten there a few minutes earlier, not enough time to move through that line. Maybe she'd never made it. Maybe the Guardians snatched her outside. Fear rushed through him and changed to rage. He would kill the assholes, every one of them. He would tear Helm to pieces.

When someone touched his arm, he jumped back and his fists came up. Then he saw Nina, wide-eyed, her fright mirroring his. He folded her in his arms.

"Let's get out of here," he said. "I'll order a takeout pizza. We can pick it up on the way to a hotel."

Animal forked over three hundred bucks for a room at the Boulderado, figuring Nina would be safest there. They rode the elevator and walked to her room together.

"Coming in?" she said and jutted her chin, challenging him. If he accepted the invitation, she would make it hard for him to leave.

"I wish I could."

"Okay then." She grabbed his wrist, pulled him down, and planted a kiss in his mouth, her tongue flickering over his, thrilling down his spine to his cock. "You be careful."

"Yeah. Call you in the morning."

While he drove to the Cascade, his imagination rested in a soft bed with Nina. By the time his Mustang rolled into the club's parking lot, he was pissed at Tyson and sick of the whole twisted scene. One more paycheck and they were splitting for Eugene. They'd scrape together the money somehow.

The snow had stopped. The empty parking lot glowed, more psychedelic than ever beneath flood lamps. The Cascade was dark. Animal parked to the side of the building near the old pickup used for deliveries. At the employees entrance, he had the key ready, but the doorknob turned without it. He knew he'd locked it—he was careful about security.

He opened the door a crack and slipped into the employees lounge, reached for the light switch, and froze. The place stank like a butcher shop. Air whooshed from a heating vent, and the engine for the freezer whirred, too loud. The door into the kitchen was open. That dumb shit Jingo could have left meat out of the cooler. Still, Animal felt safer in the dark. He padded through the lounge and entered the kitchen. The recessed ceiling lights were dimmed, as they usually were overnight. The grill was scraped, the counters cleared and washed, but the butcher-shop reek grew stronger. He felt stickiness underfoot. His boots made a sucking sound with each step.

He found the rheostat and dialed up the lights. The blood trail began at the stairwell door and led through the kitchen and the lounge to the exit. Blackening the indoor-outdoor carpet in the lounge, the splatter pulsed with the rhythm of the bleeder's heartbeat.

Get the hell out.

He stumbled back to his car and sat, breathing hard. He was being played. Tyson had dangled the manager job and sixty grand and expected him to risk his ass fighting Welch or whoever else had fled the Cascade bleeding. But Animal had no other option except the cops, and he wasn't ready to give them control of his life.

Cash the Cop was okay. Maybe. But most of them were lazy and stupid like the dumbasses in Heber. Animal had thrown a few punches in the bar fight, but he never touched the guy who went to the hospital. He stuck around and talked to the cops, trying to be a good citizen, and they busted him for aggravated assault. They had to nail someone and he was a handy suspect.

He grabbed a flashlight from the glove box, returned to the door, and tracked the blood splatter across the ice to its end, where the bleeder had gotten in a vehicle and driven away.

His instinct told him to pick up Nina and blow town tonight, but they couldn't scrape together the cash to make it to Reno, let alone the West Coast.

And he had a deal with Tyson.

Hundred to one, no attackers had stayed behind, but he couldn't take the chance. He backtracked through the lounge to the kitchen, but instead of entering the stairwell there, he cut through the club and climbed the back stairs. He threaded his way between the pool tables on the mezzanine, unlocked a door marked "Private," went down a short hallway, and entered the stairwell halfway up. He peered up and down and listened. No shadows. No sound except the furnace. He crept up the stairs to the top floor, avoiding the blood.

On the left, near Welch's office, two bullet holes punctured the wall. On the right, the door frame to Tyson's office was splintered. More blood decorated the carpet. Animal was no Sherlock Holmes, but he guessed the bleeder had been standing there when he got clipped by a shot from Tyson's office. He edged toward the blasted door frame, hanging back in case Tyson was jumpy enough to shoot. "Boss?"

"Where the fuck were you?"

He entered the office. "Yount's guys busted into my apartment."

Tyson had his feet propped on his desk. He held a Ruger 9mm semiautomatic by its butt, the barrel resting against his thigh. Behind him, the devil in the creepy painting loomed like his guardian. "Why would they do that?"

"Nina was hiding there. Yount knows I care about her. Maybe he was looking for a way to leverage that."

Tyson's eyes glittered, radioactive in his skeletal face. It was hard to tell whether he bought the story. "So you checked her into a hotel and hung around for a quickie."

"I wish," Animal said. "Who'd you cap?"

"Welch."

"You let him go?"

"Feel like disposing of a body?"

"Not really."

"Me neither. Hopefully, Yount will be busy with that and we won't be disturbed again tonight. But we'll stand watch just in case."

"Why's Yount coming after you?"

Tyson opened a drawer and took out another gun, a 9mm Glock, and offered it butt first.

Something big was going down, a fight between Tyson and Helm. Maybe Cash the Cop was right and the boss had Kelly stashed somewhere. She might come in handy as a bargaining chip since Odette had told her dangerous secrets.

Animal wouldn't get sucked under. He meant to protect Nina and bail when he got the chance. He took the gun.

Joyce Carmichael sat up straight behind a glass desk without drawers. "You have property belonging to the museum."

"It's part of our investigation," Cash said.

"The art has nothing to do with what happened."

"It was in Kelly's car."

"I told her to pick up those pieces and deliver them here. Instead, God knows why, she went home."

She was decked out in a silly Cleopatra necklace made of silver and glass beads, but Cash couldn't see much of her face, thanks to sun glare from the window behind her. Either the museum was too cheap to pay for blinds or, more likely, she'd had them taken down because she enjoyed dazzling the peasants who stood before her. He moved to the side of the room to escape the glare. Shelves of oversize art books covered the entire wall. Georgia O'Keeffe was the only name he recognized. Welcome to Kelly's world—silent and dust-free, ruled by this rigid woman.

She kept talking at him. "They're going to be auctioned at our fundraiser tonight. They're in the program."

Joyce Carmichael had suck with somebody. Cash had ignored her demands until he'd received orders to drop by the museum and smooth her ruffled feathers. Fine. He had a few questions for her anyway. "Annie Laible has disappeared."

She waved her arm. "The other officer said Annie couldn't be contacted. She's probably out of town."

She could at least fake some concern.

Realizing he was gritting his teeth, Cash relaxed his jaw. "We have evidence that Ms. Laible may have been kidnapped, too."

"What evidence?"

"Her glass sculpture could be relevant to the investigation."

"You opened the crate? You had no authorization. The piece has been appraised at ten thousand dollars. Someone's going to pay if—"

"This is a murder investigation."

Joyce stiffened her shoulders and lifted her chin.

Annie Laible's upstairs living quarters had been ransacked, but not the studio downstairs. The searchers had either found what they were looking for—more photos?—or been interrupted. Under the circumstances, the crate had to be opened, but Cash didn't owe this woman an explanation. "How well do you know Gregory Tyson?"

"I demand that you return the sculpture and Leonard Proud's collage. I suppose you unpacked it, too."

"According to a witness, you and Tyson used to date."

"Your witness is spreading gossip. Gee is on the museum's board and also a contributor. Sometimes we go to lunch together on business."

"What about Kelly?" he said. "Does she spend time with him, too?"

"I have no idea."

"Kelly went to the Cascade a week ago to pick up some boxes. What was in them?"

Joyce opened her mouth, ready to huff that she had no idea, but instead she got shifty-eyed. To lie or not to lie?

He nudged her toward the right decision. "You can go to jail for lying to an officer of the court."

"Photographs. Gee donated them to the museum and I sent Kelly to pick them up." She chose the truth, probably figuring he already knew.

"Whose photographs?"

"Day Randall's. I thought they'd be safer stored here."

"Then they're worth something."

Joyce sniffed. "Day has talent but no reputation. I doubt she ever will. She's one of those self-destructive people who sabotage themselves."

"Then why bother with her photos?"

"Gee admires them. He's a donor, so if I can do him a favor . . . Besides, he'll buy one back at the auction."

"What time's it start?"

"It's invitation-only."

"We'll do our best to blend in."

She blinked rapidly, a flickering of panic. "We?"

"My partner and me."

"I won't have you questioning the guests."

"We'll be just another couple at your party." He smiled. "Unless you try to throw us out."

Cash savored the memory of her face, frozen in constipated outrage, while he passed through the art galleries and down the stairs to the lobby where Bridget was gazing at three huge oil paintings that together depicted one scene, Custer's Last Stand. The painter had done a good job of capturing the madness in the general's blue eyes and the wetness of the blood-soaked ground. "Finally," he said. "Art that even I can understand."

Bridget shook her head. "The room's too narrow. You have to stand a lot farther back to really appreciate the triptych."

"The what?"

"Triptych. Three paintings that show different parts of a scene."

"Great. You'll fit right in."

She looked up at him, eyebrows raised.

"They're having a party here tonight. Gregory Tyson's coming. And so are we."

"Shit. El's parents are flying into Denver tonight."

"El?"

"My partner."

"Oh." He recovered from the surprise. "I thought I was your partner."

"Very funny," she said. "I'll explain—"

"No. I'll be attending this thing unofficially, so maybe it's better if I go alone."

"You sure?"

"Yeah." They headed for the door, Bridget in the lead. "Learn anything from the receptionist?" he asked.

"Not much. Kelly's nice and Joyce is a pain in the butt."

"I could've told you that much."

"You're taking this personally. You have feelings for Kelly, don't you?"

Cash wanted to snap back with a denial, but her faint smile stopped him. "I have feelings for all of them. Sometimes I wish I didn't."

Bridget looked away as if she'd caught him at an awkward moment. They started across the museum grounds, bent to protect themselves from a cold wind.

He'd married a woman who wasn't his type, and after a year she ran off to film school in New York. He didn't need a repeat of that heartbreaker. But Kelly didn't seem ambitious and self-centered like his ex. Even though they had little in common —on the surface anyway—Cash wanted to know her better.

If he was able to save her life.

"Here's some good news," Bridget said. "We got permission to search the public land behind Helm's property. The state police are taking dogs up there tomorrow."

"Helm's men have dug up the body by now."

"They can't dig up everything and they know it. Helm's left the country."

"Where to?"

"Thailand."

"Is Odette with him?"

"Not sure," Bridget said. "He hired a private jet."

"Well, there's plenty of room for another grave in the mountains. And we won't have directions to that one."

She sucked in breath like a diver surfacing. She spun through darkness, and then the stink of the mattress grounded her. The Cascade. The room where she was trapped. She sat up. Then she froze. There was a sketch of a nude woman on the wall opposite the table, done with a ballpoint pen. The woman sprawled, legs open and eyes closed. The sketch reminded Kelly of Egon Schiele—the elegance of line, the unapologetic frankness of the woman's labia and nipples. Tyson wasn't as masterful as Schiele—not even close—but the sketch radiated erotic energy. Her gaze settled on the woman's face. It was Day. Tyson had grafted Day's angular face onto a body much like Kelly's.

Her heart began hammering. Tyson could have undressed her, drawn the picture, filmed her, and raped her. Anything he wanted. She spent a nauseating minute assessing her underpants and bra. Nothing felt out of place. He hadn't taken off her clothes and put them back on. He must have imagined her naked, almost as bad.

She peed in the hospital toilet and added to the stench. After opening another bottle of water, she rummaged in the grocery sack and found an energy bar and chomped it down. She hated the taste of those things. She was more in need of some aspirin.

While she'd fought with Tyson, some of the knockout drug squirted from the syringe. The lower dose wore off sooner than he'd planned. He wouldn't admit—even to himself—that killing her was his only hope of staying out of prison, but somewhere in his coked-out brain he understood, and when the moment came he would kill her.

She checked the time on the laptop: 7:44 p.m. December 16. Saturday. Two days since Tyson had kidnapped her. Cash must be looking for her and hunting for the murderer of the locksmith. He already suspected Tyson. Why hadn't the cops searched the Cascade by now? Maybe they had, and the room was hidden where they couldn't find it.

The furnace rumbled and whooshed behind the wall. On her last visit, she'd passed a door marked "Furnace" halfway up the stairs to Tyson's office. The mezzanine level. The room where she was imprisoned was beside or behind the furnace. She had to reach the furnace room somehow. Then she could escape down the stairs and through the kitchen into the nightclub, where the presence of customers would protect her. Unless the place was closed. She heard no music, no voices, nothing but the furnace.

She stared at the laptop screen, at the ceiling reflected in its angled glass, and tried to break through the fog of the drug hangover. The ceiling. Thanks to her father, a building contractor, she knew something about construction. The ceiling tiles were installed on a frame attached to the joists, and she could crawl between the frame and joists to the furnace room. If she put the tiles back in place, it would be like disappearing in a puff of smoke. She climbed onto the table and pushed up a tile. Scratch that idea—the aluminum frame looked too flimsy to support her weight. Even if she wanted to try, the space between it and the joists was four inches at most.

She climbed off the table and uncapped another bottle of water. No matter how much water she drank, her mouth was dry. She studied the door. Pine, hollow-core, bolted. It could be kicked in from the outside. Kicking it out from inside took more strength because it was stopped by the jamb.

Most prisoners never escaped. Sometimes they tried and failed; sometimes they were too scared and hopeless to try. She couldn't let herself become that scared. She couldn't give up hope.

The door and the ceiling were impassable, which left the floor and the walls. Beneath the carpet were sheets of plyboard underlayment, and beneath the underlayment were the joists and ceiling on the bottom story of the Cascade. The carpet would conceal a hole, but she couldn't break through plyboard without an ax or a crowbar, so it had to be the wall. When she'd broken up with her boyfriend in high school, he punched the wall of his mother's living room so hard that his fist dented the plasterboard.

She could break through the wall. She needed someplace inconspicuous. The furnace noise came from the middle of the wall, so the escape hole should be on either side. The hospital toilet was in the corner near the door, and she could move it and stack the water and groceries there, but Tyson would be suspicious. The long table occupied the other corner. He wouldn't spot a hole under the table, not if she made it high enough.

She removed the groceries from their sack and put it under the table near the spot where she meant to break through. Now for a tool. Unlike her old boyfriend, she needed more than her fist. She surveyed the room. The camera tripod. Telescoped and folded, it became a ram.

Kelly took down the video cam and two lights and stowed everything except the tripod under the table where it would help to conceal the hole. If Tyson asked why she'd moved the equipment, she'd say she bumped the cam and almost broke it. Crouched under the table, she rammed the tripod, legs first, into the wall. It made a loud thud and left three shallow dents. She hoped the furnace rumble drowned out the noise. The third blow deepened the dents and crazed the plasterboard. The fourth collapsed the three holes into one and revealed the second wall a few inches away on the furnace side.

She kept hammering until the hole in the plasterboard merged with the yawning pain in her skull. Plaster chips and dust coated the floor around her knees. Every so often she wet a fistful of toilet paper and swabbed the floor and then pushed the chips into a pile and scooped them up. She put the debris in the grocery sack.

Sooner than she'd hoped, the hole was big enough to crawl through. She opened another bottle of water and took a swig. She still had to bust through the furnace room wall. It would be awkward thrusting the tripod through the first hole, but the debris would fall mostly between the walls. She wouldn't have to stop and clean as often.

She picked up the folded tripod and got back to work. The second wall turned out to be easier. By sliding the tripod along the bottom edge of the first hole, she spent less energy holding and aiming it. She could angle the tripod up or down, left or right, whatever way she needed. Her shoulders cramped, but the work went fast. The second hole was a foot wide when Animal yelled, "Who's there?"

Kelly froze. Her ragged breathing almost drowned the whoosh from the furnace. She trusted Animal. He'd delivered Odette's message and helped her escape Yount's men in Estes Park. But he couldn't help her with Tyson there. Tyson might be attending the MOR fundraiser or fleeing to Mexico—or holed up in the Cascade. She waited for footsteps outside the door. Minutes passed in silence. Finally she went back to work, punching into the plasterboard.

❖

Animal was reading a romance book someone had left in the bar. The girl hero got magically transported back in time and fell in love with a warrior who, going by the cover illustration, could have been Animal's brother. The stupid story kept his mind off his arrangement with Tyson and the danger Nina faced because of it. He could have used her company right then, but she was safer at the hotel.

What the hell was that?

He took his feet off the manager's desk and sat up, listening. The club had been closed all day, and alone in the building he heard noises he usually tuned out—the wind's howl, the roof's creaking, the knocking of pipes, the humming and throbbing of the furnace. The pipes bothered him most. Once this shit was over, he meant to tell Tyson the plumbing needed to be fixed. He went back to reading.

At nine thirty, he headed downstairs to make coffee and double-check the doors. He brought the Glock. He heard the thumping as soon as he stepped into the stairwell. A steady beat, every few seconds. From his office it sounded like bad plumbing, but from here it sounded more like someone pounding a wall. Wanting out. He followed the noise to the landing. It was coming from the furnace room, which was locked.

"Who's there?" he yelled.

The thumping stopped. Animal waited. Maybe Cash the Cop was right and Tyson had Kelly locked up in there. The dude was crazy, destined to crash and burn. The thumping started again.

The furnace-room key was probably in Welch's desk. *His* desk now. He backtracked to the manager's office, where he found five big-ass key rings with about thirty keys on each one in a drawer. No tags were attached to the rings, and he had no clue which key opened the furnace room. Then his phone rang.

The screen displayed a number he didn't recognize. "Yeah?"

"Look out the front entrance," the man on the phone said.

"Who's this?"

"Just do what I say."

"Fuck you."

On the other end of the phone someone yelped in pain. Then a shaky voice said, "Beau?"

Nina.

The man came back on. "Get out here or I'll fuck her up."

Animal put his jacket on. Gripping the Glock inside his right front pocket and carrying the phone in his left hand, he hurried down the stairs and into the club. He peered out the vestibule window. Nina stood twenty feet away, her hands tied in front, flanked by two of his former co-workers. Butt-Ugly had the muzzle of a gun jabbed against her neck.

With the floodlights outside and the darkness inside, Animal could aim and shoot without being seen, but the bullet had to kill Butt-Ugly before he pulled the trigger. Too risky. Even if Animal were Super Sniper, which he wasn't. He retreated to the arcade and stashed the Glock in the narrow space between two game stations. Then he switched on the vestibule light and stepped out where they could see him.

The second Guardian waved his phone, a nasty smile slashing his face.

Animal called him back. "What do you want?"

"In."

"Let her go first."

"I don't think so." Smiley sounded like Yount, crisp and menacing.

Animal imagined the Guardians undergoing a throat implant so they had the same voice. "I let you in, you're gonna kill us anyway."

"Possibly. But if you don't, she dies right now."

A pair of headlights floated along the highway. Even if the driver heard the shot and called the cops, Nina was dead. "Okay, I'm unlocking the door."

"Slowly," Smiley said. "Then stand back and put your hands where I can see them."

Animal turned the bolt and backed off. He held up his arms so his forearms protected his head, and he shifted weight onto his rear foot. He had a brown belt in tae kwon do—if they rushed him, he meant to fight.

Smiley held the door while Butt-Ugly dragged Nina into the vestibule. Animal tried meeting her eyes, but they had a scared-rabbit look that seemed blind. "Hands in front, Grasshopper," Smiley said. "Nina's counting on you." Reluctantly, Animal stretched out his arms and allowed the Guardian to cuff him with plastic handcuffs and pat him for weapons. He hated feeling helpless. He expected to be kicked in the knee or cold-cocked with the gun. Instead, he and Nina were herded to the bar.

"Have a seat," Smiley said.

Nina stood there, beyond hearing.

"Help the lady to her seat."

Butt-Ugly holstered his gun and lifted Nina like a child and placed her on a stool. Animal sat next to her.

"Where are the lights, Beaumont?"

"Bar lights are by the register. The others are in back."

Smiley found the rheostat and a ghostly glow surrounded the bar. "Your girlfriend needs a drink. What's she like?"

"Just let her go."

"Go where? Out in the freezing cold? She'll wander onto the highway and get run over. She's too pretty for roadkill." Smiley scooped ice into an old-fashioned glass and grabbed a bottle of Rhum Barbancourt from the top shelf. He poured two shots over the ice, added Coke, and held the glass to Nina's mouth. "Drink." The dark liquid dribbled over her chin until she opened her mouth and swallowed. She coughed, but the booze flushed the ashen terror from her face.

"We're professionals." Smiley set the glass on the bar. "No unnecessary killing."

"What do you want?"

"Welch tells me there's a hidden room upstairs."

"I wouldn't know. I'm just the bouncer." The thumping would lead them straight to the furnace room. "By the way, how is Welch?"

"Feeling no pain." Smiley's mouth twitched as if he were holding back laughter. He exchanged a knowing look with his partner.

No way would they leave him and Nina alive. If they were separated, he could possibly jump one of them. "There's a bunch of keys in Welch's office. I'll show you."

"I think I can find them." Smiley headed for the kitchen.

He knew the way to the stairs. Welch must have given them directions before they wasted him.

Animal rested his arms on the bar. The cuffs were rubbing his wrists raw. He might be strong enough to break them, but they would cut him to the bone first. Nina's were slightly looser. He was glad for that. "You hanging on?"

She nodded.

"How did they grab you?"

"I went out for dinner."

"You left the hotel?"

"Their restaurant's too expensive."

Animal felt an impossible tangle of exasperation and tenderness. "It's okay. We're gonna make it to Oregon."

For Gee, the MOR party was mostly déjà vu. Joyce had on the same emerald-green Vera Wang number as last year. Coeds in black miniskirts and white shirts threaded among the guests with trays of canapés and dribbles of Champagne in plastic flute glasses while a string quartet sawed away at Vivaldi's greatest hits. The same monkey chatter competed with the music. The same faces floated around him—Danny Boy and the other board members, museum patrons, guards, Joyce's secretary.

The only novelty was the cop.

Cash Peterson strolled around the room checking out the art. He studied Day's portrait of Kelly as if it held a clue to her whereabouts. And it did. If he were smarter, he could track down the shop where Gee had had it framed—a rush job that cost too much—before donating it to the auction just a few hours ago.

Joyce had accepted his donation with a frown. "What else did you keep?"

"Nothing." He'd stolen the photograph from Kelly's house, not from the boxes he'd given the museum, but Joyce didn't have to know that.

Gee watched her drift from one cluster of guests to another. As curator, she had a lot of kissing up to do. Every patron and donor had to feel like the most important person in her world. And Joyce was a skilled ass-kisser. He admired her for that. Tonight, though, the smile would drop from her face as soon as she would turn away from someone. She was dog tired from doing the work she usually dumped on Kelly and pissed at Kelly for getting kidnapped. Gee wished he could be there when she found out he was the kidnapper.

He slipped away from the party, took the stairs to the lobby, and rode the service elevator to the one-stool restroom opposite the exit to the underground garage. The door locked, making it a safe place. He cut two lines on the fake-marble counter by the sink and sucked powder into the vortex at the center of himself. The Big Nothing. Too many cosmic explosions had blown his soul to radioactive dust. He cackled like a lunatic. In some parallel universe, a woman might have loved him, taken care of him, and seen him through. Yeah, right. He snorted the other line and lifted his face to the unforgiving image in the mirror. There could be no starting over, no second chances after Day.

When Gee got back to the party, Peterson was bent over the bid sheet for Kelly's portrait. He waited for the cop to move and then upped the bid by a hundred dollars. Nobody would have the portrait except Kelly. He meant to buy it himself and return it to her. Ripping something off and then giving it back—how stupid was that? But it was one of the best photographs Day had ever made, and he wanted it to be seen. He wanted to own it for a little while.

He snatched a glass of Champagne from a tray, took a swallow, and grimaced.

"Not up to your standards?" Danny Boy strolled up to him, grinning. He wore a tuxedo jacket over a T-shirt and jeans.

"Piss water."

"Joyce must've ordered this time. She's always cutting corners on the important shit."

"So fire her."

Danny tipped his chin upward and laughed. "Funny, she wants me to fire you. She said you're strung out and stink of B.O. Seriously, Gee. Look at your fingernails. You're worse than Leonard."

Halfway across the room, Leonard was standing alone—as usual—eyeing them as if deciding whether they were worth his time.

Do it! Get over here and save me.

"When you can't maintain anymore, it's time to check into rehab," Danny said.

Leonard made his decision and walked over to them, clutching a fluted glass of water. Specks of lint decorated his uncombed hair, and his flannel shirt sported a dark stain that looked like motor oil. "Who invited Five-O? Son of a bitch came to my house and questioned me for over an hour."

Cash Peterson bent over the console table, placing another bid on Kelly's portrait. Screw Peterson and his devious cop games.

"The cops impounded my collage along with her car," Leonard said. "Without it there's one Native American artist represented in this auction. One. What's that tell you about Joyce?"

"Her taste is up her ass," Danny Boy said.

Leonard narrowed his eyes at Gee. "The cop intimated you had something to do with it."

Gee's heart pounded and air dragged through his lungs like syrup. His head floated above his body. Too much blow. But his body kept insisting he was terrified. "You know cops. They need a suspect."

"I'll never see my collage again."

"Every cloud has a silver lining." The words came out of Gee, out of nowhere.

A scowl knotted Leonard's face. "Screw you, too." He stalked off toward the refreshments.

"Way to go, Gee. That's one more vote to toss you off the board."

"What about you? You gonna vote against me?"

"Maybe not—if you get a manicure. And Leonard won't, either. It would rankle his ass to support Joyce." Danny Boy blathered on, speculating how each member would vote, oblivious to how little Gee cared.

He imagined Kelly pacing the Box, her heart pounding as desperately as his, shuddering in its cage of flesh and bone. Wanting out. Wanting nothing but the end. Somewhere he had a daughter. She would be nearing college age by now. He hadn't seen her in fifteen years and wouldn't recognize her if they passed on the street. Once he must have known her smell, known her shape and weight from cradling her in his arms, but he couldn't remember anymore. His life shrank to a pinpoint.

Danny was no longer talking. He studied Gee, his eyes agleam with amusement and pity. "What? Do we have to do the intervention tonight? Me and Joyce. And that toad-like dude who manages your bar. What's his name?"

"I fired him."

"Too bad. That leaves Stuart. Hard to imagine that ruthless scumbag putting anyone on the road to sobriety. Who else?"

He paused, knowing there wouldn't be an answer. "So Joyce and I are your only friends. Sucks to be you, Gee."

"It's almost ten," Gee said. "I have to get some bids in."

"Yeah, me, too." Danny leaned close and whispered. "Not that I want the shit. But you know, noblesse oblige."

Cash Peterson had upped the bidding on the portrait to eight hundred dollars. The asshole was pushing Gee, testing how high he would go, how much Kelly mattered. It would serve him right if Gee let him win the auction and shell out the eight bills on his pitiful cop's salary. Unless the Boy Scout earnestness was an act and Peterson was on the take.

Time to end the game.

Gee jumped the bidding to two large. He was spending too much with no income from Stuart. But chances were he wouldn't be around anyway when he ran out of money.

Somebody whistled, sudden and loud. Gee jerked like an idiot with his finger in an electric socket. He turned and found Peterson in his face.

"Two grand," Peterson said. "That's out of my price range."

"Good."

"How come you're bidding on this photo, Gee? Why donate something then turn around and buy it back?"

How had he found out? The donation was labeled "anonymous."

"Only my friends call me Gee."

Peterson shook his head. "Everyone who knows you calls you Gee. Is Stuart Helm your friend?"

"We're business partners."

"Your business partner flew off to Thailand. Guess he didn't invite you. Why not?"

"I hate to fly."

"The state police are searching the public land behind his property."

So Stuart was a fugitive. Gee wanted to grin, but not with the cop there. "Whatever they're looking for, it's got nothing to do with me."

"Where do you get the money for investments like Wildcat Construction? You and Stuart are partners, right? The Cascade doesn't generate that kind of income."

"You're asking me? I'm guessing you know more about my finances than I do." He pressed his hand against his chest to keep his heart from busting through the bone.

"Your phone," Peterson said.

Gee scooped the phone from his pocket. "Yeah."

"Mr. Helm wants to talk." Yount's voice poured through the distance, smooth and volatile.

"Wait." Gee stepped away from Peterson. "I need to find somewhere quiet." He slipped down the stairs to the museum's first level, glancing behind him to make sure Peterson wasn't following. "I thought he left the country."

"He's with me. We're parked in front."

"The main entrance?"

"I'm guessing. It's a rather unconventional building. There's a banner over the entrance. 'Holiday Gala.'"

Near the lobby, Gee edged toward the wall opposite the reception counter. Too close and the display lights from the gift shop would make him visible through the glass doors. He stayed hidden in the shadow of the triptych behind him. Custer's Last Stand. And maybe his. He would make an easy target crossing the floodlighted expanse to the curb where Yount waited. He spoke into the phone. "Come inside. It's warmer. And there's Champagne."

"Mr. Helm can't afford to be seen."

"Then I'll come out." And he would, but not through the front.

Gee checked the stairs again before dropping to his stomach and elbows and crawling past the doors. He felt the gravestone coldness of the tiles through his shirt. On the other side of the lobby, he climbed to his feet and hurried downstairs to his favorite restroom, where he took a leak and snorted a few more lines.

In the parking garage, he listened through the hum and whoosh of ventilation and the echo of his footsteps. Yount might anticipate his plan and lie for him there. Floating above his body, he watched himself creep between vehicles, crouching to stay out of sight. He reached his car and retrieved the Ruger from the glove box. The butt felt colder than the gravestone tiles and brought him back to himself. He clutched the gun hard and made its coldness his.

Tyson was headed for the stairs. Sneaking off to the john to use drugs. Maybe. The way he moved suggested purpose, not desperation. Cash started to follow.

"Detective!" Joyce Carmichael tottered toward him, hobbled by four-inch spiked heels. He considered ignoring her, but her yelling might alert Tyson.

He stopped. "What is it?"

"You're bidding. We need you to register."

"Does it have to be now?"

"It would be very helpful." She slipped her arm around his and set her face in a big phony smile.

Reluctantly, Cash allowed her to guide him to the auction table.

"Marta, this gentleman needs a registration form."

The museum receptionist, the meek woman Bridget had questioned that afternoon, scurried to the table. She plucked a form from a nearby stack and set it in front of Cash. Joyce could have reached the form herself without taking a step, or simply instructed him to take one. She was drawing out the process, no doubt to keep him from following Tyson. She knew about Tyson's drug habit and didn't want her party to be wrecked by a bust.

He took a ballpoint from his pocket and scanned the form. "You want my credit card number. I haven't won anything yet."

"Oh, that's optional." Joyce beamed. "It helps us process the sale faster if you do win."

"Then it can wait." Cash scrawled his way through the form. "Here's your paperwork." He turned to go.

"Have you made any progress finding Kelly?"

"Nothing I can talk about." He started walking.

She tailed him, talking fast. "That's an amazing photograph of her. Here you are bidding on a portrait of the woman you're searching for. Just like *Laura*, with Gene Tierney and Randolph Scott."

"Dana Andrews," he said without breaking stride.

"Oh, of course. You're right. I always get those two mixed up."

He was outpacing her. The tick-tick-tick of her heels sped up and she began to pant. But she hung on. At the stairs he wheeled. "Why are you following me?"

Her garishly red mouth formed an *O* as she gave an offended gasp. "I'm sorry!" As if Cash were out of line, not her. "I just thought—if you're looking for the restroom, there's one up here."

He started down the stairs to the darkened lobby. No Tyson. Outside the glass door, the beam of a floodlight pooled on the snowy ground in front of the building. A sidewalk made a straight line from the entrance to the curb, where a lone set of headlights illuminated the street. Someone was parked out there, waiting.

"I'm sorry," Joyce called after him. "The lower level is closed."

He kept going.

"Detective—" Then she cried out.

He whipped around.

Several stairs above him, she flung out her arms and listed forward. She thrust one leg in front of her, ripping the narrow skirt of her dress, and landed on a lower stair. Her ankle twisted in the ridiculous shoe. She crumpled and began pitching forward. He charged up the stairs and caught her, mashing her face against his shoulder. He couldn't afford to be gentle—her weight could bowl him over and send them both tumbling to the bottom.

He lowered her onto the stairs. "Are you okay?"

"My shoes are ruined." She sniffled. "And I twisted my ankle."

The headlights still waited in front of the building. Cash made out the silhouette of a large SUV, but no sign of Tyson. "You're lucky you didn't break your neck."

"The auction. I have to go back. And I can't, not like this."

"You took a nasty fall. Someone else will have to run the show."

"There is no one else," she said bitterly. "Kelly got herself kidnapped."

"Then you're on your own." He descended the stairs and crossed the lobby. At the door he caught sight of Tyson, a shadow beyond the pool of floodlight, approaching the SUV from the rear, crouched and moving fast. Cash drew his gun.

"What's going on? Are you going to shoot someone?"

He went outside and sidestepped into the darkness of a covered walkway. "Police!" he shouted. "Stay where you are."

Tyson hitched his stride but kept going. As he closed on the passenger side of the SUV, gunfire flashed and a shot rang out. A window shattered. Tyson went down and Cash ran toward the scene. Suddenly, Tyson popped up and fired four shots into the vehicle. The driver returned fire, a single shot that knocked Tyson off his feet, this time for good.

By then Cash was almost across the snow-covered lawn. He zigged right and aimed through the windshield, but he held fire. The driver was slumped against the dash, his shoulder wedged between the steering wheel and door. Tyson was sprawled several feet from the curb. No need to check him for signs of life—at least a gallon of blood soaked the snow around the body. The second bullet had severed an artery. Cash peered into the SUV, a Land Rover. Another easy call. The top of the driver's skull was gone. Cash stepped away from the window and let himself feel the wind chilling his face and the snow leaking into the dress shoes he'd dusted off for the occasion. He exhaled steamy breath and inhaled the smell of blood.

28

The second hole was big enough. Kelly squirmed through the two holes, arms outstretched. She scraped her shoulders and knees on the plasterboard and bumped her knee against the concrete of the furnace-room floor, but she was out.

She peered up and down the stairwell and then crept downstairs and opened the door a crack. The kitchen, dark and empty. She breathed in grease and a meaty stench. Filthy. Tyson no doubt paid off the health inspector. She moved to the swinging door.

Almost there.

A dash from the kitchen to the front entrance and she'd be out of this hellhole. Halfway through the door, she froze. A voice drifted from the bar, where crimson light glowed against the darkness. A big man in a leather coat lumbered toward her. Yount, she thought for an instant. But it wasn't him.

She stepped back, careful to stop the door from swinging, ducked into the stairwell, and scuttled to the landing. Her heart pulsed in her throat as the man's footsteps echoed on the stairs. She grabbed the knob on the furnace-room door. Locked. It had locked automatically when it closed.

She fled onto the mezzanine and groped through a dark hallway to another door, this one unlocked. Dimmed lamps spotlighted the pool tables. She skirted the tables to the back of the mezzanine. Crouched at the top of the back stairs, she peered over the balustrade.

Animal sat with his forearms resting on the bar, his hands tied together. Nina huddled on the stool next to him. A hulking man with a gun stood behind them. "Where's Yount?" Animal said. "He should be here for this."

"He's busy."

Hidden by the balustrade, Kelly lowered her butt from one step to another until she was halfway down. About twenty feet from the bottom step, straight ahead, a lighted sign marked an emergency exit. She could dash for freedom and hope the gunman was a slow runner and a bad shot.

Something thudded on the far side of the mezzanine, where the hidden room was. Another thud, more violent. The Yount look-alike was smashing something. Probably a door. When he found the hole, he'd guess someone was loose in the building. As she scooted up the stairs, her foot slipped and she grabbed the edge of the balustrade.

"Shit!" Animal said. She guessed by his pained laugh that he saw her hand.

The next thud ended in an explosive crack. She scrambled across the mezzanine.

Wherever she hid, they'd find her.

She had to get out of the building.

She fled down the stairwell, past the metallic hammering from the furnace room and into the dark kitchen. There should be another emergency exit. She visualized the kitchen in relation to the rest of the building. It occupied the northwest corner, so there were two external walls where an exit might be. She felt her way around a turn and started along the north wall. The hammering stopped, and a hum filled the silence. Her fingers touched the cold vibrating metal of a walk-in refrigerator. She came to a counter and followed its edge past a sink that smelled unclean.

Rapid footsteps drummed in the stairwell.

She froze.

Her pursuer charged into the kitchen and slammed through the swinging door into the bar. "She's loose! Watch the front—she could run for the door. Don't forget, Yount wants her alive."

Somehow that wasn't much of a relief.

When he slammed the swinging door coming back into the kitchen, terror mushroomed at her core. If he turned on the lights . . . But he went back upstairs. He would probably begin on the top floor and work his way down. Flushing her out. She drew a shuddering breath and moved faster. She rounded another turn. If she had the layout right, she'd come to the west wall, the side of the building. The exit would most likely be here.

She groped across a bulletin board thick with papers and then a calendar hung from a nail. Calendars were near doors, usually. She touched a wood jamb.

Yes!

She stretched out her arm, and her fingers brushed a metal screen.

Not a door.

She lowered her hand to the sill.

A window. Almost as good.

She felt along the sides of the screen and found the latches. She knew what to do: slide the latches simultaneously and lift the screen from its grooves. But her fingers slipped off the narrow grips. One side unlatched but not the other, and the frame came partway out and jammed.

A wave of dizziness struck her, an after-effect of Tyson's drug, worse in the dark.

She could break through the screen and open the window—or shatter the glass—but there would be noise. They would be right behind her. She left the window and groped past a metal cabinet to the corner.

The fourth wall faced the interior. She stood near two ovens, one stacked on the other, and beyond them were a stove top with gas burners and a grill. A counter paralleled the grill, forming a narrow corridor. At its end was the swinging door, edged with light.

The stairwell door opened. Kelly flattened herself against the wall beside the ovens.

"How much time do we have?" The Yount look-alike listened. "All right." He pushed into the bar and called out. "Yount's been shot."

"Is he hurt bad?"

"Not your concern. The cops will be here. There's no time to look—we have to flush her out." His voice dwindled as he moved farther from the kitchen.

"How?"

"Give me some booze . . . No, dummy, not the fucking merlot. The Everclear. Over there. And the vodka."

"What about these two?"

"Don't shoot them. It's going to be an accident."

Nina started keening. There was a scuffle and a sharp bang as something struck the floor. "Sit the fuck down!" the gunman yelled.

"She's got no part in this!"

A thud with a mushy finish, like a melon bursting.

Nina screamed until a slap silenced her.

Fear squeezed Kelly's throat. Even if she made it outside, they would run her down in the parking lot. If she could distract them, buy some time for the cops to get there . . .

"Go outside and cover the back," the Yount look-alike yelled, his voice close. "I'll take the front and side." He barreled into the kitchen, straight at Kelly. She pressed her back against the wall. He yanked drawers open and slammed them shut and made ripping noises. The gas burners whooshed on and the flame light danced on the ceiling.

She peeked around the ovens. He was already gone. Before turning on the gas, he'd soaked towels and wads of paper with alcohol and strewn them over the burners. White flame spread over the stove top and crawled down the front of the stove. The wood floor, primed with more alcohol, began to burn.

She had to circle the kitchen, back the way she came. She paused at the window. A way out—except that she could burn to death while wrestling with the jammed screen. She went on. By the time she passed the walk-in fridge, the fire was climbing the wall and lapping at the door. She staggered, head down, coughing. The heat took her breath. She charged out the door, ankle-deep in flame.

Her slacks were on fire.

Drop and roll, she remembered from somewhere.

Her breath huffed and whooshed inside her head as she rolled on the plank floor. The fire was out, but her legs hurt. Good—with the worst burns, the pain came later. She got to her feet. Yount's henchmen could have grabbed her without a fight, but they were gone.

Animal sprawled on the floor beside the bar, his hands tied to the foot rail. Nina was tied to a thick chrome rail at the servers station. Kelly ran toward them.

◈

Animal coughed, his mouth full of blood. He called to Nina. No answer. He focused on the bar stool knocked over during his scuffle with the Guardians. When he moved his arms to sit up, pain flared in his wrists. Twisting his neck around, he found another plastic cord looped between his cuffed wrists and around the footrest under the bar.

"Cut us loose," Nina said. "The lime knife. On the cutting board there by the fridge."

She was tiny but fierce. Nothing made her lie down and quit. One way or another, he meant to bring her out of there safe. Fire shimmered on Tyson's picture of the miners riding the waterfall. In a minute it would reach the Christmas decorations and spread across the ceiling in a flash.

Kelly knelt beside him. The lime knife's blade barely fit under the plastic circling his wrist. She sawed in a half-ass way, scared of hurting him.

"Just cut it," he said. She twisted the blade against the plastic tie, digging the blunt edge into his wrist. He sucked air through his clenched teeth. "Harder." She jerked the knife and snapped the tie. "Give me that." He cut the other tie and hoisted himself on to one knee and then lurched sideways. He steadied himself and gave Kelly the knife back. "Cut Nina loose."

On the third try, Animal made it to his feet. His entire head throbbed. He stumbled to the arcade and retrieved the Glock. A gobbet of burning plastic dropped inches ahead of him. He hurried to the women as fast as his spastic legs would carry him. "Let's go." They started toward the back exit.

"He turned on the gas burners," Kelly shouted behind him. The whole building could blow.

Flaming tinsel icicles rained down on them. "Beau?" Nina's voice trembled, but she wasn't on fire. He was. He brushed the fire off his shirt and pulled her the last few steps to the exit.

He stood with his back against the wall and stretched his arm along the metal bar that unlatched the door. His other hand held the gun ready. "We're gonna run to my car. Stay behind me. And don't open the door more than you have to. The air's gonna draw the fire."

The winter air shocked him awake and set the nerves in his nose howling. It was broken for sure. He crept to the corner of the building, his brain pumping out chunks of thoughts that he fumbled into some kind of sense. His Mustang was maybe fifteen feet away, the pickup twice that far. The two vehicles were the only cover. Otherwise the ground lay open to the highway.

Butt-Ugly would be squatting behind the pickup, waiting for Kelly to rabbit for the Mustang. It was her only move. He wouldn't expect Animal. Or the gun. Animal meant to pop off a few shots and startle him while they dashed for the car, but he needed to go first, and if Nina or Kelly lagged behind, Butt-Ugly could pick them off.

Two hundred yards away, headlights floated on the highway, as distant as spaceships. In a few minutes the fire would be visible from the highway. The Guardians needed to grab Kelly and get out of there before someone called 911. They would circle the building, one from each direction.

"Change of plan," he said. "We run for the highway."

"They'll shoot us," Nina said.

"Shoot at us. Don't mean they'll hit us. The one in back won't even see us, not if we run that way." He pointed to a path angled slightly toward the front of the building.

"There's the other one in front," Kelly said.

"He'll be on the other side of the parking lot."

Nina shrieked.

Animal turned, already knowing. He pivoted rightward toward the building, raised the Glock, and squeezed the trigger. The flash from its barrel mirrored the star-burst of Butt-Ugly's gun. The bullet slammed Animal's arm and he went down. A floating feeling came over him. It was done. Fine with him.

Nina knelt beside him. "Beau?"

"He's dead," Kelly said.

"Not yet." He barely heard his own voice.

"No—him." Her voice shook with cold and shock. "You—killed him."

"Run!" He threw all his strength into the command. "Now!"

Kelly hesitated and then took off, but Nina stayed.

"Go on."

"I'm not leaving you."

"He'll see you. Go." His shirt and jeans were damp with sweat. He began to shiver. "Get the hell out of here."

Nina scrambled to her feet, grabbed his ankles, and began pulling. She meant to drag him clear of the building before the gas exploded. *Stupid.* He was twice her weight. More than twice. *It's no use*, he wanted to say, but his voice no longer worked. Next thing he knew, she was pushing his chest and hip with her little hands, grunting with the effort. Even her grunts were cute.

The world turned over. He felt dizzy. And happy. He could have ended a lot worse. Then his broken nose grazed something hard and he gave a feeble yelp.

"Oh, Beau, I'm sorry."

She kept pushing, rolling him into the field. Face up again, he saw the Cascade with its roof on fire. An explosion lighted the sky and shook the ground and his hearing stopped. Nina kept going. *How the hell* . . . She heaved him on to his side and then pushed him on to his back again. The Cascade's back wall loomed over them. Protected from the blast by distance and the mezzanine, the wall had shielded them. Then the ground slanted downhill. Not by much, but enough to give his body momentum. He rolled faster. She kept pushing. His Nina. She could move mountains. It would break her heart if he died anyway.

She was the one they wanted.

They would chase her and leave Animal and Nina alone. They wouldn't have to chase her far, though. In the dark beyond the fire, she couldn't see the ground. Hallucinations blossomed, shapes like silver flowers. Tyson had drugged her too many times. Her feet dragged through the snow and her lungs clenched against the frozen air.

Light swept over her. A motor roared and she turned to see headlights sweeping toward her. She stopped and waited, imagining her body crushed beneath the wheels and not caring. But the Land Rover slowed and pulled alongside her. The window on the passenger side slid down. "Get in," the driver said.

Kelly shook her head.

"Come on, make it easier for both of us."

His face was a shadow, but she knew the voice. The man who'd set the fire.

He got out and circled the hood, in no hurry. Kelly lurched away from him. He caught her in seconds. With his thick forearm wedged under her chin, pressing her throat, he dragged her to the Land Rover. He yanked open the passenger door and shoved her in.

Braced against the seat, she kicked blindly and struck somewhere soft. He grunted. He lunged and punched her ribs, three sharp blows that left her stunned and breathless. The door slammed, loud and final like a sprung trap. He took a few seconds to reach the door on the driver's side—an opportunity to run if she weren't gasping for breath. He slid behind the wheel and pulled the door shut, put on his seat belt, and shifted out of "park." The Land Rover bumped across the field.

"Keep your head down." He seized a fistful of her sweater and yanked her down until her cheek pressed against the console. Her spine was twisted, with her legs in the foot well, so she curled up on the seat. Every jolt stabbed her ribs. Sirens howled, too far away to save her or the Cascade. She'd be dead before the firefighters extinguished the embers.

"Where're you taking me?"

"You've caused a lot of trouble. People are dead because of you."

"Who?" She thought of Odette.

"Your boyfriend, for one."

"I don't have one."

The man laughed from his throat, an ugly laugh. "Why are you holed up with him if he's not your boyfriend?"

"Did you kill Day?"

"I have her," the man said to his phone.

She heard the voice that answered, a flat voice, flat like the head of a snake, pronouncing her fate in words she couldn't understand.

"Okay." The man listened to more. "I think Beaumont shot him. Both of them were down when I went after Kelly."

She hated the way he spoke her name, as if she amounted to nothing.

"Maybe he's dead. I don't know, I couldn't get to him. The cops are here."

Kelly raised her head and glimpsed lights flashing through smoke. He slammed her face against the console and pain exploded in her skull.

"Shut up and stay down."

Her face pulsed along with her heart.

"She wanted to have a look around," the man said, back on the phone. "I doubt Beaumont knows squat anyway."

She fought the pain, tried to think. Squad cars had reached the Cascade. They were off to the left, which meant the Land Rover was heading away from Boulder. Away from any hope of rescue. The ride was bumpy and slow—her kidnapper was staying off the highway. Lying low until they were farther away.

"Yeah, too bad," her captor said. "Yount had skills."

The snake voice on the phone said something.

"I appreciate your confidence, sir."

Bootlicker.

So Yount was dead.

Good. Yount deserved to be dead.

The Land Rover swung right and began climbing an embankment. A few more seconds and they'd reach the highway. He'd take her to some isolated place, kill her, and dump her body. He'd probably question her first. Find out how much Odette had confided and whether she'd told anyone. She would disappear like Day. Cash might guess what happened, but he wouldn't have proof. Stuart Helm was long gone, maybe halfway around the world, giving orders to this thug in a snake voice.

Kelly thought of her parents. Mom had already checked out of life. With both their daughters dead, Dad would give up, too. The man's elbow brushed her head as he pocketed the phone.

Her chance.

She grabbed the wheel and yanked. The Land Rover crested the ditch, accelerating. For an instant it hung, balanced on two wheels, engine howling, and then it crashed on the passenger side and slid, grinding and shrieking against the asphalt. Kelly bounced off the door and struck her head on the roof. Then the airbags pushed against her. The Land Rover skidded to a stop and the engine stalled.

At first Kelly hurt too much to move. She lay with her shins against the bottom of the dashboard and her cheek pressed against the window frame. Her right arm was pinned beneath her. She twisted toward him and managed to free her arm and unlatch her seatbelt, and then she pulled her shoulders free of the airbag. She moved sluggishly, as if connections between her brain and limbs were damaged.

Suspended above her, the man reached toward his armpit. Where the gun was. She caught his forearm in her left hand and clung. Only a few inches separated his right shoulder from her torso, so he couldn't wrench his arm free. Hanging, caught between the seat and airbag, he couldn't use his body strength either. He thrashed and jounced in the harness of the seat belt. Both of them huffed with effort. His jacket hung open and the gun was right there. She seized the butt with her right hand and pulled the gun from its holster.

She knew a little about guns from long-ago hunting trips with her father. She curled her finger on the trigger and thumbed the safety. Already off. He grabbed her wrist and squeezed hard to make her drop the gun. She clutched her left hand over her right hand and they wrestled in the cramped space. The agony in her arm forced every other thought from her head—her wrist was about to snap.

The gun fired.

She saw the flash, heard the explosive crack. The recoil torqued her wrist. He wasn't gripping it anymore. The world was silent. She couldn't hear her own cries of pain or any sound from the man. His arm flailed and then dropped, limp. Hot wetness dripped onto her face.

Blood. He was hit.

Kelly waited a minute, maybe five. More blood soaked her face and sweater. His body hung above her, blocking the driver's door, the only way out.

If she shifted him against the seat back, she might be able to squirm between him and the airbag, then open the door like a hatch.

She inched her feet along the foot well, downward to the passenger's door. When they were beneath her, she straightened her back as much as possible in the cramped space, wedged her left shoulder and arm against him, and pushed with her legs. She pushed until she was gasping and her heartbeat filled the world. Then she fell back, exhausted. All her strength shifted his body only an inch or two. He and his airbag still blocked the door.

Hopeless.

The ringing in her ears (when had it started?) became faint and faraway. A separate thing. Like her pain. The darkness took her breath and she began to float.

She forced her eyelids open. *Not like this, frozen beneath the corpse of this thug.*

Then how—tortured to death like Day or killed in a random accident like her sister?

Beth's face, Day's face . . . She tried to form images in her mind, but the memories drained away like blood from a wound.

It doesn't matter how you die. Every way is just as gone.

She let herself go.

Strobe light flashed at the edge of her vision. Brain damage. She wanted to laugh. Like it mattered now. Then a light struck her face, blinding her. Above her, the driver's door opened and two men set to work unstrapping her kidnapper's body and lifting it out. She waited as they worked in eerie silence. Someone touched her cheek, and she jerked awake and saw the shadowy face of a man above her. His mouth moved, but she couldn't hear. She grabbed the rearview mirror and tried to lift herself. The man was saying something, shaking his head. She understood. Hold still. Just wait and they'd get her out.

She closed her eyes.

When they lifted her from the wreckage, a freezing wind swept through her. She was lowered onto a gurney, covered with a blanket, and wheeled toward an ambulance. Then the sting of a needle. This time she welcomed it.

And darkness.

Kelly looked at the image in her bathroom mirror. Only an inch of her hair remained after the singed ends had been trimmed, not enough to need combing. She fluffed it with her fingers, but why bother? Her face seemed naked without eyebrows. The bruises had faded, but a second-degree burn cut an angry swath from her temple to her jaw. Another burn covered the top of her forearm, and another twisted over her leg. All on her left side where her clothing had caught fire. Her sprained right wrist needed a bandage. Her cracked rib hurt when she breathed too hard. Clumsily, she applied the cream the doctor had prescribed, the damaged skin hard and slick against her fingertips. It might scar. But at least her hair would grow back.

The doctor, the nurses, Cash—everyone said how the burns could have been much worse, how she was lucky to have survived.

She spent more time in front of the mirror since the fire. She never considered herself vain, but now she understood she'd taken her looks for granted. She tried to accept the image smiling back at her, a lopsided smile that tugged at her burned cheek. She massaged her skin until it absorbed the cream and then went into her bedroom and got dressed. Slowly. Her cracked rib stabbed her when she moved wrong. She wore silk underwear beneath a polyester sweater and pants with an elastic waistband. Old lady clothes. Her skin couldn't tolerate anything that scratched or rubbed.

She noticed the time and went downstairs. Cash had called to say he was running late. He could show up any minute.

She set her bag and coat on a nearby chair and washed down two pain pills with a mouthful of cold black tea. Cheery sunlight illuminated the traces of bloodstains on the kitchen's vinyl flooring. Stupid—rushing headlong into the house instead of waiting for the locksmith to get out of his van. Cash hadn't lectured her, though. She appreciated that.

The flooring would have to be replaced before the house went on the market. Kelly hated staying in the house, but she couldn't recuperate in a hotel.

The doorbell chimed, and she carried her bag and coat to the front and peered through the side pane. He waited outside, breathing steam into the frigid air. She opened the door and stepped out.

He took her arm gingerly. "Doing okay?"

Kelly nodded.

"Careful on the ice," he said as they walked to the driveway. "Let me have your coat." After folding it on the backseat of his Outback, he opened the passenger door and steadied her while she maneuvered into the bucket seat.

"Thanks." Kelly wished he wouldn't fuss over her. She hated feeling like an invalid.

"I called Beau. Their plane's on time. We won't have a lot of time with them." He backed the car into the street.

Cash and Animal had bonded one afternoon at her bedside while the Broncos played on the hospital-room TV and she drowsed in a morphine haze. They traded stories about the jerks and crazies they'd encountered. It seemed cops and bouncers met the same kinds of people. Cash explained how Animal could get his record expunged and be bonded for security work. "Just not with the Guardians, okay?" Their camaraderie seemed like a drug-fueled fantasy of happy-ever-after, and Kelly couldn't stop herself from giggling.

"Was I that funny?"

"Nah, she's just high."

Kelly smiled at the memory. Houses floated past the car window and the Flatirons reeled overhead. "Will he and Nina have to come back for Helm's trial?"

"There probably won't be one. His lawyers will fight extradition and the case isn't airtight. There's your testimony and Beau's. There's Day's photographs and evidence a body was buried behind Helm's estate, but so far nothing proves it was Marcus French. For Annie Laible, we got nothing. We just know she's missing."

The medicine made her woozy. She squeezed her eyes closed and opened them again. "Where do you think the bodies are?"

"Bridget has a theory they're buried on land owned by the Wildcat Construction Company. Helm has a controlling interest, but with him hiding and Tyson dead, Daniel Jorgenson is running the company. He doesn't want us messing with his profits."

She imagined Day buried under someone's house, her wandering finally over. "You can't get a warrant?"

"The company owns a dozen parcels of land in the Denver area. Their lawyers are arguing the state needs evidence a body is buried on one parcel in particular, rather than seeking a warrant to search everywhere. I don't think they'll prevail, but—"

"At least you caught the guy who tried to kidnap me."

"You'll have to testify at the trial and so will Beau and Nina." Cash aimed a smile in her direction. "You should have shot to kill. Now you'll have to stick around."

"I don't have a job anymore." Joyce had made that clear even though the board hadn't officially fired her yet.

"I'll help you find one. Something to tide you over."

"The doctor says I can't work for at least a month. I have money saved, but . . ." Depression overwhelmed her. One moment she was slogging through the muck of pain medication, the next moment sinking fast in quicksand. "My parents want me to come home."

"Do you want to?"

She'd been too woozy when Dad called to remember much of their conversation, but his voice carried the message: They loved her and wanted to have her close by. "For a visit. But not permanently."

"Then don't. Let me help you, Kelly."

Cash had been kind since the night the Cascade burned, like a friend hoping for more. But they hardly knew each other. Nina's chirpy voice echoed in her memory. *Beau's the one. I knew the second I set eyes on him.* Nina had come to visit her in the hospital, jubilant to be striking out for Oregon with her beloved Beau. Trusting her choices in a way Kelly never could. Kelly wasn't the type to fall instantly in love. She had to build love from scratch with the right someone, and she was anything but sure about Cash. He probably felt guilty about failing to save her, but his tenderness seemed genuine. And the way he looked at her sometimes, as if she were beautiful in spite of the burns. She needed that the way a parched plant needs rain.

She was tired, too tired to think anymore. Her grainy eyelids shut out the daylight.

"Are you awake?"

She lifted her head and opened her eyes. They sailed along in a stream of traffic, surrounded by Denver. "How long was I asleep?"

"Half an hour or so."

"Thanks for driving me."

"No problem. How long do you need to keep taking that stuff?"

"Another week, maybe longer."

His phone rang. "Hey." Kelly guessed from his tone that it was his partner. "We're on our way to the airport now." He listened for a minute. "Good. One less scumbag in the world. And a load off Nina's shoulders." He chatted a little longer before pocketing the phone. "Welch's body was found north of Helm's property. It was spotted by a truck driver a ways off the road."

"They hid the others. Why not him?"

"There was probably no time. The Guardians cleared out in a hurry after Tyson shot Yount."

Maybe Tyson had meant to save her after all. In Day's close-ups, his face kept changing, attractive from one angle and ugly from another—the closest she would get to the truth about him. The photos belonged to her if she wanted them. Without Tyson's patronage, Joyce had no interest in Day's work. She'd informed Kelly it would be discarded after the holidays unless someone claimed it. Tomorrow was New Year's Eve.

"I have another favor to ask. Day's photographs are at the museum, and they'll be thrown out unless I pick them up in the next couple of days."

"Sure, I'll drive you." Cash paused. "I'd like to look through them first, in case there's something relevant to the investigation." He set the turn signal blinking and moved into the right lane. The airport exit was a quarter mile ahead. "I was wondering about Day's photo of you at the auction."

"Of me?" She couldn't imagine Joyce choosing an image of her from among the hundreds of prints available.

"Tyson and I had a bidding war going on it. Joyce told me he donated it the day of the auction. He was bidding on his own donation."

Kelly tried to swallow. Her mouth always felt dry. "He could have stolen it the day he killed that poor guy and kidnapped me."

"I figured as much." Cash descended the exit ramp and merged into the traffic on Peña Boulevard. "Anyway, I got a call from Joyce. Since Tyson's dead, I'm the winning bidder. How do you feel about me having it?"

Just like Joyce to collect the money in spite of everything. She'd probably try to claim Annie's sculpture, too. "Don't pay her. It's my photo. I'll get it back and give it to you."

"I don't mind making the donation."

"Well, I mind."

He winced and then smiled with a trace of smugness. "I'm not sure if you're sticking up for me or sticking it to Joyce. But thanks."

"The photo belongs to me. It's mine to give, not hers to sell. And I want you to have it."

They passed the notorious *Blue Mustang*, which had killed its creator, Luis Jiménez, when a piece of the sculpture fell on him. The cobalt horse towered over thirty feet high, its red eyes gleaming with hellfire when the sun caught them. Kelly couldn't help asking. "What do you think of *Blue Mustang?*"

Cash laughed. "Blucifer? It's one of those things, even the people who hate it get attached to it." His gaze swung to her and then back to the road. "You like it, don't you?"

The sculpture reminded her of the painting in Tyson's office, the devil choking on a crucifix. Another vision of the demonic, ashes now. "I admire it."

He found a spot in the short-term parking garage and helped her out of the car. The air stank of exhaust fumes and she swayed, suddenly nauseated. His hold on her arm tightened. "Are you okay? Do you want to wait a minute?"

"I'm fine."

They rode a crowded escalator and entered the airport's main building. She peered over the colorful balustrade at the throngs of travelers pulling suitcases and lining up at car-rental and ticket counters. The noise was hushed, absorbed by the baffled roof. They rode another escalator to the bottom level. "There they are."

Nina stood and waved. Beside her Animal rose slowly, his left arm in a sling. His shorter hair revealed an elegantly shaped skull that made his face more distinctive and his blue eyes more intense. Transformed by the haircut, a collared shirt, and something more—a scrubbed wholesomeness—he looked ready to meet his future in-laws.

"How's the arm?" Cash said.

"Better." Animal grimaced. "I hope to hell I never get shot again."

Cash sat next to Animal, and Kelly sat on the other side of the couple, next to Nina.

"The burn looks like it's healing," Nina said.

As if on cue, Kelly's face began to throb and itch. "It could scar. But the doctor thinks laser treatments might help." Her attention drifted to Cash's voice assuring Animal that the Mustang's new owner loved the car and would treat it right. Cash had brokered the sale.

Nina touched her arm and offered a tentative smile. "I'm sorry about Day. I know you and her were really close." She paused. "About that day at Angkor, I didn't mean to be such a bitch."

"You just wanted to be left alone."

The silence between them filled with airport noises and Animal's telling Cash about a park in Oregon, how awesome the hiking trails were supposed to be.

"Detective Farrigan called while we were driving down here," Kelly said. "A truck driver found Welch's body."

"Who killed him? Yount?"

"Probably."

"Well, that's a relief. I wouldn't be much use at a trial. I don't remember anything. Just the next morning, it hurt so much to pee I wanted to scream. At least I won't have to talk about peeing to a courtroom full of people." Nina stared into her lap, where she was winding and unwinding the webbed cloth strap of her bag around her index finger. She rifled in the bag and pulled out her phone. "Give me your number. I'll call you so you have mine."

Kelly recited her phone number, wondering if they would stay in touch. Their bond was the harrowing night at the Cascade, a past they both wanted to leave behind.

"We better get going," Animal said. "There'll be a line at the security checkpoint, and last time they gave me some extra attention."

The two men stood and shook hands. "If you need anything, you know how to reach me," Cash said.

"I won't forget you saved our lives," Nina said and hugged Kelly, avoiding her injured side but pressing on the cracked rib.

Kelly winced. "And Beau saved mine."

Nina missed the wince, but Cash noticed and shot Kelly a sympathetic look.

As they walked toward the security checkpoint, Animal grinned and winked. "Hey, Kelly, thanks for not giving me up to this cop."

Cash snorted. "Her loyalty almost got you all killed."

As Animal and Nina took their place at the end of a long winding line, Kelly's body set off alarms. Her face throbbed steadily, and the silk underwear brushing against her burned leg triggered bolts of pain. She needed more medicine, but she lingered to wave another good-bye. Animal towered over Nina, his hand gentle on her shoulder, and she tilted her head and smiled up at him.

It gave Kelly hope to see them so happy.

Acknowledgments

Few books are the work of the author alone. I couldn't have finished *Darkroom* without the support and valuable criticism of the Writer Babes—especially Letitia Moffitt, Daiva Markelis and Angela Vietto—who urged me to continue writing when when I wanted put the manuscript aside and forget about it. And I owe a great debt to my editors, Peter Gelfan and Doug Wagner of the Editorial Department, whose imput made *Darkroom* a far better book. Beta readers Stephanie Hill and Alexandra John provided frank and helpful feedback as well as the encouragement that every writer needs to keep working. Finally, special thanks to Seeley James for his fresh insights and specialized knowledge.

About the Author

M ary Maddox is a suspense and horror novelist with what *The Charleston Times-Courier* calls a "Ray Bradbury-like gift for deft, deep-shadowed description." Born in Soldiers Summit, high in the mountains of Utah, Maddox graduated with honors in creative writing from Knox College, and went on to earn an MFA from the University of Iowa Writers' Workshop. She taught writing at Eastern Illinois University and has published stories in various journals, including *Yellow Silk*, *Farmer's Market*, *The Scream Online*, and *Huffington Post*. The Illinois Arts Council has honored her fiction with a Literary Award and an Artist's Grant.

Visit her online at marymaddox.com.